"DELIGHTFUL"

The New York Times Book Review

"Packed as full as a good fruitcake, including the nuttiness. Just consider: Time, the 1930's, so there's an international secret touch; scene, a Stately Home, with everyone simply whizzing around in the dark; murders, a jewel thief called The Wraith; charming young women, impersonations, a pair of antique pistols (priceless) ... and a surprise finish. ..."

San Francisco Chronicle

"FUN A-PLENTY"

The London Times

"All-in-all a real whodunit in the old fashioned style, a pleasure in these days of long psychological novels ... moves fast with a new twist offered in every chapter."

West Coast Review Of Books

"CLEVER ... SATISFYING ...

A JOLLY GOOD READ."

The New Republic

THE AFFAIR
OF THE
BLOOD-STAINED
EGG COSY

James Anderson

AVON
PUBLISHERS OF BARD, CAMELOT AND DISCUS BOOKS

AVON BOOKS
A division of
The Hearst Corporation
959 Eighth Avenue
New York, New York 10019

First Avon Printing, April, 1978

Contents

Principal Characters

George Henry Aylwin Saunders, 12th Earl of Burford

The Hon. Richard Lestrange Saunders, MP, his brother

Mr. Hiram S. Peabody of Texas, a multi-millionaire

Martin Adler, a foreign envoy

Nicholas Felman, his aide

Lieut-Commander Giles Deveraux, RN (Rtd.)

Algernon Fotheringay, Esquire, a young man about town

Stanislaus Batchev, a stranger

John Evans, secretary to Mr. Peabody

Merryweather, butler to Lord Burford

Detective-Inspector Wilkins, CID

Detective-Sergeant Leather

Lavinia, Countess of Burford

Lady Geraldine Saunders, her daughter

The Baroness Anilese de la Roche, widow of a French aristocrat

Mrs. Hiram ("Carrie") Peabody

Miss Jane Clifton, an impoverished young lady

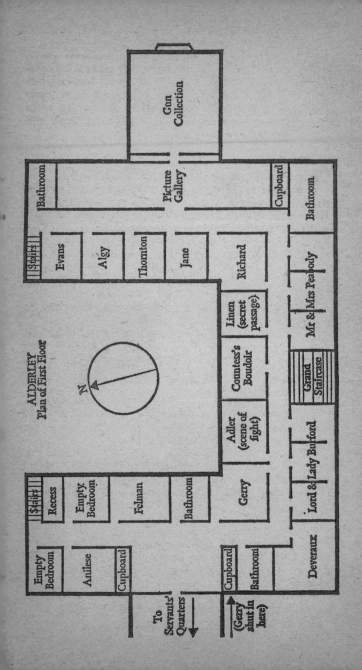

ALDERLEY
Plan of First Floor

N

To Servants' Quarters

Empty Bedroom

Anilese

Cupboard

Stairs

Recess

Empty Bedroom

Felman

Bathroom

Gerry

(Gerry shut in here)

Cupboard

Bathroom

Deveraux

Lord & Lady Buford

Adler (scene of fight)

Countess's Boudoir

Linen (secret passage)

Grand Staircase

Mr & Mrs Peabody

Richard

Jane

Thornton

Algy

Evans

Stairs

Bathroom

Picture Gallery

Gun Collection

Cupboard

Bathroom

Prologue

"**H**OW well do you know Adolf Hitler?"

The man who asked the question was short and dapper and wore a military uniform heavy with insignia. He turned away from the window of his office as he spoke and surveyed the only other occupant of the room with a look of slight distaste.

This was an older, somewhat seedy-looking man in a blue serge suit and a dirty collar. He was smoking a cigarette and lazily blowing smoke rings towards the ceiling.

"Not well at all," he said. "I've met him twice. Why do you ask?"

"Last week your department supplied me with the transcript of a speech he had just made to a secret meeting of Nazi party officials."

"Concerning the Duchy?"

"Yes."

"What about it?"

"I just wondered if you were able to read between the lines of that speech."

"Well, it's obvious he wants the Duchy."

"That has been obvious for a long time. On this occasion, however, he laid considerable stress on her strategic importance—and on her military weakness."

"Indicating that he intends to act soon—to annexe her?"

"We believe so. Which would, of course, be disastrous to our interests."

"Would it? Well, if you say so."

"I do. It was decided many months ago that if any country was to annexe the Duchy, it had to be ourselves. But there was no great urgency. Because there is an obstacle."

The older man sucked at his cigarette and puffed three or four smoke rings upwards. "England," he said.

"Precisely. Or Britain, to be more accurate. Britain recognizes the importance of keeping the Grand Duke on the throne and the Duchy, to put it crudely, on her side. She will certainly be prepared to act to ensure this. Just how much she will be willing to do we've never known. However, Hitler's speech has changed the situation entirely. Now it is essential we act quickly. As the American cowboy films so quaintly put it, we must beat him to the draw. But first of all we have got to find out just how far Britain is prepared to go in the Duchy's defence."

"Which, I suppose, is why I was so peremptorily summoned here this morning."

The short man sat down in a chair near the other, leaned forward, and spoke in a low voice. "There is shortly to be a secret meeting between a representative of the Grand Duke—probably Martin Adler himself—and a British government minister. Can you discover where and when that meeting is to take place—and what is decided at it?"

The older man's eyes narrowed and he eased himself slowly upright in his chair. "That," he said, "will not be simple."

"Of course it won't be *simple*. But can you do it?"

"Perhaps." The older man was silent for a moment, then added: "There is one agent—and one agent only—in the world who might succeed. Not one of my own people—a freelance. If this agent is available, then the answer is probably yes. But it will cost a great deal of money."

"The cost is immaterial. Just find out what we want to know."

"Which is—precisely?"

"Exactly what arms and equipment Britain agrees to supply, and—most important—how soon she can deliver: we must know how quickly we have to act. Also, what Britain would do in the event of the Duchy being invaded: would she intervene directly by sending troops? On the answer to these questions depends our course of action. It is entirely up to your department to get them."

The civilian was still for a few seconds. Then he stubbed out his cigarette and got to his feet. He brushed a few specks of ash from his waistcoat, and ambled towards the door. "I'll be in touch," he said, and went out.

I

A Resignation

JANE Clifton was fuming. Some customers were absolutely intolerable. And Mrs. Amelia Bottway just about took the cake. Jane replaced the red dress on the hanger, took down a green one, and returned to Mrs. Bottway.

"Perhaps you would care to try this one, madam."

"Oh, really, you are the most stupid girl! I told you distinctly not green." She had a piercing voice.

Jane reddened, then swallowed hard. "I'm sorry, madam. I didn't hear you. I'm afraid this is the last one of your size in a bright-coloured satin."

"Well, it's no good to me at all. None of them 'ave been. You've been wasting my time. It's disgraceful."

"I've shown you nine gowns, madam. I'm sorry if none of them is suitable, but—"

"I shall 'ave to try h'elsewhere. Somewhere where they keep a adequate stock—and employ some h'intelligent girls." Mrs. Bottway struggled to her feet and fixed Jane with what was plainly meant to be a withering glance.

Jane looked back at her with revulsion, her face fixed in what she called her painted-doll expression. The foul-mannered, ugly old barrel, she thought to herself. How dare she speak to me like that?

"You foul-mannered, ugly old barrel," she said loudly and distinctly, "how dare you speak to me like that!"

She hadn't meant to say this: the words had just come. But they were out now, and Jane suddenly felt very much better.

For several seconds Mrs. Bottway did not react at all. Then slowly her face started to go purple. Jane suddenly realized that she was the centre of attention. There were

11

three or four other customers in the shop, and, together with the assistants, they were all staring at her speechlessly.

Mrs. Bottway, whose complexion by now resembled an over-ripe plum, at last got her mouth open. "You—" she said, "you—you—you 'ussy."

Jane watched her with a cool and curiously detached air. She marshalled her thoughts: might as well be hung for a sheep as a lamb.

"Mrs. Bottway," she said, "you and your sort sicken me. You are insolent, bad-tempered, and arrogant. You've got pots of money and not the first idea how to spend it. You ask for a satin dress in a bright colour. I ask you— with your figure! You'd look even more grotesque than you do now."

She got no further. For from behind her came a voice raised in a screech. "Clifton!"

Jane swung round to confront the proprietor of *Mayfair Modes*, Monsieur Anton. "Clifton—you wicked, wicked girl. You will apologize to madam this instant." He was almost hopping with rage.

Jane interrupted quietly. "I shall apologize to nobody. I meant every word of it. Don't bother to say any more. It's too late. You can't fire me. I resign!"

And she strode to her cubicle, jammed her hat on her head, grabbed up her coat and handbag, and made for the door. Just inside it, she turned.

"Mr. Anton," she said loudly, "I have a week's wages due to me—three pounds, seven shillings and sixpence exactly. But don't bother to send it on. Put it towards the cost of a new wig." And with her head held high, Jane marched out into Bond Street.

She walked off briskly, struggling into her coat as she did so, and cursing herself for a prize idiot. Fancy throwing up a steady job, walking out without a reference— and no hope of getting one now!—not even claiming what was rightfully hers; when she had just £9 18s 7d in her bank account and 11s 3¼d in her purse.

But it had been worth it. Their faces! Jane suddenly laughed out loud—greatly to the surprise of a plump, bowler-hatted little man she happened to be passing.

"Jane—wait!" The voice came from behind her and Jane spun round to see a small, red-haired girl darting along the pavement towards her.

"Gerry!" she exclaimed.

Lady Geraldine Saunders, only daughter of the twelfth Earl of Burford, rushed up to Jane and caught her by both hands. "Jane—darling—what a simply devastating performance!"

Jane stared. "You were there?"

"You bet I was there. I called in to ask you to lunch. I was just waiting quietly for you to finish with that ghastly person when you suddenly blew up. It was magnificent. Jane, tell me, does that funny little man really wear a wig?"

"Not that I know of. But everyone will think he does now, won't they?"

Gerry gurgled happily. "Oh, how priceless. Jane, you must come and lunch with me at the Ritz. It's ages since I saw you. I've got tons to talk about."

"You'll have to treat me, Gerry, if you really want the honour of my company. I'm absolutely stony broke."

"Who isn't, darling? But I can just run to it. Come on. Let's hail a cab."

In the taxi Jane reflected ruefully that her friend's idea of stoniness was quite a different thing from her own. To Gerry it meant trying to stretch to the end of the year an annual allowance of fifteen hundred pounds. It was ironic that there should be such a contrast between the situations of two girls whose families a few generations previously had been of about equal standing—two girls who had gone to the same school, been "finished," and come out together. But whereas the present Earl of Burford was still the proprietor of estates in the West Country and Scotland, a series of disasters and blunders over a period of sixty or seventy years had gradually eroded the Clifton fortune. So that Jane had to fend for herself.

She sighed. "Oh, Gerry, why am I such an ass? Why do I keep throwing over all these jobs? I know it's irresponsible, but I can't seem to help it."

"Well, nobody could put up with being spoken to like that. You had no alternative."

"Oh, but I did. To bite my lip, keep smiling, and say I was very sorry if I hadn't given satisfaction. That's what any of the other girls would have done. It's what I've done—often."

"I don't know how you stood it for so long."

"Because I wanted to eat. It's as simple as that."

A minute later the taxi pulled up outside the Ritz. "Come along," Gerry said, "you'll feel better after a good lunch. No banting today. Let's forget our figures and have a real blow-out."

It was while they were drinking their after-lunch coffee that Gerry suddenly said: "I say, I've just realized you're a free woman. You can come down to Alderley for a bit."

"Oh, it would be heavenly. But I must start job-hunting again."

"Bunkum! You needn't begin straight away. You need a breather first."

"But, Gerry, I explained, I'm practically on my beam ends. I can't afford—"

"You're not going to be any worse off by spending a few days with us. It won't cost you anything to live while you're there. Look, I'm motoring down in the Hispano-Suiza tomorrow—oh, of course, you haven't seen her, have you? She's absolutely my pride and joy. She's got a nine and a half litre V12 engine. Does over a hundred miles an hour. Pushrod ohv, two twin-choke carbs— sorry, I'm being a bore. Where was I? Oh, yes, you must come with me, you must, you must."

Jane laughed. "All right. It's terribly sweet of you. Thanks awfully. But I can't come tomorrow, really. I must put in a few days job-hunting first. Next Thursday OK?"

"Lovely."

"Actually, it's just what I need. Who else is going to be there?"

"Oh, some Americans called Peabody. He's a fabulously rich Texan. Oil, I think. We've never met them, but he's got one of the biggest collections of old guns in the States and he wants to see Daddy's. No doubt they'll both be excruciatingly boring the whole time about frizzens and multiple matchlocks and things. Then Richard's bringing down a couple of foreign diplomats, and a man called Thornton from the Foreign Office. I gather they're all going to be engaged in some sort of government talks. Richard asked if it would be all right and of course Daddy agreed, though why they've got to use Alderley, I don't know."

"How—er, how is Richard?"

"Fine. He comes down about every fourth or fifth week

14

on average. It must be quite a long time since you've seen him."

"Over two years."

"Really? Yes, of course, the two last times you came he was abroad. He'll be thinking you've been avoiding him."

"Anyone else expected?"

"Well, I'm afraid—and you must brace yourself, darling —that Algy is."

"Algy Fotheringay? Oh, Gerry, no! What on earth possessed you?"

"Not me—Daddy. Algy buttonholed him at the Eton and Harrow match. You know how he's always trying to cadge invitations. Daddy swears he couldn't get out of it. I've just about forgiven him. But I'm afraid we're all going to have to spend merry hours listening to Algy talk about himself, his rich and fashionable friends—and food."

"If you go on like this," said Jane, "I may well change my mind."

2

Ten Downing Street

THE Honourable Richard Saunders sat in the ante-room to the Prime Minister's private study and wondered again why the Old Man had picked him, a junior minister, for this job.

It had happened just two weeks ago. He had been unexpectedly summoned into the Presence and given a surprising little lecture.

"It is highly important that a stable democratic state friendly to Britain be maintained in central Europe as a bulwark against both Fascism and Bolshevism," the Prime Minister had ended. "The Duchy fills that rôle admirably. Now, however, she is extremely weak militarily and is threatened by invasion from several directions. The Grand Duke has approached us for assistance. We want to help; it will be in our interest to do so. However, in the present political climate we cannot be seen wantonly distributing British arms to small states, or committing British troops to war in Europe, without something tangible to show in return. The Grand Duke has indicated his willingness to cede to the British crown certain so far unspecified colonial territory, where rich mineral deposits have recently been discovered, but which the Duchy herself is not in a position to exploit. He is sending an envoy to negotiate a treaty whereby we will supply military aid in exchange for this territory. What has to be determined is precisely what aid we supply—and how soon—and exactly what land is given in return. Until we can announce full agreement, the negotiations must remain secret. Clearly, neither the Foreign Secretary nor I can be involved. We want you to handle them. Think you can manage?"

Richard, of course, had said yes. But still he wondered —why him? Today he was determined to find out.

"The Prime Minister will see you now, sir."

Richard rose and entered the private study.

"Ah, come in, Saunders."

The Prime Minister got to his feet and held out his hand as Richard went forward. "Do sit down."

Richard sank into a deep leather chair and waited silently as the Prime Minister lit his pipe, leant back and eyed him keenly from under bushy eyebrows. "All set?"

"I think so, Prime Minister."

"The Foreign Secretary and the War Minister have briefed you fully?"

"They have."

"Splendid. There are just one or two points I want to emphasize. Firstly, the importance of speed: this matter must be settled quickly. Intelligence sources tell us that the threat the Duchy faces is very real, and growing. Fortunately, we are in broad agreement with the Grand Duke. Naturally, their envoy will try to obtain from you more than we are able to give, earlier delivery of the equipment, and so on; and to keep the extent of the territory they hand over to us to a minimum. They may also want British troops stationed permanently within their borders. But we wish to avoid this: you must keep it in reserve as an ultimate concession. Your task is really going to be extremely delicate: obtaining the best possible deal for Britain consistent with assuring the security of the Duchy."

The Prime Minister reached into his drawer and took out a large envelope, which he handed to Richard. "Here are the blanks for the draft treaty. Simply fill in the details in accordance with the agreement you reach. The final terms are entirely your responsibility: we will stand by whatever arrangements you make. You'll have Thornton from the FO present as your adviser throughout, of course. You've met him?"

"Yesterday for the first time. He seems very able."

"He is extremely able. Highly experienced, and with a full knowledge of our capabilities."

"Which is something I conspicuously lack, I'm afraid. Needless to say, I'm deeply honoured, but I cannot help wondering why you asked *me* to undertake these negotiations."

"Why do you think I asked you?"

"Well, obviously if outsiders weren't to realize the im-

17

portance of the talks, you had to pick somebody fairly junior; yet it's patently too important a matter to be handled at Embassy level. But I can't help feeling there are others better qualified than I to deal with it. The only real asset I have seems to be—" He broke off.

"Seems to be what?"

"Alderley."

"How do you mean, Saunders?"

"Well, I do spend a certain amount of time there with my brother and his family. My sister-in-law gives frequent house parties. Then there are the Alderley collections—foreign visitors do call now and again to examine them. So the visit of two men from a small European country, at the same time as I'm there myself, will cause no talk; while at the same time they will be well out of sight of the press and the diplomatic corps. In addition, the house is extremely secure. From the moment the Foreign Secretary asked if my brother would be willing to entertain a couple of strangers for a few days, I had in mind that that might have been the reason I was chosen."

The Prime Minister shook his head firmly. "No. Those factors did enter into our calculations and Alderley did seem an eminently suitable venue. However, there were others equally suitable. I did not select you because your brother happens to be Earl of Burford, but because you are the best junior minister for the job. All right?"

"Very much so. Thank you."

"Please convey to the Earl and Countess our gratitude for their co-operation. I shall, of course, write when the talks are concluded. There are to be some other guests present, I understand?"

"Yes, an American couple by the name of Peabody. He's in oil, I believe."

"They are the only ones?"

"The only ones I know of. My niece, Geraldine, may have some friends of her own down. Why—do you think she ought to be asked to put them off?"

"By no means. We do not want to give the impression that anything out of the ordinary is taking place there. By the way, how much do you know about your opposite number?"

"Adler? Only that he's been very much the power behind the throne in the Duchy in recent years."

"Comparatively few people know even that much. The

18

general public have barely heard of him. Have you realized how rarely you see his picture in the papers?"

"No, I hadn't. But, of course, it's quite true."

"He's an American, you know."

"Really?"

"Well, half-American. His mother was American and he lived there most of his life until about ten years ago. He met the present Grand Duke at Harvard and returned to the Duchy with him. Since then he's never looked back —even though he's reported to be a highly unconventional kind of diplomat. Apparently he's the one man in the country who's got all the facts necessary to conduct the negotiations at his finger tips—without even having to consult notes."

"Remarkable. Who is this man Felman who is accompanying him?"

"Oh, just a young aide or secretary of some kind. We are not, at their request, laying on any official welcome. We do not even know by what means they are travelling to this country. They will make their own way to Alderley."

The Prime Minister rose. "Now I must wish you luck— and assure you that if you succeed in bringing these negotiations to a satisfactory and speedy conclusion, I will not let the fact go unrecognized."

3

Guests

"**I**'D just like to see any doggone jewel thief try to lift my Carrie's diamonds. Even this guy they call the Wraith." And Mr. Hiram S. Peabody looked pugnaciously up from the magazine out of which the faces of himself and his wife stared at him.

His secretary, John Evans, who had been the one to bring the magazine to him, gave a sigh. "I'm afraid you might get your wish, HS."

"Let him. I'll be ready. My daddy didn't make half a million bucks, and I didn't turn it into fifty million, by backing down to cheap crooks."

The two men were in the sitting-room of Mr. Peabody's suite at the Savoy Hotel in London. Evans, a thin young man, with hornrimmed glasses and a small toothbrush moustache, was looking harassed. "The Wraith is hardly a cheap crook, sir, And I'm not suggesting you should back down to anybody."

"Tell me, John, how long have you been with us?"

Evans looked surprised. "Nearly twelve months."

"For the last four of those we've been travelling all over Europe—Athens, Rome, Venice, Paris, and a whole lot more. All that time Mrs. Peabody has had her necklace with her. You've never worried about it before. Why start now?"

"Well, for one thing, your exact movements—and the facts about the necklace—have never been publicized in advance before."

"But if this Wraith character moves in society, as he's reputed to, he doesn't need a newspaper to tell him where the wealthy are, does he?"

"There's more to it than that. This magazine lays down a definite challenge. It's not the sort of thing the Wraith will want to ignore. He's been inactive for some time now and he's probably ready for a comeback. This is thoroughly irresponsible journalism, if you ask me."

"I'm with you there. Guess I was a mite foolish to speak so freely to that reporter."

Just then the door opened and Mrs. Peabody sailed in. A smart woman of about fifty, with a round, good-natured face, she was followed by four package-laden page boys. They put down their burdens, were lavishly tipped, and departed. Carrie Peabody turned a beaming face towards her husband. "Hiram, you really should have come. I've had a dandy morning. And I don't suppose I've spent more than two thousand dollars, either."

"That's swell, Carrie. Come and look at this." He held out the magazine to her.

Carrie took it and gave an exclamation of pleasure. "My, isn't that nice? You look truly distinguished, honey."

"Read what it says."

"Read it to me, will you? Save me putting my eyeglasses on." She passed the magazine back.

Peabody read aloud: "Mr. and Mrs. Hiram S. Peabody, who arrived in London this week on the final stages of a European tour. Mr. Peabody is the well-known Texas oil millionaire, and the owner of one of America's largest collections of antique firearms. Mr. and Mrs. Peabody will be staying for some days at Alderley, the country seat of the Earl and Countess of Burford. His lordship is, of course, well known as the foremost collector of old weapons in England, and Mr. Peabody is anxious to inspect the Alderley collection—and to show Lord Burford one of his own prize possessions, which he recently purchased in Rome.

"Mrs. Peabody is here seen wearing her famous diamond necklace, which is insured for five hundred thousand dollars. It is perhaps fortunate that Alderley has one of the most elaborate burglar-alarm systems in Britain. Otherwise, we feel the necklace might make an almost irresistible target for the notorious Wraith!"

"The Wraith?" Carrie Peabody said sharply. "That's that society jewel thief, isn't it—the one who always leaves a calling card?"

"That's it. A drawing of a sheeted ghost. John figures we should deposit the necklace in the bank before we

21

go to Alderley—just to be on the safe side. What do you think?"

Mrs. Peabody shook her head firmly. "Oh no. Definitely not. I've never stayed with the English aristocracy before. Our hosts may have a title going back hundreds of years and a famous stately home full of art treasures and antiques. But they don't have a diamond necklace worth half a million bucks. I must have something to keep Uncle Sam's end up. I'm taking my necklace—and wearing it."

Her husband chuckled. "Good for you, Carrie. That's just what I figured you'd say. Something else our hosts lack, too, is a unique, personally-engraved Bergman Bayard 1910/21 semi-automatic pistol, custom-made as a gift for Tzar Nicholas II just before his assassination. I'm sure looking forward to seeing the Earl's face when I produce it."

In the smoking-room of his club, Algernon Fotheringay was talking.

"Then, of course, next week I'm toddling off down to jolly old Alderley for a few days. You ever stayed at Alderley?"

His listener, the laziest member, and the only one who hadn't made a hasty withdrawal within moments of Algy's appearance, yawned and shook his head.

"Oh, it's an absolutely topping place. The Earl and Countess are ripping people. So's Gerry, their daughter. I met the Earl at Lord's the other day. He almost begged me to go down. They're having quite an exclusive party, and he said that it wouldn't be the same without me at all."

"I'm sure that's true."

"I had several other invitations outstanding, of course, including one to Cliveden. I was tempted, but when it came to making a decision, Alderley won. The grub there's ripping. The cook does a perfectly spiffing steak and kidney pie—and she's a dab hand at soufflés, too, don't you know. The only possible fly in the ointment is that a little bird tells me there are going to be a brace of foreigners there. Some Americans, too, but I don't bar Americans. No these are a couple of *real* foreigners. Of course, if they turn out to be too hairy at the heel, one can steer clear of them. It's a pretty big place. But the danger is that Lady Burford might be tempted to dish them up some of their national dishes. I was staying once at a place in Norfolk, don't you know. Of all things they had a bally Arab staying there. A sheikh or something. Well, you know, the chief delicacy among those johnnies are sheep's eyes. Well, would you believe it—I say, old man, are you all right?"

But the laziest member was asleep.

4

The Richest Man
in Europe

IN a large house on the outskirts of Paris, in a big
curtained room lit only by a flickering log fire, a little
wizened, bald old man sat in a high-backed armchair. He
was holding an open atlas and studying a map of Africa.
Eventually he raised his head, revealing a hooked nose
and deep set eyes, which burnt with a fierce light. His
lips were thin and his jaw long and pointed. His hand,
which now moved slowly to press an electric buzzer set
into the low table beside his chair, was scrawny, like a
claw. The old man looked frail, almost lost in the big
chair, dwarfed further by the high vaulted room, and by
the huge old-fashioned grate, the flickering light from
which barely reached the distant recesses of the room.
Yet in spite of his frail appearance, there was strength
in the old man—strength in the talon-like hand, strength
in the jaw, above all strength in those dark and darting
eyes. The old man dominated his surroundings, as for
forty years he had dominated the lives of thousands of
people all over the world—people who had never even
heard his name.

That name was Jacob Zapopulous. It was a name which
was spoken of with something like awe in the financial
centres of the world; the name of a man who, through a
combination of financial genius, treachery, graft and
blackmail, had made himself the richest man in Europe.

Jacob Zapopulous had no friends and no partners, for
he trusted nobody. There were, however, half a dozen
men in his employ in whose efficiency and sense of self-
interest he had confidence, and it was one of these who

now entered the room in response to the buzzer. He was a man of about forty, with a pale face, light blue eyes, and blond, short-cropped hair. He was a Dane and his name was Bergsen. He crossed the room silently, his feet sinking into the sumptuous Persian carpet, stopped in front of his master, and stood waiting impassively. Thirty seconds passed. Then in a high-pitched, cracked voice, Zapopulous spoke—slowly, quietly, and distinctly.

"I have a task for you. It is for you alone. Succeed in it and you will become a rich man." He held out the open atlas. "Take this."

Bergsen did so.

"Look at the territories shaded blue."

"May I switch on a light?"

"Yes, yes."

Bergsen crossed to the mantelpiece, switched on a lamp, and stood under it with the atlas in his hands. "Yes?"

"How many are there?"

Bergsen was silent for a few seconds. Then he said: "Thirteen."

"Yes, thirteen—scattered throughout the entire length and breadth of the continent. An absurd empire! Each individual colony isolated, not one of them large enough ever to be of any importance. The fools in the Duchy could never even afford to develop them slightly, to exploit them in any way. Not one of those colonies has any industry to speak of, no large-scale commerce, no great city. They are peopled almost exclusively by primitive native tribes and poor white farmers. A few of the people are tolerably prosperous, most of them just scratch a living. The territories are backward, moribund, useless. Or they have been until now."

Bergsen looked up, but said nothing.

"In one of those primitive, useless colonies, something has been discovered," Zapopulous said, and his voice was harsh. "What it it, I don't know: gold, diamonds, oil. And I don't know in which one. But I do know that the Duchy is quite unable to take advantage of the discovery. She is weak, threatened from all sides, desperate for military aid. And in return for this she is prepared to cede that entire territory, her only negotiable asset, to the British."

Zapopulous sat up. His voice grew higher. "Some people in one of those little blue patches are sitting on a fortune.

And they do not know it. Their land will shortly become immensely valuable. Whereas now—now, most of those people could be bought out for a comparative pittance."

Bergsen nodded. "If we knew who they were. You want me to find out?"

"You are quick, Bergsen. That is just what I want: ascertain what mineral has been discovered and the precise location of it. Bring me the information when you have it; later you can handle the actual purchasing of the land on my behalf."

"You don't think that there might be a risk? If the whole colony—whichever it is—is going to change hands, might not individual landowners lose their holdings?"

"Pah! Nonsense!" Zapopulous made a gesture of contempt. "Whatever government is in control of the territory, it will not affect the legal standing of individuals. The British government are not Bolsheviks. They will respect the rights of landowners. I intend to be the biggest landowner. And the first essential is to discover which land is involved. Find out—and ten per cent of everything I make will be yours."

He was being offered the chance of a fortune, but Bergsen displayed no emotion—and offered no thanks. He waited, aware that there was more to come.

"Very shortly," Zapopulous continued, "a representative of the Grand Duke, a man named Martin Adler, is going to England to discuss the deal with a British government minister. Who this minister is to be and where the meeting is to take place, I do not know. How you make use of this information is entirely up to you. But obviously if by some means you can learn what is said at the meeting, your job will be done. Now go. Do not come again until you have all the information I require. Turn the light out before you leave."

5

Misgivings

"WHAT'S the matter, Nick? You looked worried."
Martin Adler's companion in the first class compartment of the Orient Express looked up and gave a smile. "Why do you speak in English, Martin?"

"Good practice for you, pal. Frankly, yours sounded a bit rusty when you were speaking with those Britishers at the reception the other day. So I think we'll stick to English for the rest of this trip. Nothing makes an English-man feel more superior than to hear another guy talking broken English."

Nicholas Felman hesitated for a moment; then: "OK, you are the boss," he said carefully. "How did that sound?"

"Not bad. Keep trying. But you didn't answer my question: why the anxious visage?"

Felman shrugged. "Just nervousness. I have never had experience of anything so important as this. I cannot help wishing that you had not asked for *me* to accompany you, Martin. You need someone older—someone more prac-tised at negotiations of this nature."

"Don't be such a hick. I didn't want one of the old guard of stuffed shirt diplomats—all hot air and protocol. I wanted someone I could talk to, who understands me, and whom I understand. You know just as much about the situation as any of those old buffers."

"Yes, I believe I do, and I do not want you to think I am not grateful for your confidence. It is merely that I cannot bear the thought that I might fail my country. The situation is so perilous—"

"You don't need to tell me that, old buddy. But I don't see in what way you *could* let the country down. If we should fail, I'd be to blame. But the British aren't our enemies. They want to help. These are just going to be cosy, informal talks to decide the precise details of how best they can help—and how we can best repay them."

"You make it sound very easy. But I have this feeling that things are not going to proceed quite as smoothly as you anticipate."

"You're a natural-born pessimist," said Adler.

"Blasted foreigners." George Henry Aylwin Saunders, twelfth Earl of Burford, muttered the words as he sat in a wicker chair on the terrace at Alderley, gazing out across the tree-dotted parkland, baking under the summer sun.

A few yards from him, a hammock had been slung from a hook on the wall of the house to the spreading branch of a nearby tree. At that moment the only indication that Lord Burford was not simply soliloquizing was a bulge in the underside of the hammock; but after a quarter of a minute his daughter's voice from inside it murmured: "Which ones? Richard's? What's wrong with them?"

Ten seconds passed before Lord Burford said: "Coming here. Disturbin' things. Having to be entertained. Shown round. Talked to. Not understandin' English all over the place. Deuced unsportin' of Rich to foist 'em on us. I blame your mother, I'd have said no."

"You wouldn't—any more than you did to Algy."

"Well, no, p'raps I wouldn't. But I'd have said yes in a grumblin' manner. Algy Fotheringay's different. No one can keep him away when he decides to pay a visit. He's like a 'flu germ."

"Well, what about the Peabody's? You invited them, too."

"Couldn't very well get out of it. Been correspondin' with the feller for donkey's years. When he wrote saying they were coming to England and he'd like an opportunity of examinin' me collection I had no choice. But I didn't *want* 'em here."

"You'll thoroughly enjoy having them. You love showing off your guns."

"Not to Peabody. I know these Americans. He'll keep insistin' how much better his stuff is, and crowing over this new piece he's picked up in Italy. Yankees!"

"I thought he was a Texan."

"He is. Why?"

"I don't think he'd take very kindly to being called a Yankee."

"Why not?"

"A Yankee's an American from the northern states. Even you must know Texas is in the south."

"Oh, I can't be bothered with these fine distinctions. Americans—Yankees—foreigners: they're all the same. I don't mind entertainin', but I like to choose me guests. And I like 'em to be English. But when the party consists of two central Europeans, two Yankees, and the only two Englishmen are some septic civil servant and Algy Fotheringay, it makes a chap feel like emigratin'."

"Perk up. Jane's coming too, remember? You like her."

"Course I do. Charming gal. Wish all your chums were as presentable. She doesn't make up for the others, though. I think we're in for a ghastly few days; and you know one of the worst things about it? However gruesome things get, I won't be able to blame your mother. She didn't invite one of 'em."

"Perhaps she'll meet somebody up in town today and ask them down."

"If she does, it'll be somebody absolutely charming, who'll be personally responsible for saving the weekend from complete disaster. You mark my words."

"Excuse me, but it is Lady Burford, isn't it?"

The Countess of Burford paused in her leisurely examination of Messrs. Harrod's furnishing fabrics and surveyed the speaker through her lorgnette. He was a tall, bronzed young man with deep-set blue eyes, and he was smiling at her engagingly.

"It is." She looked for a few seconds, then her face cleared. "Of course. You're Lucy Arbuthnot's nephew."

"My word, you've a good memory."

"For faces. I can never remember names."

"Giles Deveraux."

"Of course. We met at her Yorkshire place about three years ago."

"That's right. How are you, Lady Burford?"

"I'm very well, thank you."

"And the Earl—and Lady Geraldine?"

"They're both in excellent health, I'm thankful to say. You're looking extremely fit. Been abroad?"

"Yes, for several months."

"Lucky you."

"It was far from pure pleasure. My work keeps me on the move."

"Oh, of course, you're in the Navy, aren't you?"

"Was. I left a couple of years ago. I'm by way of being a writer now."

"Indeed? What sort of things do you write?"

"All sorts. Bit of freelance journalism. Travel books. Guide books."

"And what is the current project?"

Deveraux hesitated. "Um, well, I'm about to start on a hectic series of country house visits in connection with a commission I've received."

"Oh?" Lady Burford fixed him with an enquiring gaze.

Deveraux seemed a little embarrassed. "Actually, I've been asked to write a book on famous British houses—one of a series. Each one will cover a different period—Elizabethan, Queen Anne, Georgian, and so on."

"And which period are you dealing with?"

Deveraux cleared his throat. "Er, late Stuart."

"I see." Lady Burford looked at him somewhat grimly. "And why isn't Alderly being included? It's the finest smaller Carolean mansion in England."

"Unfortunately, the houses have been more or less selected by now—"

"Which ones?"

"Well, Eltham Lodge, Ramsbury, Honington, Belton—"

Lady Burford interrupted with a snort. "You must be out of your mind! Some of those places aren't in the same class as Alderley."

"Well, that's a matter of opinion—"

"Fiddlesticks! It's not a matter of opinion: it's a matter of fact. You ever been to Alderley?"

"No, I've seen pictures of it."

Lady Burford dismissed pictures with a gesture of contempt. "You definitely committed to include certain houses and no others?"

"Not really. There's nothing about it in the contract."

"Then you must come and see Alderley. Don't make up your mind until you've been. I guarantee that afterwards you'll agree Alderley's got to be included. How about it?"

"It's very kind of you. But I'm afraid my time has been very carefully allocated. At the end of next week I'm off to Eltham, and from then on it's a different house every few days until the end of October—and my publishers want the manuscript by the New Year."

"I see." Lady Burford thought for a few seconds. Then she said: "What about this coming weekend?"

Deveraux hesitated again. "I haven't made any firm arrangements. I was hoping to do some sailing . . ."

"You must come to us. Now don't argue. You'll be under no obligation to include Alderley afterwards if you don't want to. But you must see the place and talk to my husband before you make up your mind. Will you?"

"Well," Deveraux smiled, "if you insist."

"That's settled, then. We are giving a small house party, anyway, so it'll fit in quite nicely. Thursday suit you? That's when most of the others are arriving."

"Thursday will be admirable."

"Trains at quarter-past ten, twelve, two, and four from Paddington. Takes about two hours. Tell the guard to stop at Alderley Halt. It's an old right we've got."

"Actually, I shall probably motor down."

"Well, it's easy enough to find. Look forward to seeing you. "Bye."

"Good-bye, Lady Burford. And many thanks."

Deveraux watched Lady Burford walk briskly away. Then he strolled off in the other direction. He gave a little smile to himself. "Well, my boy," he muttered under his breath, "congratulations. I must say you arranged that very nicely indeed."

Richard Saunders eyed the man who was sitting opposite him, fastidiously sipping coffee out of a Crown Derby cup. Then he pushed an open box of cigarettes across his desk. "Cigarette, Thornton?"

"Thank you, no, Minister. I do not smoke."

Richard took one himself and lit it before saying: "I asked you here this morning because I thought it would be a good thing if we got together for a chat about the weekend. I wondered if you have any advance thoughts about these talks."

Edward Thornton put down his cup, took out a white linen handkerchief and carefully wiped his lips. Then he said: "None of any importance, I'm afraid, Minister."

He was a tall, thin individual, wearing pince-nez and a wing collar. There was little in his personality to impress.

Yet Richard knew him to have a reputation as one of the Foreign Office's best negotiators—a man of icy logic, decisive speech, and prodigious memory.

Thornton said: "As I see it, the negotiations should be relatively straightforward. After all, there is no clash of interests involved. HMG and the Grand Duke want basically the same thing."

"The details may be tricky, though. That's where you're going to come in especially."

"I feel confident I am adequately prepared and can advise you with a high degree of accuracy."

"Good man. Just talking to you makes me feel happier. As you know, I'm very much a new boy at this sort of thing. But I don't think you'll let me make too many floaters."

Thornton smiled thinly. "I do flatter myself that I have saved the reputation of more than one minister in the past. But I do not expect to be called upon to do so on this occasion."

"I hope you're right," said Richard.

Merryweather, Lord Burford's venerable and stately butler, sat in his pantry and ticked names off his list. Mr. and Mrs. Peabody, the Royal Suite; the European gentlemen, the Cedar and the Blue bedrooms; Miss Jane her usual; Mr. Fotheringay, the Green; Mr. Deveraux, the Grey; Mr. Thornton, the Regency; and Mr. Evans, the Dutch. All the rooms ready. Everything done.

Merryweather read through the list once more, and suddenly a strange feeling of uneasiness smote him. There was something wrong with this house party. It was in a way different from any of the others, the many, many others, which he had supervised at Alderley. The guests were too diverse, too disparate. Most of them were strangers to each other, and even to the Family. There weren't enough ladies, either, which made the seating at table awkward. And speaking of that . . .

Merryweather made a quick count of the guests. Yes, there would be thirteen to dinner. It was the last-minute addition of this Mr. Deveraux that had caused it. The Family wouldn't mind; but it was to be hoped none of the guests was superstitious. Had her ladyship realized? Perhaps he should point it out to her.

Merryweather got to his feet. He found himself hoping

her ladyship would find an additional guest. For thirteen to sit down this evening would somehow set the party off on quite the wrong foot. And he couldn't help feeling that the weekend was handicapped enough already, without further troubles being added to it . . .

6

Jane's Journey

IT always gave Jane a kind of thrill to tip the guard and loftily instruct him to have the train stopped at Alderly Halt. It seemed so delightfully feudal and anachronistic. So it was with a slight disappointment that she heard him reply cheerfully: "That's all right, miss. We're stopping there anyway. There are some other passengers for Alderly on the train."

But he took her hard-earned shilling none the less. Jane found an empty compartment and leaned back in a corner seat, reflecting that it was a pity she'd mentioned it. On the other hand, she was forewarned now. For one of the other passengers for Alderley might well be Algy Fotheringay, and it would be ghastly if he spotted her and she was stuck with his company all the way. But she probably didn't need to worry: Algy would certainly be travelling first class and wouldn't deign to enter her humble third class compartment. In fact, she thought, with a momentary and uncharacteristic twinge of bitterness, it was probably rare for any but first class passengers to have the train stopped at Alderley.

It was horrible to be poor. Especially when your family had once been rich and influential. It had been in her grandfather's day that things had really started to go wrong. It was almost frightening, looking back, to see how quickly a family fortune could shrink. Her father, an only child, might have been able to retrieve the situation. But he had been a charming and impractical dilettante, who had never really woken up to the fact that he was becoming poor. His wife and family had not realized it, but the cost of giving Jane and her younger sister Jennifer a good education, and enabling them to do the London season, had almost bankrupted him. He had died suddenly, almost penniless and uninsured.

Mrs. Clifton and her daughters, then twenty and eighteen, had found themselves in great difficulties. They had raised some capital by selling both the country home near Bath and the town house, and had rented a smaller one just outside London. But it had been clear that they would not be able to live on this money for long, and that at least one of the girls would have to get a job.

Jennifer had been fortunate. She had been the beauty of the season the previous year, and at school had shone in theatricals. She had decided to try her luck on the stage. She could afford no formal training, but her looks and a natural talent had stood her in good stead. After a few months in provincial repertory, and a cameo part in a talkie by the promising young director Alfred Hitchcock, she had got her big break: the chance of going on a long tour of the United States with a leading Shakespearian company. Jennifer had jumped at the opportunity.

With the tour half over, she had died suddenly.

It had fallen to Jane to break the news to her mother that Jennifer had succumbed to a rare disease and been buried in the mid-west of America.

Mrs. Clifton had never really recovered from her husband's death, and the new shock had been too much for her. She suffered an immediate heart attack and died eight weeks later.

A distraught Jane, who in a little over eighteen months had seen her whole world collapse, had tried to drown her grief with gaiety. She had joined up with a set of the so-called bright young things and had lived wildly for twelve months.

She had gone through about half her money when, one day, on a visit to Somerset, she had run into one of her father's ex-gardeners. He had told her that his young son was dangerously ill. There was no hope for him—unless by a miracle he could be taken to Vienna for a new operation perfected by an Austrian surgeon.

Jane had seen the family's doctor, checked with her bank, and agreed to pay all the expenses.

The operation was completely successful. But Jane had been cleaned out: she had no choice but to get a job.

This, however, had not turned out to be so easy. She was without qualifications, and she shied away from the usual sort of position taken up by girls of her class in similar circumstances—nursery governess or paid companion. Eventually she had obtained a post as a hotel receptionist—only to walk out after one week when the manager made a pass at her. Then she had moved to the country to become an instructress at a riding school. This had gone well until one day she had seen a pupil, the seventeen-year-old daughter of a rich company promoter with a large family of potential clients, viciously beating a troublesome horse. Jane had snatched the whip and used it to give three or four vigorous thwacks across the back of the girl's riding jacket.

In London again, Jane had got work with an antique dealer. This had lasted until she had discovered she was expected to ask certain customers to pay with two cheques—but to enter only one in the books. Finally had come *Mayfair Modes*. It was not the sort of job Jane had ever imagined herself doing—but she had been getting desperate. Almost from the first, however, she had known she wouldn't stick it long. In a way the blow-up with Bottway had come as a relief—even though she had put herself in a terrible stew financially.

But she wouldn't think of that this weekend. She was going to enjoy herself, pretend she was accustomed to ease and plenty—and forget that in a few days she'd have to start looking for a job again.

It would be good to be back at Alderley. Like going home. Her visits there, and her friendship with the family, had been the one unchanging feature of her life. And, thank heaven, the weather had cleared up. After a long hot spell it had rained heavily that morning and Jane had feared that a wet period had set in; but now it was lovely again, and all the fresher for the rain. Jane stared out of the window and watched the city give way to suburbs, and the suburbs in their turn to soft green meadows.

When at last the train puffed into Alderley Halt, Jane heaved her two small cases down from the rack, jumped out, and, without waiting for a porter, ran awkwardly with them to the barrier. She stopped, and glanced back; she wanted to see who else alighted. Two men were getting down from a first class compartment. Jane gave a puzzled frown, then her face changed, as from another compartment the figure of Algernon Fotheringay emerged. He was wearing a blazer in two-inch wide red and yellow stripes and the most voluminous plus-fours Jane had ever seen. She turned and hurried out to the sleepy station yard.

Lord Burford's Rolls Royce was waiting there, the liveried figure of the chauffeur Hawkins, an old ally of Jane from her schoolgirl days, standing beside it. Jane walked across. "Hullo, Hawkins."

Hawkins touched his cap and permitted himself a discreet smile of welcome. "Good afternoon, Miss Jane." He came forward and took her cases from her.

"How are you, Hawkins?"

"Nicely, thank you, miss."

"Hawkins, who were you expecting to meet?"

"Yourself and three gentlemen, miss: two foreign gentlemen—Mr. Adler and Mr. Felman—and Mr. Fotheringay."

"They'll be out in a minute. I think I'd prefer to walk. I'll take the short cut. Tell her ladyship I'm on my way, will you?"

"Very good, miss."

Carrying just her bag, Jane started off briskly. The station was about a quarter of a mile from the quaint, old-world village of Alderley itself. Jane walked along the single street, passing the *Rose & Crown,* Jenkins's Garage, and the half dozen shops, and out the other side onto a quiet country lane. Shortly she came to a stile on the left. She clambered over it and set out across the field along a footpath—just as the Rolls passed along the lane behind her.

Five minutes later Jane topped a rise, climbed over a low wall that marked the boundary of the Burford estate, and looked down on one of her favourite sights—Alderley itself, solid and serene, flanked by its outbuildings and surrounded by the tree-dotted park, the lake, which at one point came within thirty yards of the house, the beech copse, and the home farm half a mile beyond. All was spread out below her like a perfect miniature model, and Jane just stood looking down in sheer pleasure.

From here the house, which was built basically in the form of three sides of a rectangle, looked like a reversed capital E with the centre bar missing. It was three storeys tall, but outwards from both top and bottom bars of the E—the east and west wings—a two-storey extension projected.

Jane started down the slope. Another ten minutes' brisk

walking and she came to the higher wall which flanked the park. Somewhere the other side of the wall she could hear the sound of a car engine, getting closer. It was noisier than the Rolls, and Jane wondered if it was Gerry in the Hispano-Suiza. She followed the wall until she came to a small door. She stopped, opened her bag, and took from it an old key. This had been given to her by Lord Burford many years previously—an act considered a special mark of esteem—and had been treasured by Jane ever since. She opened the door, passed through, and locked it after her. As she did so, she realized the sound of the car engine had stopped. Just in front of her stood a row of trees, flanking the drive. Jane passed between two of them—and was instantly splattered from head to foot by a thick spray of cold, dirty water.

She stood gasping, rubbing the water from her eyes. She heard a squeal of brakes, got her vision cleared, and looked up to see a bright red two-seater open car, which had pulled up a few yards along the drive, facing the house. The young man in the driving seat was looking back over his shoulder, an expression of dismay on his face. He hurriedly put the car into reverse and backed down the drive until he was level with her. In spite of herself, Jane could not help noticing that he had blue eyes and very brown skin.

"I say, I'm most terribly sorry," he said, in a pleasant voice. "I didn't see you until it was too late. Are you in a frightful mess?" He broke off. "Oh dear, you are, aren't you?"

For five seconds Jane was speechless. Then she let fly. "You blithering idiot! Do you always dash along private drives at ninety miles an hour in complete silence?"

"Well, no. Actually, I was only doing about thirty. And it was so beautifully peaceful I just switched off the engine to coast a little way and enjoy the quietness."

"Not caring two hoots that you might knock down some poor footbound pheasant—"

"Footbound pheasant? Is there one of those around here? How very sad. What's the trouble? Rheumatism of the wings?"

Jane breathed deeply and clenched her fists at her sides. "I meant peasant," she hissed. "You didn't care what footbound peasant you knocked down."

"Oh, I assure you there was never any danger of that.

I could have stopped very quickly if anybody'd stepped out. I mean, I didn't hit you—"

"Thanks for that, anyway."

"Everything would have been all right but for an unfortunate combination of circumstances. There's a hollow in the road just here, you see, and it's right in the shadow. Also it was full of water. It must have been left from the heavy rain this morning—"

"I didn't think it had been left from last January's snow!"

"I'm trying to say that I'm not really all to blame. I was simply cruising quietly along. I couldn't see the hollow or the water or you. And you know, you did step straight onto the drive without pausing."

"Oh, that's right. Motor like a lunatic, half-drown me, and then blame me."

"I was not motoring like a lunatic and I am not blaming you. I'm merely exonerating myself. It was an accident." He was starting to sound cross.

"I sincerely hope it was an accident! Because if I thought you did it on purpose—"

"Oh, don't be such an idiot." He swallowed and, apparently with something of an effort, said quietly: "Are you going up to the house? If so, can I give you a lift?"

"No thank you. I think I'll be safer if I stay a considerable distance from you."

"Just as you wish." He slammed the car into gear, accelerated, and let in the clutch—just a little too rapidly.

Now, while they had been talking, the water from the puddle, having spread itself over a larger area when the car first passed through it, had been soaking into the surface of the drive around the rear wheels. The result could have been anticipated: as the wheels spun fiercely Jane was comprehensively sprayed by a fine cloud of muddy specks.

The young man looked round, realized what he had done, made as if to stop again, seemed to think better of it, and roared away.

Jane stood quite still. The only word she managed to get out was a long drawn out "O—oh." Then she started to march up the drive, muttering imprecations against all motorists. After a few minutes, however, her anger gave way to misery, and she found herself blinking back tears. Absurd to get so upset. And she'd made a bit of a fool

39

of herself, too, by flying out at him like that. But she hadn't been able to help it. She was going to arrive at Alderley looking like a drowned rat. Moreover, her feet and legs had taken the worst of the deluge, and in her traps, now presumably at the house, reposed the only other pair of silk stockings she possessed in the world. She would have to change into them as soon as she arrived; and if they should ladder before she had a chance to get the ones she was now wearing washed and dried, she would have to borrow a pair from Gerry. Humiliating.

Before Jane got in sight of the house she stopped, cleaned her face as best she could with her handkerchief, applied some powder and lipstick, and ran a comb through her hair. Having done this, she felt a little better. But not a lot.

When she approached the house she was tempted to avoid the front and to enter by a rear door. But this would entail a long march, round the stables and orangery and through the kitchen garden—and then she would have to find a servant to notify her hosts of her arrival. So she strode up the shallow steps, past the huge Doric columns, to the great front doors, and rang the bell.

The door was opened almost immediately by the pontifical Merryweather. "Good afternoon, miss."

"Hullo, Merryweather," Jane said, going into the big, oak pannelled hall. "How are you?"

"I am in my usual excellent health, thank you, miss. May I take the liberty of enquiring after your own?"

"Oh, I'm pretty fit, but as you can see wet and dirty. I had a contretemps with a—a—" Jane gulped, "a *gentleman* in a red tourer."

"Yes, miss. Mr. Deveraux explained there had been a slight accident."

"Oh dear," Jane said. "Tell me, Merryweather—is he a guest here?"

"Yes, miss."

"Crumbs. I hoped he was just calling about the drains or something. Do you know if he's a great friend of the family?"

"I believe not, miss. He is here professionally rather than socially. I understand he is writing a book on the stately homes of England and is considering including Alderley in it."

"I see. That's something, anyway. I'd like to go straight up to my room now."

"Certainly, miss. If you will just follow me."

"Is it my old room?"

"Yes, miss."

"Then don't bother to take me. I know my way. Have my traps been taken up?"

"Yes, miss. You should find Marie unpacking."

"Fine. Tell Lady Geraldine I've arrived, will you. Merryweather?"

"Certainly, miss."

"Thank you." Jane made her way up the grand staircase. At the top she turned right along the main corridor, and at the end left into the east wing. She opened the second door on the left and went in. This was a small but pleasant room, overlooking the courtyard. Gerry's maid, Marie, a pretty, dark girl, had just completed the not very arduous task of unpacking. She gave a shriek of horror upon seeing Jane.

"Mille tonnerres, mademoiselle! What 'ave they done to you?"

"Not they, Marie. One man in one car."

She took off her tweed coat and skirt and gave it to Marie for sponging and pressing. Then she removed her precious stockings and handed them to her too, with a request to have them laundered with the greatest possible care. After Marie had left, Jane washed her face and hands, and gingerly put on her other stockings. This operation completed without mishap, she was just struggling into her dress, when Gerry burst in.

By the time she had given an account of her misadventure with Deveraux, Jane felt more cheerful. Gerry proved a most satisfactorily sympathetic audience, exhibiting just the right amount of indignation on Jane's behalf. When they'd talked the subject out, she said: "Now, tell me: have you got a job yet?"

Jane shook her head.

"Good. Then you can stay as long as you like."

"I wish I could, but honestly I must get fixed up soon."

"Jane, darling, can't you marry money?"

"Lead me to it."

"Perhaps I have. Perhaps there's somebody here. Pity you got off on the wrong foot with Giles Deveraux. He's not exactly good looking, but he's rather attractive. And

I should imagine he's pretty well-heeled. His car looks expensive."

"Probably stolen."

"Then how about one of our mittel Europeans? I don't know anything about them financially, but these continental diplomats usually come from ancient aristocratic families."

"Somehow the idea of being married to an ancient European diplomat doesn't really appeal to me."

"No, honestly, they're not at all bad. I was very agreeably surprised. I was expecting terribly stiff and formal old buffers with thick accents and monocles and little imperials, bowing and kissing my hand all over the place. But actually they're both quite young. They speak very good English—in fact one of them could be an American. The secondary one—Felman, I think—is a bit quiet, but the chief one, Adler, has really got a lot of charm—and SA."

"Sorry, darling, but I'm not keen. What about this oil millionaire? Any chance for me there?"

"I don't know. He hasn't arrived yet. He is bringing his wife with him, though."

"Perhaps I can entice him away from her. Alternatively they might have an eligible son."

"If they have, he's not coming with them. Just a secretary. Name of Evans."

Jane applied lipstick. "I'm not interested in secretaries unless they've got double-barrelled surnames if English, have "Van" in front of them if American. Is that the lot?"

"There's somebody Richard brought. From the FO. I don't know if he's married. Nice enough, but a bit of a stick. Then there's Algy—"

"Stop. There's no need to be obscene. I must say, none of them sound awfully promising. It seems likely that in the immortal words of Amelia Bottway, I shall 'ave to try h'elsewhere—somewhere where they keep a adequate stock. However, I will inspect what you have."

"Then if modom will follow me to the terrace, she can do so at her leisure while taking tea."

7

Tea on the Terrace

THE two girls went downstairs and onto the terrace. After Lord and Lady Burford had greeted Jane, the Countess started on introductions.

"May I present Mr. Alder? Miss Clifton, a very dear friend of the family."

Alder smiled easily, stood up and held out his hand. He was pleasant-looking in a quiet, inconspicuous way, slightly below average height, slim yet nonetheless with a look of latent strength.

"Miss Clifton, I'm very glad to make your acquaintance."

Jane suddenly knew what Gerry had meant by charm. Adler had oodles of it and, without meaning to, Jane found herself smiling more broadly then she usually did on meeting anyone new.

"Mr. Felman," said Lady Burford.

Mr. Felman was tall, fair-haired, with finely-moulded sensitive features; he was also plainly ill at ease. He murmured a few words of greeting as he shook hands, then backed away quickly, glancing at Adler as he did so; it was almost as though he were seeking approval.

Lady Burford moved on. "Mr. Thornton."

Thornton gave a severe little bow of the head and shook hands with stiff, cold fingers.

"And Mr. Deveraux," Lady Burford said.

Jane turned towards the fourth man. She had decided to be very magnanimous, to make no mention of the incident on the drive. She was all ready, therefore, to be extremely pleasant to Mr. Deveraux. But as he looked at her, she clearly saw his lips twitch and she knew at once that he was remembering her as he'd seen her last, standing, dripping and furious, on the drive. At that second all her good intentions went to the wall.

So as Deveraux stepped forward, she extended her hand, smiled sweetly, and said: "Mr. Deveraux and I are acquainted, Lady Burford. How are you, Mr. Deveraux? Have you assaulted any other young women since last we met?"

And as Lady Burford stared blankly, Jane turned away to where Algy Fotheringay was still sitting, a cup of tea in one hand and a chocolate éclair in the other, and greeted him in a tone of great warmth. "Hullo, Algy. How delightful to see you. How are you?"

Algy got hurriedly to his feet, knocking over his chair as he did so, held out half an éclair to Jane, tried to transfer it to his left hand, couldn't do so because of the cup, popped the éclair into his mouth, swallowed, and gave Jane limp and sticky fingers.

"I'm in topping form, thanks, Jane. How's yourself?"

"Very well, thank—"

"I've had a really ripping year, Jane. In January I went to Le Pinet as a guest of Lady Masters. Do you know her? Charming woman. She said I was the most unforgettable guest she'd—"

"You must tell me all about it, sometime," Jane interrupted firmly. "I shall look forward to it." And she moved away towards the last member of the party. This was a tall, slim man, impeccably dressed, with a moustache and dark hair touched with grey at the temples; he was twinkling at her out of deep-set eyes.

"Hullo, Jane. It's been a long time."

Jane held out her hand. "It has, hasn't it?"

"I've been here often enough, but you never seem to have come then."

"I am a working girl, you know. Anyway, it's very nice to see you again Unc—er, Rich—" She smiled. "What do I call you now?"

"I think you should follow Gerry's lead, and call me Richard. Come and sit by me and let's have a chat."

He pulled forward a chair for her. She sat down. Richard looked at her with pleasure. He saw a tall girl, very slim, with ravenblack hair, a generous mouth, clear grey eyes, and a straight, steady gaze.

"It was Gerry who started me calling you uncle," Jane

said. "We were at the share-everything stage—and that had to include you."

"I insisted on her dropping the uncle part a long time ago. It's nice to be called it by a schoolgirl, or even by a debutante; but once she'd grown up it just drew attention to my advanced age."

"Advanced age my foot!" Jane accepted a cup of tea from a footman, added milk, and selected a cucumber sandwich from a laden trolley wheeled up by a maid. "You are sixteen years older than me. I know that because when I was sixteen Gerry and I worked out that you were twice my age. I am now twenty-four, so you are forty."

"You are superbly diplomatic, Miss Clifton. Actually, I'm forty-one."

"All right, forty-one. And a future Prime Minister, according to at least one paper."

"Oh, that. They talk a lot of rot. But you didn't come to Alderley to talk politics. Tell me, what was the meaning of that cryptic remark you made to Deveraux?"

"Oh, don't let's talk about it now. I'll explain later."

"As you wish, madam."

Jane gave a mock groan. "Why does every conversation I have today remind me irresistibly of *Mayfair Modes?*"

"Ah yes, the job from which you so magnificently departed. Gerry told us about it. Have you got another one yet?"

Jane shook her head.

Richard frowned. "I wonder if I could help to fix you up. What sort of thing do you want to do?"

"Anything at all. But I've no qualifications."

"There must be jobs going where you don't need formal qualifications."

"Do tell me what. I can't type or do shorthand, I've got no academic degrees or certificates, no artistic or acting talent. I talk in the right sort of accent, know the right sort of people, wear the right sort of clothes. I speak passable French and good German, ride moderately well and play a reasonable game of tennis. And there are thousands of girls who can say exactly the same thing. So what do you suggest?"

Richard pursed his lips. "Nursery governess?"

"Can you honestly see—"

He interrupted with a laugh. "All right. I wasn't serious. Doctor's receptionist?"

"No thanks. I don't want anything to do with medicine or illness."

"Some other sort of receptionist?"

"I've already tried it at an hotel—without great success."

"Hm, you're a problem, aren't you? A nice problem, but a problem nonetheless."

"I'm a problem to myself. It's no good. I shall have to become an adventuress."

"Well, I'll keep my eyes and ears open for something else all the same—just in case you don't take to it."

"Thank you. But enough of me. Tell me about your foreign friends." She nodded towards Adler and Felman, who were talking to Lord Burford and Geraldine. (She noticed with satisfaction that Deveraux had been cornered by Algy.)

"Oh, they're not really friends. They're over here on official business and the PM thought it would be nice to give them a taste of a typical English country house party."

"I see. And what about Mr. Thornton?"

"Oh, he's just a chap from the FO I've got friendly with lately. Nice fellow. We're all going to take the opportunity to do a bit of work, actually. Just some routine business."

"Is this your first visit to England, Mr. Adler?" Gerry asked. By dint of some complicated conversational manoeuvres, she had at last managed to divert her father and Felman into one channel of discussion and had then gently detached Adler from it.

"Yes, Lady Geraldine, it is."

"Too soon to ask how you like it, I suppose?"

"What I've seen so far I've liked very much. Particularly your charming house."

"It is nice, isn't it?"

"When was it built?"

"Commenced 1670. One of the genuine, if smaller, stately homes of England. Complete with secret passage."

"Really?"

"Yes, I'll show you later, if you're interested."

"I'd be fascinated. I've never seen one. They're such wonderfully romantic things."

"After dinner tonight, then. I'll take you to the room

where one end of it comes out, and I bet you half a crown you can't find the entrance."

"You're on."

"There are quite a lot of interesting things here, actually— if you can afford the time off from your talks."

He smiled. "Don't you have a proverb in this country: something about all work and no play being a bad thing?"

"Something like that."

"Then I'll certainly find time for as many conducted tours as you're able to give me, Lady Geraldine."

He looked steadily at her. Gerry seemed to find this disconcerting. "Er, another cup of tea, Mr. Alder?" she said hurriedly.

"Thank you."

Gerry signalled to the footman, then watched Adler surreptitiously as he took a fresh cup and added lemon. Strange; his features were quite ordinary really. But he certainly had something. And she felt sure he could tell a few stories. She was starting to look forward to the next few days . . .

"Personally," said Lord Burford, "I'm very attached to the good old-fashioned cesspit."

He had been finding Nicholas Felman a most admirable listener. The young man did not initiate much conversation himself, but he was splendidly attentive and sympathetic to the trials and tribulations of an English landed proprietor: the iniquities of county council and government, and the insatiable demands of tenants—the latest of these being for modern sewage disposal.

His last remark, however, was overheard by the Countess, who interrupted firmly: "George! I'm sure Mr. Felman has no desire to converse about such a matter. Kindly desist."

"Oh. Sorry, m'dear."

"It's clearly time to change the subject. Tell me, Mr. Felman, is this your first visit to England?"

Felman gave a little start. "I beg your pardon? Oh— yes, it is."

"Have you been long in the diplomatic service?"

"Yes. Since I left University."

"Always stationed at home?"

"No. I did—let me see—two, yes, two years in Stockholm."

"That must have been enjoyable. A delightful city."

"Yes, very pleasant."

"We were there ten years ago. Tell me, do you know a charming little restaurant called Olsen's in Storkyrkobrinken?"

"No, I'm afraid not."

"Oh." Lady Burford fell silent. Strange that a professional diplomat, good-looking and presumably intelligent, should seem so gauche, so ill at ease, so, frankly, dull. Still, the Countess was not a person to give in so soon.

"I expect your family have been in the diplomatic service for generations, have they?" she asked next.

"What? Oh no. Actually, I'm the first."

It was hard work but the Countess persevered, gradually eliciting from Felman the information that he was unmarried and that his only close relative was a younger sister, Anna, a medical student. Then he appeared to make a great effort.

"You have a wonderful home, Lady Burford."

"I'm glad you like it."

"You seem to have quite large stables."

"Fairly. Do you ride?"

"A little."

"Then you must talk to my daughter. She's the keenest these days. Geraldine!"

"Yes, Mummy."

"Come and talk horses to Mr. Felman. Excuse me, Mr. Felman. I must go and speak to cook about dinner."

She got up and walked away. Gerry, who'd been getting on famously with Adler, looked a trifle put out, but she made her apologies and went across. Lord Burford, who had been listening to her conversation, leaned over and tapped Adler on the shoulder.

"Tell me all about this country of yours," he said.

"That's quite a tall order, sir. What exactly do you want me to tell you?"

"I don't know anything about it hardly. Tell me what I ought to know."

"Well, we're small, peaceful, and prosperous. The people are free and on the whole happy. We have what I suppose you'd figure was a pretty measly little empire, but which we're kind of proud of. I guess our main aim is just to keep things pretty much as they are."

"And you think Britain can help, is that it?" Lord

Burford spoke in a quieter voice. "And you needn't worry," he added. "I know this is all hush-hush. Me brother got the OK to give me an outline of what'll be going on. I do sit in the House of Lords and I have taken the oath of allegiance."

"Oh, I'm well aware nothing needs to be kept from you, Lord Burford."

"Keep as much from me as you like, my dear fellow. This sort of thing's not my cup of tea at all. Good luck to you, though."

"Thank you."

"You've spent most of your life in America, I understand."

"A good part of it."

"Would it be bad form to call you a Yankee?"

"On the contrary, I'd be honoured."

"Oh, capital. You must tell my daughter."

Adler looked a shade puzzled at this somewhat enigmatic remark, but he got no enlightenment, Lord Burford then asking: "How did you come to take up a political career in another country?"

"Well, I was born in the Duchy, of course. But my mother was American, and after my father died when I was eight, she returned to the States. The only connection I retained with the old country was a knowledge of the language. Then when I was at Harvard, the then Grand Duke, the present one's father, sent his son there to finish his education. Shortly after he arrived, he discovered that there was a solitary compatriot of his there also. He invited me to visit him. The short of it was we struck up a friendship, and when we finished he asked me to go back with him and become his aide. My mother had died about a year before and my best girl had just jilted me. I had nothing to keep me in the States. So I went. Over the years I've worked my way up. That's just about it. Rather a boring story, isn't it?"

"Have we ever met? Your face looks definitely familiar to me."

It was Edward Thornton who spoke, and Giles Deveraux turned with relief towards the source of the precisely enunciated words. He had been listening for what seemed like hours to a lengthy discursion on some of the More Memorable Meals served to Algy Fotheringay by his aristocratic hosts, and the interruption had come opportunely in one of Algy's few pauses for breath.

"Is that so?" Deveraux said. "I fear that it's merely that I've got that sort of face. I can't say I reciprocate."

"In the war, perhaps? I was with the Somerset Light Infantry."

"I'm sorry to say I missed the show—by about two months. I was in the Navy afterwards, but not until after all the shooting had stopped. Frustrating. Still, I've seen a fair amount of the world since—both in and out of the service."

"You've travelled extensively?"

"I've got around."

"Whereas I have never been farther than four or five European capitals."

"And you with the FO!"

"That is the precise reason. I am attached to the European section."

"Ah, then it's unlikely we met abroad, anyway. Probably we've just sat next to each other at Wimbledon or Twickenham."

"I think not. I have little interest in games. You are a writer, I understand."

"Of a sort."

"I have to admit never recalling having seen any of your books."

"Probably because I write under various pseudonyms."

"May I ask what names?"

"Oh, G. K. Chesterton, Ernest Hemingway, Virginia Woolf."

For a split second Thornton looked startled. Then he smiled icily. "I'm sorry. You think I'm being too inquisitive."

"Not at all. Merely a feeble joke. No, I'm not a best-selling author. Mine are mostly travel and guide books. And I write magazine articles. I use the names Jonathan George and Andrew Lewis mainly."

"Oh, I am familiar with the name Jonathan George. A work on Malaya, I believe?"

"One of my slightly better-known efforts."

"Surely a far cry from the stately homes of England, is it not?"

"I believe in casting my net wide."

"Who are to publish this book?"

"It's for the American market, actually. A New York firm. I doubt that the name would mean much to you."

"What other houses are to be included apart from Alderley?"

"I'm not quite sure Alderley is to be included yet," Deveraux said. He listed some of the other houses.

"I see," Thornton said. "Your plans seem to be far advanced."

"Far enough, I think," said Deveraux. "Far enough."

8

The Secret Passage

MR. and Mrs. Peabody and Evans arrived about six. Jane, who'd had vague expectations of meeting the caricatured Texans of fiction, was pleased to find the Peabodys pleasant, unassuming people. She took to them at once.

The only person, in fact, who seemed not to like them, was Lord Burford himself. This puzzled Jane until Gerry explained the Earl's fears and suspicions about the guns. "He'll be all right in a few hours, though," she added, "when he realizes how nice they are."

However, this wasn't to be. During the pre-dinner drinks, Gerry found her father standing alone, looking glum.

She poked him in the ribs. "What's wrong?"

"Don't. Him." He gave a jerk of his head.

"Peabody?" Gerry glanced towards the millionaire— a squarely-built man of about fifty-five, with a pugnacious jaw and rimless glasses. "I thought you'd be happier now you'd seen how pleasant and quiet and intelligent he is."

"That's the trouble. I was hoping he'd be a brash, self-opinionated fool, who'd just used his money to buy blindly. But I've got a horrible feeling he's going to turn out to know more about guns than me."

"Oh really, Daddy, don't be ridiculous. I'm sure you'll get on like a house on fire when you really know him. Now go and talk to him."

"Oh, all right." Lord Burford squared his shoulders and ambled across. He tapped Peabody on the shoulder. "Tell me all about Texas," he said.

In spite of Merryweather's forebodings, dinner that evening was a very successful occasion.

The food—clear soup, dover sole, saddle of lamb with garden peas, strawberries and cream, and a fine Cheddar cheese—was superb. Lord Burford, having talked to Peabody, had, temporarily at least, got over his apprehensions and was a jovial host. Lady Burford, who, after Merryweather's warning had spent a hectic time trying to find an unaccompanied lady to invite at short notice, had at long last succeeded in getting hold of a Mrs. Carpenter, the relict of a former bishop of the diocese, who usually dined at Alderley a couple of times a year. So the Countess was happy, and determined not yet to worry about the same problem at future meals.

The guests seemed to get on well together. Mrs. Peabody wore her famous necklace, and the magnificent stones were an immediate talking-point. Peabody and Adler found a common interest in baseball. Felman seemed less ill at ease than earlier. Algy was eating too eagerly to bore anybody greatly. And Jane and Deveraux, finding themselves seated side by side, had caught each other's eye, hesitated, then both smiled tentatively. Thereafter—much to the relief of Gerry, who had arranged the pairing—they talked, formally at first, but later more cordially.

So the atmosphere was in every way thoroughly satisfactory, and as Merryweather supervised he wondered why he had earlier felt so uneasy. The house party was clearly going to proceed swimmingly.

After dinner, when the men joined the ladies in the drawing-room, Lord Burford made a short speech. "While everybody's here I'd like to explain something about our security system. As you know, there's a lot of very valuable stuff here—paintings, silver and personal jewellery, as well as quite famous collections of stamps, first editions, and coins. In addition, of course, there are my firearms and ammunition, which mustn't fall into the wrong hands. So to be on the safe side we've had a unique and, we think, foolproof burglar alarm installed. The drawback is that not only can nobody get in without setting it off, but nobody can get out either. Your bedroom windows will open six inches only. If you should force them wider—and, of course, you can do that quite easily in an emergency—or open or break any other window, unlock or force a door, you'll trigger the alarm off. Merryweather switches on—or if we're having a late night, I do—last thing after locking up, so I'm afraid that it's just not possible to go for a stroll in the grounds after that. Sorry."

Peabody said: "You can turn it off, I suppose, Earl? There is a master switch?"

"No. We wanted to be as secure as they could make us, and we had to think of the possibility of a really serious burglar—"

"Like this Wraith guy, huh?"

"Exactly. We had to think of the possibility of a thief like that bribing a servant to turn it off. So the thing's on a time switch. After it's primed it stays on until the morning, when it switches off automatically—at six-thirty this time of year."

"What would happen if a door had to be opened at night?" Adler asked. "To let a doctor in, say, if someone was taken ill."

"We'd just have to put up with the alarm bells for five minutes or so. Actually, they wouldn't cause too much of a disturbance. There's one in my bedroom, one in the butler's, and one in the hall. Unless you were a very light sleeper or left your door open, I doubt if you'd hear it in your room. Now, who's for bridge?"

Two games were soon started, one involving Lord Burford, Peabody, Felman, and Thornton; and the other Carrie Peabody, Richard, Algy, and Evans. Lady Burford sat with Mrs. Carpenter, who did not play.

Meanwhile, Gerry took Adler off to hunt for the entrance to the secret passage. Deveraux also expressed an interest in seeing it and went along too. Jane made up the fourth.

Gerry led the way across the great hall to the breakfast-room, which was at the eastern end of the main block. She went in, switching on the lights. The room was oak panelled and had french windows leading onto the front terrace. Heavy velvet curtains were at present drawn across them.

Gerry perched herself on the edge of the mahogany table and smiled at Adler. "Right. It's all yours."

He stared round. "I don't know where to start."

Deveraux said: "Can I help?"

"Sure. I figure I'm going to need it."

"If we find it, I'll expect a half-share of your winnings."

"I'm not at all sure that's fair," Jane said. "Mr. Deveraux is an authority on English country houses. He'll know just where to look. I think they're out to break you, Gerry."

"I'm no authority, I assure you," said Deveraux. "I haven't started to write the bally book yet. My entire knowledge of secret passages is drawn from the storybooks of my misspent boyhood."

The room itself was sparsely furnished. Apart from the table, there was only a large sideboard and a dozen or so upright chairs placed round the walls. A large cupboard was built into one wall. For over ten minutes, while Gerry and Jane sat on the table, smoking and making unhelpful remarks, Deveraux and Adler examined the room. They tapped at panels, twisted, pulled and pushed at each small protuberance, and stamped on every accessible inch of the floor. Eventually they were forced to give up.

Gerry stubbed out her cigarette, got off the table, and crossed to the cupboard. She opened it wide, then twisted the knob twice in each direction. Suddenly there was a click, and to the right of the fireplace one whole panel slid silently aside, revealing a black square, just large enough for a man bending low to pass through.

Adler stared. "Holy smoke."

"Well, well, well." Deveraux shook his head. "Most remarkable."

"It only works," Gerry told them, "when the cupboard door is wide open and the knob turned right-left-right-left. We think the cupboard was only put in as a sort of *raison d'être* for the knob."

"Fascinating." Deveraux walked across to the hole in the wall and peered in. "Can't see a thing."

"Allow me." Gerry pushed past him, stuck an arm into the blackness, fumbled for a moment, and withdrew it, holding an electric torch. "Don't let it be said that the Saunders are unprepared. Coming?"

"Where does it lead?"

"Wait and see. Mr. Adler?"

"Oh, sure. I'm not backing out at this stage—whatever terrors are in store."

"Then I'll lead the way. Are you coming, Jane?"

"Not this time, darling, thanks. Not in the only evening dress I've brought with me."

"I think it's pretty clean in there, actually. It's com-

55

pletely enclosed, so it can't get very dirty. Still, perhaps it would be a bit risky in white."

"Have a lovely time," said Jane.

Gerry disappeared into the opening, saying as she did so: "Keep your heads down."

Deveraux and Adler followed her. Jane heard Gerry's voice, muffled: "Mr. Adler, if you reach upward with your left hand you should feel a sort of handle. Will you pull it downwards?"

There was a slight rumbling sound and the panel slid into place. Jane left the room and made her way upstairs to the first floor, turned right along the main corridor, and then went through a door on the left into another large panelled room. It was filled with shelves, which were stocked with sheets and other household linen. She waited for a few minutes, then heard a bumping sound behind the wall, a panel slid back, and Gerry emerged, followed by the two men. They looked around them, blinking.

"Welcome back to civilization," Jane said.

"Where are we?" Adler asked.

Gerry told them. "Did you both enjoy it?"

"Well," Deveraux brushed a speck of dust from his cuff. "As secret passages go, I'm sure this one is one of the most delightful. But, frankly, if I should again have the occasion during my stay to proceed from the break-fast-room to here, I shall ask Miss Clifton to guide me by the overland trail—no matter what dangers we may face from hostile natives."

"I think you're a soulless beast," Gerry said. "I'm sure Mr. Adler appreciated the romance and mystery of it."

"Indeed yes, Lady Geraldine. In spite of having banged my head at least a dozen times, I consider it to have been one of the most deeply satisfying experiences of my life. And I must congratulate you on never once losing your way."

"What on earth was the passage built for?" Deveraux asked. "Isn't the house rather late for a thing like that?"

"Yes. Nobody really knows. My great-grandfather's chaplain is reputed to have said that it was to be assumed it had been installed in order to facilitate an irregular liason, but as Alderley was built by the first Earl, and it must have been included at his instructions, that theory hardly holds water."

"Something of a puritan, was he?" Adler asked.

"Precisely the opposite. He was the most notorious profligate in the county. And utterly brazen withal. He didn't care who knew about his activities—and the sort of ladies he entertained were hardly likely to have cared either. So a secret passage would have been rather an unnecessary expense. Probably he just wanted a secret passage for prestige, in the same way he wanted a—a lake, say."

"How does that sliding panel downstairs work?" Deveraux asked. "It's very ingenious."

"Oh, it's a highly complicated system of levers and springs and weights. It was added much later, by the fifth Earl, who was very mechanically minded. Before that it was just a matter of sliding the panel aside with your hands—as you still do this end. Incidentally, I hope you're both paying attention. You will be examined on the subject before you leave."

9

Friday Morning

FRIDAY dawned another glorious day.

At ten a.m. the official talks commenced in the small music-room, which was soundproof and had been set aside for the discussions. At the same time Lord Burford finished breakfast and ambled somewhat gloomily out to the terrace, where Hiram Peabody, who'd breakfasted earlier, was reading.

Lord Burford spoke heartily. "Mornin', Peabody. Lovely day."

"Good morning, Earl. It sure is." He folded up his paper.

"Sleep all right?"

"Fine, thank you. Actually Carrie and I are both notoriously heavy sleepers. But who wouldn't sleep well in a place like this?"

"Where's your missus got to?"

"Oh, she's exploring the house. The Countess kindly told her to feel quite free to go anywhere. She'll be happy as a cricket for hours just poking round on her own. It'll be the furnishings chiefly that'll take her attention, I guess."

"Capital, capital." Lord Burford coughed. "I was thinking, p'raps you'd like to come and take a dekko at my little collection now."

Peabody got to his feet with alacrity. "Lead me to it, sir. This is something I've been looking forward to ever since we arrived in Europe."

"Well, I hope it comes up to expectations, that's all. Come along, then. I'll take you up."

He led the way up the stairs and turned right. They went along the main corridor and at the end turned left into the east corridor; about half-way along it, Lord

Burford opened a pair of imposing double doors on the right and went through. Peabody followed. They were in a long gallery, which ran most of the outer side of the east wing. It was lined with paintings.

Lord Burford said: "These are our pictures. Supposed to be very fine, if you're interested."

"Oh, I'm sure they are. They certainly look beautiful. But I'm afraid I don't—I'm not . . ."

"Nor me. Come along." He crossed the gallery to another door, almost exactly opposite. This was the entrance to the top floor of the eastern extension, the ground floor forming the ballroom. Lord Burford took a bunch of keys from his pocket, unlocked the door and opened it. Four feet beyond this was another door. This was not locked. Lord Burford opened it, then stood back and ushered his guest in. Peabody went through—and stopped dead.

He was at the end of a long, high-ceilinged and delightfully-proportioned room, with tall french doors leading onto a balustraded balcony at the far end. Through these could be seen the beech copse and the lake. The room had a finely-moulded gilded ceiling, elaborately panelled walls, and a highly-polished floor.

But Peabody had eyes for none of this. For the room was crammed from end to end with hundreds of guns. They were of every shape and size, from tiny pistols up to several huge cannon at the far end. He looked round reverently for ten seconds, before turning to his host.

"Earl," he said. "During the last four months I've seen most of the sights of Europe—the Parthenon, St. Peter's, Notre Dame, the Tower of London—you name it. But this for me is the highlight. Now, where do we start?"

"Well, suppose first we have a quick survey of the whole collection, then later on you can examine the pieces that particularly interest you in greater detail."

"Lead on," said Peabody.

While Lord Burford was showing his collection, his wife had begun her task of impressing the glories of Alderley on Giles Deveraux. Determined he should miss none of the finer points, she had swooped on him shortly after breakfast and swept him off on the start of a detailed guided tour.

They commenced in the hall. "Right," the Countess

said, "let's first take a look at the staircase. We're quite proud of it. It's an early example of a type introduced at about the time Alderley was built. As you can see, the balustrades are composed of these pierced and carved panels in four-inch pine. The craftsmanship is considered particularly fiine. If you look closely at the acanthus foliage . . ."

Jane and Gerry had gone riding.

"I was frightfully glad you made it up with Deveraux," Gerry said. "It would have been awfully awkward if the two of you had kept up a running feud all over the weekend. He's really much too nice to fight with, anyway, don't you think?"

She spoke casually, but cast a glance sideways as she asked the question, searching her friend's face.

The two girls had dismounted to rest their horses on the extreme southern border of the estate and were sitting on the bank of the little meandering river which eventually fed the Alderley lake.

Jane was lying back with her eyes closed. "He's nice enough, I suppose, but he's not really my type. And you needn't use that innocent tone with me. I know just what's going through your scheming little mind."

"It's not a little mind."

"All right, your scheming big mind. Use it to scheme yourself into getting off with Martin Adler."

Gerry screwed up her nose. "I'm not sure I really want to. I could understand someone falling for him in a big way—I think I would have myself three or four years ago. But he's just a little too charming. I'm not sure I don't like Nick Felman better. He's nice I think. Even though he is like a cat on hot bricks most of the time."

"He's worried about something."

"Yes. Now and again he manages to throw it off—but he can't keep it up. I wish I knew what was wrong."

"Why don't you ask him?"

"Oh, I couldn't."

"Why not? I would."

"You might get away with it. He'd probably tell me to mind my own business."

"I don't know why you should think that. He hasn't given the least sign of being interested in me."

"And, of course, he's not really your type, is he?"

Jane laughed.

"In fact, none of them are, are they? You'll have to try elsewhere, after all."

Jane hesitated fractionally before saying: "Looks like it, doesn't it?"

The pause lasted only a second, but it was enough for Gerry. She gave a squeak, grabbed Jane by the shoulders, and stared into her face. "Jane—there is someone. There is, isn't there?"

"No, don't be silly." Jane sat up and looked away.

"There is. I can tell. Who? Oh lor'—not Martin Adler—not after what I said?"

"Of course not."

"Evans, then, the secretary? But you've hardly spoken to him. And it couldn't possibly be Thornton."

"Oh, Gerry, really!"

"Algy! Not Algy—I just won't believe it. But there isn't anybody else. I don't understand. Apart from them, Daddy, Mr. Peabody and Richard are the only men—" She broke off with a gasp as she noticed Jane's eyes flicker. "Richard! Not Richard? Darling, you're not in love with Richard?"

Jane didn't answer.

"Jane, I just don't believe it!"

"Nobody's asking you to." Jane spoke snuffily.

"But he's so much older than you."

"He is not. He's sixteen years older. Which is nothing. Not that it would make any difference if it was a hundred and sixteen years. There never has been, and never will be, anything between us, so just shut up."

"Darling, I'm sorry. I honestly had no idea you felt like that." Gerry sounded rather dazed. "How long—I mean, when did you first . . ." She tailed off.

"When I was about seventeen." Jane's voice quavered a little.

They both sat silently for a few minutes. Then Gerry said: "I think it would be ripping."

"What would?"

"For you and Richard to team up."

"You don't sound as though you thought that."

"Well, it sort of took me on the hop. But now I've had a chance to think about it, I'm beginning to *see* you together."

"Well, forget it. It's never going to happen."

"But for heaven's sake, why not?"

"Because he just doesn't think of me that way, that's why not. To him, I'm just his little niece's little friend."

"Then it's up to you to open his eyes."

"Never." Jane shook her head firmly.

"Oh, don't be silly, Jane. I don't mean you've got to *vamp* him."

"What else would it amount to?"

"You've just got to make him see you for what you are—a fully mature and very attractive woman."

"Thanks for the compliment, but nothing doing. He's either interested in me, or he's not. I did hope that after such a long break he might see me in a new light. I've avoided him, you know, for over two years. But when we met yesterday, nothing happened. He was pleased to see me, friendly, interested, helpful. And that was all. So let's just leave it at that, shall we, and talk about something else."

"No, let's not. I think you'd be crazy to let things stop there. Look, why don't I have a word with him—"

She broke off and winced as Jane grabbed her fiercely by the arm. "You dare, Gerry! I swear I'll never speak to you again if you so much as hint to him how I feel."

Gerry tried to unwind Jane's fingers from her arm. "Jane, let go, you're hurting."

"Promise me you won't ever mention it."

"All right—I promise."

"To Richard—or to anybody else."

"All right."

Jane let go, dropped down onto her back again and stared at the sky. Gerry rubbed her arm.

"Your trouble, Jane, is that you're just too proud."

"Maybe. But I will not make myself cheap—for anything or anybody. Besides," Jane rolled over onto her stomach and spoke a little less vehemently, "he's probably got a girl already."

"I don't think so. Not a regular one, anyway. There are women he takes out, of course, but no special one, I'm sure. I believe there was a girl once he was in love with, but that was a long time ago."

"Oh? When?"

"During the war, when he was in France. I've got an idea there was some sort of tragedy about it. I don't know any details. He's never talked about it. But I vaguely remember hearing him telling Daddy some story when I was quite a little girl."

"I suppose she died, did she?"

"I honestly don't know. Probably. I just remember him and Daddy sounding rather grim, then seeing me and shutting up. I could try to find out."

"No don't bother. There's no point in dragging up the past."

Jane got to her feet and brushed down her jodhpurs. "Come on, let's give these beauties of yours a really good gallop."

Richard Saunders was feeling a little worried. The talks were not going quite as he had anticipated. It was not that, so far at least, any real differences had arisen between the sides; but matters were certainly not proceeding as smoothly as they should be.

The trouble, to Richard's mind, lay in the attitude of Adler. He appeared to expect the British to make a number of firm commitments, yet seemed unwilling to reciprocate himself. He repeatedly asked for facts and figures regarding the proposed military aid, but so far had been strangely unwilling even to mention the existence of the land which was to be handed over in return— let alone discuss it in detail. Already Richard had made concessions—had promised the delivery by a certain date of specific equipment. But no corresponding concession had been forthcoming. It was very puzzling. Richard wondered if he had said anything which might have led Adler to distrust him. If so, he would have to find out what it was and put things right as quickly as possible.

Now Adler was giving a long, repetitious and quite unnecessary peroration about the great peril faced by his country. When he eventually stopped, Richard suggested a coffee break. He rang the bell and the coffee arrived a minute or so later. After the footman had left, the two sides drifted to different ends of the room.

Richard cocked an eyebrow at Thornton. "Well?"

"Odd, Minister. Very odd."

"I'm glad you agree. I was beginning to think it was *me*!"

Thornton shook his head. "No, it's Adler. He's behaving

very strangely. There's something here I don't understand."

"It's almost as though they're trying to go back on their government's word—trying to avoid ceding any land."

"I know."

"Do you think they could have discovered that these territories are much richer than they originally estimated?"

"I would say there's more to it than that. Something peculiar is going on here. I've never known anyone conduct negotiations in the way Adler is."

Richard looked at him keenly. "Then what is the explanation?"

"I don't know—yet."

"Well, what's our next move? Concede a little more?"

"That would not be my advice."

"You thought I was wrong to give in just now, didn't you?"

Thornton hesitated. "Well, frankly, I would not have done so."

"Maybe you would have been right. I simply thought it was time for somebody to make a gesture of good will."

"Oh, I appreciate your motive, Minister. And you've certainly put yourself in the right. But I would recommend firmness now—press hard for more details of this territory. That I think is vital."

Adler said to Felman: "What do you think?"

"Saunders is worried."

"I know. I'm getting to feel quite sorry for the guy."

"Sorry for him!"

"Yes, he seems a decent fellow. I don't want to louse up his career."

"Then you know what to do."

"Talk sense. Anyway, if he does strike out over this business, at least you won't have to blame yourself. Because, to be frank, Nicholas, you haven't been a great deal of help this morning."

"What do you expect? I'm not exactly used to this sort of situation."

"I'm not used to it myself. I've never handled anything like it before. I'm not enjoying myself, you know. I like these folk—Saunder's brother and his wife, those two girls. Nothing would give me greater pleasure than to spend another two days here, inspecting the old boy's collection, seeing over the house, playing tennis with the chicks, then shake hands all round and go home. But I can't and you can't either. So I'm afraid you're going to have to make the best of it."

Before Felman could reply to this, Richard spoke from the other side of the room. "Well, gentlemen, shall we get down to business again?"

"Here's a rather nice fourteen-barrel volley gun," said Lord Burford. "Made by—"

"Dupe & Co., around 1800?"

"Yes, but let me tell you—"

"Remind me to tell you something about Dupe's later on. Now, let's have a look at that case of percussion pistols."

"Oh, the Devillers." Lord Burford picked up the case. "About 1830?"

"Twenty-nine, actually." He handed the case to Peabody.

"What a beautiful pair of gold-damescened duellers," Peabody said reverently.

"Calibre point—"

"Point fifty. I know. Multi-groove rifling, right?"

"Right. The two pocket pistols—"

"Point four-four, I think. Folding, single selective triggers. Now, talking of double-barrelled pocket pistols, let me tell you about something I picked up in New Orleans a year or so back."

Lady Burford flung open a door and went in. Deveraux followed her meekly. "This is known as the Parlour. Note the bolection moulding of the fireplace. Nothing like black and white marble."

Deveraux peered at the fireplace. "Oh, very fine indeed."

"Also the oak wainscot. And the enriched architraves round the windows. Right, come along. We can examine everything in more detail later. I want to show you the Royal Suite while the Peabody's are out. The bedroom has an Angelica Kauffman ceiling."

"Ah," said Hiram Peabody, "what's this?" He pounced.

"A French arquebus, eh. Very nice . . . double crowned muzzle . . . brass orthoptic sight . . . about 1600?"

"That's right," said the Earl.

"I've got a similar one myself. Only mine . . ."

The morning passed peacefully.

10

Friday Afternoon

SINCE it was uncertain just when Richard and Adler would want to break off the talks, a cold buffet lunch was served that day.

The afternoon proceeded much as the morning. The talks continued in the small music-room. Jane and Gerry played a couple of sets of tennis with Deveraux and Evans. When they'd finished, Jane, prompted by a vague sense of duty, settled down on the terrace and let Algy talk to her. Gerry went to make some adjustments she claimed were necessary to the Hispano. Deveraux and Evans both went to do paper work. The Earl and Peabody spent the entire afternoon with the collection. And Lady Burford took Mrs. Peabody along to her boudoir for a quiet *tête-a-tête*.

"Tell me, Lady Burford, do you like guns?" Carrie Peabody asked the question a trifle diffidently.

"Like them? Let us say I've learned to live with them."

"Yes, one has to do that. What I really mean is, do you take an interest in them?"

"Not in the least. Do you?"

"I never have. But I sometimes wonder whether I should try."

"Well, of course, I don't know your husband well, but I'm sure George would not welcome *my* trying to take an interest in *his*. He would have to keep explaining things to me and answering my questions, and that would make him highly impatient."

"Oh, Hiram likes talking about his guns—to anybody who will listen. I think he'd enjoy educating me in the finer points. What stops me chiefly is a fear of what it might lead to."

"How do you mean, my dear?"

"They take up so much of his leisure time already. Naturally I am thankful that he has gotten this hobby. If he didn't, he'd probably spend all the time he now devotes to guns at the office, which wouldn't be good for him. His heart's a little weak—"

"I'm sorry. I didn't know."

"It's not a serious condition, as long as he takes things fairly easy. Our doctor told him some years ago that he had to learn to relax. Guns were his way. He'd always been interested in them, but it was after that that they really became a passion with him. It's only consideration for me that stops him giving even more time to them. If he thought I was an enthusiast, too, I really don't think we'd get anything else done at all, out of business hours."

"You might actually *become* an enthusiast—have you thought of that?"

Mrs. Peabody chuckled. "I hardly think that's likely. I quite like some small ones. They can be very pretty with their ivory or silver inlay."

"Oh, I don't mind the pistols and things like that. It's the cannon I object to."

"Cannon?" Mrs. Peabody stared. "The Earl has cannon up there?"

"But yes. Not many, I'm glad to say, because I managed to talk him out of going in for any more. But he's got half a dozen really big pieces."

"Oh dear." A look of consternation appeared on Mrs. Peabody's face.

"What's the matter?"

"Hiram's never gone in for anything like that. I just hope he doesn't get ideas."

Just at that moment Lord Burford was saying: "And down this end, as you see, I keep the heavy stuff."

"Which is where I guess I get a trifle out of my depth. I know very little about artillery."

"Really?" Lord Burford seemed to perk up a little at these words. "Then let me try to enlarge your education." He cleared his throat and took a deep breath.

"Now this first little job is one of the earliest machine guns. Invented in 1718 by James Puckle. Six chamber cylinder. Each chamber has to be primed through the touch hole. Fired by a conventional flintlock mechanism fitted to the barrel. Its weakness was a loose-fitting breech mechanism which allowed a lot of gas to escape. All the same, this type of gun was reported as firing sixty-three rounds in seven minutes under test conditions in 1772. Next is a British 2.75 inch mountain gun. This was the basic weapon of the Indian mountain artillery. Introduced 1914. An improved version of the original ten-pounder "screw" gun. Replaced after the war by the 3.7 inch Howitzer. Next we have a thirty-two-pounder carronade —made at the Carron foundry in Scotland, you know. This one's off *HMS Victory*—Nelson's flagship at Trafalgar. Range about five hundred yards. This next giant's a circus cannon. Used by Burundi the Human Cannonball to set up a world record of 165 feet. The barrel's sixteen feet long. Fired by compressed air. The electrical compressor plugs into the mains. Takes three or four minutes to build up pressure. Triggered by that lever and the barrel elevated by this handle. Now we come to a Maxim Nordenfeldt 75 mm. These were used by the Boers in the South African war. Hydro spring recoil system. They're light and—"

Lord Burford broke off. "Not boring you, am I, old man?"

Peabody was looking a bit dazed. "Not at all," he said.

"Good. Where were we? Oh yes. Next a Becker Semag cannon. This was a forerunner of the Oerlikon gun, and . . ."

In the music-room Richard got to his feet. "I think," he said, "that it might be a good idea if we called it a day now. I know it's early, but we don't seem to be making a great deal of progress and we may do better if we start fresh tomorrow morning. I don't quite know what's gone wrong today. There must, I think, have been some sort of misunderstanding between our respective superiors, and it might be necessary for one or both of us to take fresh instructions before the morning. I hope now we can forget our differences and spend the rest of the day pleasantly."

"Oh, I'm sure we can," Adler said with a smile. "We don't want to spoil the weekend for your brother's other guests. And I think, Saunders, that you are tending to exaggerate the differences between us. I'm sure that by tomorrow evening everything will have been settled satisfactorily."

"I sincerely hope so," Richard said.

They left the room and walked to the hall. Felman went straight upstairs. Adler paused and seemed to hesitate for a moment. Then as Richard and Thornton walked on, he called out: "May I make a 'phone call, please?"

Richard turned back. "Yes, certainly. The telephone room is along here. I'll show you." He led Adler to the door and asked: "Is it a trunk call—long distance, that is?"

Adler seemed somewhat surprised by the question. His eyebrows went up. "Yes—that is, if you don't mind—"

"Of course not. I'm sorry; I wasn't being inquisitive. I was just going to explain the procedure. You ask the operator for 'Trunks'."

"Thank you."

Richard started to move away. Then he stopped and said: "You're welcome to ring the Grand Duke himself, if you think it'll help."

Adler smiled. "I don't think that will be necessary."

Richard went back to the hall, where Thornton was waiting for him, and said quietly: "He's making a trunk call."

"Indeed?" Thornton looked interested. "His embassy, do you imagine?"

Richard nodded. "So I would guess—and probably to arrange for them to inform the Grand Duke that the ploy has failed and he's going to have to start giving away some land."

"I trust you're right. We must find out something about this territory soon. I hope I may say without disrespect that I think your firmness this afternoon was admirable."

"My dear chap, I'm sure in no circumstances could you be disrespectful. Thank you for your support. I suspect that certain of your colleagues would have been urging me to give way—anything to avoid a disagreement. Now, how about a drink?"

Jane entered the drawing-room through the french windows at the same time as Martin Adler came in by the door.

"Ah, Miss Clifton."

"Good afternoon, Mr. Adler. Business finished for the day?"

"Yes, we decided to knock off early. You haven't seen Felman anywhere, have you?"

"I'm afraid not. Mr. Saunders and Mr. Thornton are on the terrace having a drink—they may know."

"It's of no importance. A drink sounds good, though."

"I was just going to ring for one myself."

She rang the bell, then threw herself down onto a settee. "Whew! I have been acting as captive audience to Algernon Fotheringay for a full ninety minutes and I'm exhausted."

"Fotheringay likes the sound of his own voice, does he? I've barely spoken to him as yet."

"You won't get much chance to speak to *him*, either. Algy will speak to *you*, though, some time. You won't be able to get out of it, I warn you."

Just then Merryweather entered in answer to the bell. Jane said: "Merryweather, could I have some lemonade, please?"

"Certainly, miss. And you, sir?"

"I'd like a whisky, please."

"Yes, sir. With ice, I imagine?"

"Correct."

Merryweather withdrew. Jane said: "What did he mean? Oh, of course, all Americans take ice, don't they? You're only partly American, though, aren't you?"

"Half by parentage, wholly by education, but not by birth."

"And is this your first visit to England?"

"Yes, it is. I feel I know the country quite well, though. I had an English girl-friend once. She was always talking about London, and about the Cotswold hills, where she'd been born. It sounded nice. She wanted me to come back with her and settle here."

"Why didn't you?"

"Oh, I don't think I'm the type to settle down to domestic bliss."

"Love 'em and leave 'em is your motto, is it?"

"That's about the size of it."

Merryweather came back then with the drinks. Jane sipped her lemonade and watched Adler as he poured himself a whisky and added ice. The man had magnetism as well as charm.

Then Jane gave a start just as Gerry suddenly came bounding in through the french windows. She was wearing slacks and an old open-neck shirt and there was oil on her nose.

"That's fixed the brute. Gosh, I'm dying for a gasper." She took a cigarette from a box and lit it. "Oh, lemonade. Gorgeous." She poured herself a glass and sat down by Jane. "Darling, you look awfully pale. Do you feel all right?"

"I've got a bit of a headache, Gerry. I sat out there in the sun without a hat and without my glare glasses for about an hour and a half, just listening to Algy waffle. I think I'll go and lie down for a bit." She stood up. "I'll see you at dinner."

She went out. Gerry turned to Adler. "Had a good day, Mr. Adler?"

"Well, Lady Geraldine, not exactly good, but much as expected. Shall we say everything's under control?"

After the tennis, Giles Deveraux settled down in the shade of an oak tree to do some writing. He stayed there an hour, then put away his notebook, got to his feet, and brushed a few loose blades of grass from his flannel bags. He looked up at the grey mass of Alderley, standing timeless and stalwart under the August sun. It was a magnificent sight. Was it so handsome from each side, he wondered. It was time, for professional reasons, anyway, that he had a good look at it from every angle. He began to stroll round. He had nearly completed one circuit when he came upon John Evans, who was leaning against the wall next to the orangery, gazing at the house in silent admiration.

Deveraux jerked his head towards it. "Nice, isn't it? What's your offer going to be?"

"Oh, I might run to a hundred quid."

"You won't get it at that price. I'm offering guineas."

Evans smiled. "You're writing a book about it, aren't you?"

"I'm not sure yet. I'm writing a book about country houses. Whether Alderley will be included, I don't know."

"It would be a great pity to leave it out."

"I know. Unfortunately, that will apply to many places."

"I suppose so."

"I'm just going in to tea. Coming?"

They strolled off. Evans said: "Must be an interesting job, yours."

Deveraux shrugged. "I keep moving."

"I do, too, to a certain extent, with Mr. Peabody. But it's quite hard work. Voluminous correspondence follows him everywhere. I was dealing with it all the morning. Then on a trip like this I have to make all the travel arrangements, reservations, and so on. Anyway, they're going home next month. I'm not sure I shall go with them. I like England—"

"Your first visit?"

"Yes. I'd like to get a job and stay here for a while, if I could find anything suitable. You don't happen to know of a good billet, do you?"

"Not off-hand."

"Well, if you find the owners of any of these stately homes you're intending to write about are in need of a reasonably efficient tame secretary, perhaps you'll bear me in mind."

"Certainly. Give me an address where I can contact you before we leave."

11

The Baroness de la Roche

"GEORGE," said the Countess, "you are not looking well."

"Ain't I, my dear? I feel fine."

"No you don't, George. You don't feel well at all."

Lord Burford stared at her. "But I do, Lavinia."

"George—you feel a bilious attack coming on. I quite forgot to get another guest for dinner tonight and it's far too late now. Moreover, I've found out that Carrie Peabody is superstitious, so we cannot sit down thirteen to dinner. You, therefore, will have to dine alone."

Lord Burford gave a groan. "Oh, Lavinia, no! Why me?"

"Because we cannot conceivably ask one of the guests to absent himself; and for Geraldine or me to stay away would cause still greater imbalance between the sexes."

"But good gad, I'm the host!"

"Richard is quite capable of acting as host. You can recover and come down and join the men as soon as we've withdrawn. Now please, George, do not be obdurate." And with this concession Lord Burford had to be satisfied.

Reprieve, however, was to come to him unexpectedly.

At seven-forty-five, the party was beginning to assemble in the drawing-room when Merryweather entered and crossed to Lady Burford. "Excuse me, my lady."

"Yes, Merryweather?"

"Bates has been on the telephone from the lodge, my lady. There seems to have been an accident on the road outside."

"Oh dear! Has anybody been seriously hurt?"

"Reportedly not, your ladyship. The occupants of the vehicle were a French lady and her chauffeur. The chauffeur is unhurt; the lady merely shaken. But it seems the motor car has been extensively damaged. Bates has telephoned to Jenkins in the village and he is sending a break-down vehicle. But the lady will plainly be unable to proceed on her journey this evening. Her name apparently is the Baroness de la Roche. As the only accommodation in the village is the *Rose & Crown* . . ." Merryweather paused diplomatically.

"Why, of course. Send Hawkins down to the lodge and instruct Bates to give the Baroness my compliments and tell her his lordship and I shall be delighted if she will join us. Have a bedroom prepared and lay another place at table."

"Very good, your ladyship."

Lady Burford lowered her voice. "And tell his lordship not to count his chickens yet, but he'd better start dressing just in case. Understand?"

"His lordship is counselled to refrain from enumerating poultry, but is recommended to be in a state of preparedness to descend for dinner. Yes, my lady."

Merryweather went out and Lady Burford turned to Geraldine. "Baroness de la Roche. Ever heard of her?"

Gerry shook her head. "French, did Merry say?"

"That was merely Bates's guess, I imagine."

"I've got a very good friend called the Baroness von Richburg," Algy said. "She's German. Charming woman. I stayed at her Schloss in Bavaria a few years ago. Had a spiffing time. Her chef produced the most terrific *apfelstrudel*. I used to eat mountains of it. Unfortunately, after a few days the Baroness was called away suddenly to a sick relative and she shut up the place, so I had to leave. However—"

"Has anyone else ever heard of a Baroness de la Roche?" Lady Burford asked loudly and desperately.

Neither the Peabodys nor Thornton, the only others present, had, nor had Jane or Deveraux, who entered a minute later. So there was quite an air of expectancy in the room by the time Merryweather opened the drawing-room door and announced: "The Baroness de la Roche."

There was an almost theatrical four-second pause. Then there walked into the room the most beautiful woman Jane had ever seen. She had a flawless complexion, deep limpid eyes of a most remarkable violet, with thick, long natural lashes, a perfectly straight nose, and softly upcurving lips, exactly outlined in the most delicate shade of lipsitck. She was wearing a russet sports suit and a Tyrolean hat, decorated with a long feather, perched on the side of her head. At first glance she looked about thirty, though after closer study Lady Burford estimated her age as seven or eight years older than that.

The Baroness took two or three steps forward, conveying at the same moment an impression of being quite assured yet rather shaky on her feet.

Lady Burford went up to her, introduced herself and Geraldine, and said: "Welcome to Alderley."

"Oh, Lady Burford, Lady Geraldine, a thousand apologies for gate-crashing your home in this way." She spoke with the very slightest of French accents. The voice, warm, vibrant, slightly husky, had the barest trace of a tremor.

"Not at all. We're only too glad to be able to help. What a ghastly experience! You must have been terribly shocked. Come and sit down." She led the Baroness to a chair.

"Really, you are too kind. I am most grateful."

"Now, I'm sure you need something to drink."

"Well." The Baroness gave the ghost of a smile. "Perhaps a little cognac, if you have some."

"Of course." Lady Burford looked at Merryweather and raised one eyebrow. He bowed his head and withdrew.

"Are you sure you're not hurt?" Lady Burford asked.

"Quite sure, thank you. I feel just rather shaken."

"And your chauffeur," Gerry put in, "is he all right?"

The Baroness looked up at her. "Roberts? Yes, he seems perfectly well."

"Yet the car is badly wrecked?"

"He seems to think it will require considerable repair work."

"How did the accident happen?"

"I really couldn't say. I am afraid I was dozing in the back when suddenly there was a swerve and the next thing I knew we were in the ditch."

At that moment, Merryweather returned with the brandy. The Baroness sipped it gratefully and Lady Burford said: "Do you feel capable of introductions? It will make it easier to remember everybody if you can meet people in two installments, as it were."

"Yes, I am dying to meet all these charming people."

Lady Burford briskly performed introductions, carefully

76

forestalling Algy from starting a conversation with the Baroness. Then she said: "That simply leaves my husband, his brother, and two other—" she had been about to say "foreign," but with an obscure idea that it sounded vaguely insulting, amended this—"two other overseas visitors we have with us."

"I shall look forward to meeting them."

Deveraux asked: "Were you intending to travel far tonight?"

She favoured him with a flashing smile. "To Worcestershire. I am on my way to stay with some friends of mine there: Lord and Lady Darnley. Perhaps you know them?"

"You are a friend of the Darnleys?" There was a subtle but immediate change in Lady Burford's manner. The Baroness was no longer just an unknown stranger: she was a friend of friends—accredited. It made a difference.

The Baroness said: "Perhaps I might use your telephone later to let them know that I have been delayed. Heaven knows when I shall arrive now."

"Well, certainly not tonight," Lady Burford said firmly. "Tonight you will stay here. Merryweather, have you prepared a room?"

"Yes, my lady. The Spangled bedroom."

"And the Baroness's things have been taken up?"

"Yes, your ladyship."

The Baroness said: "Really, your kindness overwhelms me. I feel I am imposing on you shamelessly."

"Not at all. We are already entertaining a moderately large party. We will hardly notice one more—at least, not in any inconvenient way. Now, would you care for some more brandy?"

"Oh, no thank you."

"Then I expect you would like to go to your room and freshen up?"

"That would be nice."

"Very well, Merryweather will take you up. Or perhaps first to the telephone?"

The Baroness got to her feet. Lady Burford said: "Merryweather, after you have escorted the Baroness upstairs, send Celeste to her." She turned back to the Baroness. "My maid will attend you. I don't know whether you would like to rest in your room, or whether you feel up to joining us for dinner?"

"Oh, I feel quite recovered now, Lady Burford. I

should like very much to join you for dinner, if I may, but I have no wish to delay you."

"There'll be no question of that. We don't dine until eight-thirty. Take your time."

Merryweather and the Baroness went out. Before anyone could speak Gerry said, "Oh, excuse me," and hurried after them. When she got outside, Merryweather and the Baroness were approaching the stairs. "Oh, Merryweather," Gerry called.

He turned and came back to her, with a murmured apology to the Baroness. Gerry spoke in a low voice. "Merry, tell my father the chicks have hatched."

Merryweather's upper lip shifted about an eighth of an inch in acknowledgement of this remark. "Very good, my lady." He returned to the Baroness and led her upstairs.

Gerry watched till they'd disappeared, then signalled to a nearby footman. He hurried across to her. "William, find Hawkins and tell him I want to see him straight away, will you? I'll be in the library."

By eight-thirty the rest of the party had joined the group in the drawing-room—all agog to see the ravishing beauty spoken of by the others. Five more minutes passed. The Baroness still did not appear, and Lady Burford sent Gerry up to bring her down. A few minutes later there were voices outside, the door opened, and the Baroness entered the room, Gerry on her heels.

Lord Burford muttered "By jove!" under his breath, Algy screwed his monocle into his eye, and there was nobody in the room who did not stare shamelessly.

The Baroness was wearing a backless evening gown of shimmering gold marocain, with the skirt very tight to the knees and flaring out round her feet. Her hair was ash blonde and worn in the ultra-modern shoulder length page-boy style. Her complexion was now ivory pale and her lips vivid scarlet. Around her neck she wore a sea-green emerald necklace.

She paused inside the door, smiled, and said in her low voice: "I do hope I have not kept you all waiting."

Lady Burford stepped forward. "Not at all. My husband's only just down. He's been so looking forward to meeting you."

"I have indeed." Lord Burford bustled forward.

"Charmed, Baroness, charmed." They shook hands. The Earl said: "May I present my brother—"

He turned towards Richard, then broke off. "Rich? What's the matter?"

For Richard was standing as though turned to stone. His eyes were fixed on the Baroness in an expression of utter disbelief. He took no notice of his brother's words, but for a full five seconds just stood motionless. Then in a whisper he spoke one word.

"Anilese."

The Baroness took a step towards him. Her lovely eyes grew even larger. She started to raise her hand as if to reach out and touch him, but froze in mid-movement.

"Richard. No—I don't—I don't—"

She swayed and fell into a crumpled heap on the floor.

"I wonder—would you all mind going into dinner? Mademoiselle—the Baroness—and I will join you presently."

Five minutes had passed since the Baroness's dramatic swoon. Richard and Lord Burford had lifted her onto the settee, water had been fetched, and Mrs. Peabody, saying briskly: "I've had some nursing experience," had bathed the Baroness's face and wrists.

Within a minute she had opened her eyes and murmured weakly: "Where am I?" Then she had looked round in bewilderment, until her gaze alighted on Richard again. She had shaken her head, as if to clear it. "Richard. It is you. I thought it was a dream." She had taken his hand. "It is like a miracle."

Carrie Peabody had said: "Do you feel all right, my dear?"

"What? Oh yes. Quite all right, thank you. I'm very sorry. I'm afraid I have been a fool." She looked and sounded embarrassed.

She sat up, and then Richard made his request for dinner to be started.

Lord Burford nodded. "Splendid idea. I'm famished. Come along, everybody."

Slowly they trooped out. While the room emptied, Richard simply stood, staring down at the Baroness, unable to tear his eyes away from her face. Then as a footman closed the doors behind the end of the procession,

79

leaving the two of them alone, he dropped on his knees beside her and took her hand.

"Anilese—I can't believe it. Is it really you—after so long? I thought you were dead."

"Oui, Richard, chéri. C'est moi."

"But what happened to you? You were never seen after that bomb fell."

"It is a long story, Richard. You know how things were then."

"But surely you could have got in touch with me after the war —just to let me know you were alive? You knew how I felt. You must have realized what I thought had happened. Why didn't you?"

"There were reasons—good reasons. I will tell you, I promise. Only later."

"But why did you seek me out now—after all this time?"

Her eyes widened. "I did not seek you out, Richard. I had no idea you were here. Would I have fainted if I had been expecting to see you?"

He stared at her. "But you knew this was my brother's house."

"No. I was told by the lodge-keeper that it was the house of the Earl of Burford. But that meant nothing to me. I knew you as Captain Richard Saunders. I was aware you came from an aristocratic family, that your brother had a title; I did not remember what that title was."

Richard shook his head in amazement. "Then you're really here just by chance?"

"My car crashed outside the gates, Richard. That is why I am here."

"It's incredible."

"I prefer to think of it as—destiny."

"Destiny—chance—what does it matter? You're here, that's the important thing. And to think that when they told me the Baroness de la Roche—" He stopped short. "Of course—you're married."

She shook her head. "I am a widow. I married in 1923. The Baron died in 1928—nearly penniless."

"Oh, my dear. And—what since then?"

She looked away from him. "Since then many things, Richard. Many places. Many experiences I would prefer not to remember. Many ways of making a living. Much heartbreak."

"And—many men?"

"No one who mattered."

"No one now?"

"No one."

"Then I—do you mean I've got—"

She put her fingers on his lips. "We cannot talk now. We must go in to dinner. We will have plenty of time later."

"You're staying?"

"Overnight, at least. I shall have to go on when my motor is mended. But, never fear—I shall come back."

She took a powder compact from her bag, examined her face, and made some minor repairs. As she did so she said: "Richard, you will, of course, tell them you believed me dead. Will you also tell them I thought the same about you? I can tell *you* the truth, but not strangers."

"Whatever you wish."

She put her make-up away and smiled at him. "I'm ready. Shall we go in?"

The soup course was finishing when they entered the dining-room. The conversation stopped as they went in, and all eyes were on them.

After they'd sat down, Richard said: "We obviously owe you all an explanation. As will have been plain, Baroness de la Roche and I are acquainted. We knew each other in France during the war. Our surprise just now arose from the fact that we had each thought the other was dead. The Baroness has been married—and widowed—since I knew her, so the name de la Roche meant nothing to me. She likewise knew me only as Saunders, and was not aware the Earl of Burford was my brother. You can imagine how astonished we both were."

Carrie Peabody said: "My, isn't that too romantic."

Algy spoke loudly. "I say, Saunders, how come you both thought the other was dead? Sounds as though there might be a dashed exciting story behind that. Why don't you blow the gaff, what?"

"It's an exceedingly dull story, Fotheringay, and would bore you immensely. I'm sure we'd all much rather hear about your visit to Lady Masters."

Algy beamed. "Oh, really? Righty-ho."

Jane paid silent tribute to Richard's skill. There'd certainly be no more discussion about Anilese de la Roche during this meal.

When the ladies entered the drawing-room after dinner, Gerry waited some minutes for a good opportunity, then said to the Baroness: "You know, I'm intrigued by this accident of yours."

Anilese looked at her coolly. "Really? I assure you, intriguing is not what I found it. I doubt, too, that you would have found it so had you been in the car." '

Gerry flushed slightly. "Perhaps 'intrigued' is the wrong word. 'Puzzled' would be better. What puzzles me is the cause of it. That's a long straight stretch of road outside the gates. The light was good, the sun was behind you, the road was dry and the surface is in first class order. No other vehicle was involved. Yet your car suddenly swerved off the road and into the ditch, being so badly damaged that your chauffeur thinks it'll take a long time to repair it. Can you enlighten me?"

Anilese shook her head and gave a sweet smile. "I'm afraid not, Lady Geraldine. I have no knowledge of motor cars. But perhaps it was some sudden mechanical failure in the vehicle itself which caused us to crash. That is possible, is it not? You seem to be an expert on these matters."

"Oh, yes, that's quite possible. You could have burst a tyre, or a wheel could have come off. Except that I've been talking to our chauffeur, who drove you up here. He had a good look at your car while you were supervising Roberts as he transferred your luggage to the Rolls, and he tells me all the wheels of your car are in place and the tyres fully inflated. Your steering could have suddenly failed, I suppose. But it's a very rare thing to happen."

"I am very unfortunate then, am I not?"

"Not really. I could say you are exceptionally fortunate."

"Oh?" The Baroness raised her finely-plucked eyebrows.

"Yes. Hawkins tells me the car is at right angles to the road, facing straight into the bank, and the front is very badly smashed in—as though you'd been travelling at a pretty high speed. And that means you were both very lucky to walk away unhurt; quite apart from the fact that, having turned at right angles like that when moving at such a rate, it's almost miraculous your car didn't overturn."

The Baroness laughed, a delightful tinkling laugh. "Why, Lady Geraldine, this is fascinating. Quite like your English Sherlock Holmes stories. You really must talk with my chauffeur about it. I'm sure you'd get on famously with him. Unfortunately, nearly all you've said is completely over my head."

"I may talk to your chauffeur," Gerry said, "though I think it would be better if you were to talk to him yourself—for your own safety. However, I shall be more interested in talking to Harry Jenkins at the village garage, to ask exactly what he found wrong with your car."

The entry of the men at that moment put an end to the conversation before Anilese could reply.

That night the party broke up early, as for many of them it had been in one way or another a wearing day. Only Algy, who had slept most of the afternoon, was fresh and tried to get some dancing going. But he found no takers, and, rather disgruntled. was forced to retire early to bed with a new Ethel M. Dell novel.

After undressing, Jane slipped on a *négligée* and went along to Gerry's room. She found her having her hair brushed by Marie, and waited a few minutes, making conversation, until the maid was dismissed. Then she said: "You think Anilese's crash was faked."

"Precisely."

"For what reason? Just to provide an excuse to gate-crash this party?"

"I can't think of any other reason."

"And you think she knew Richard was here—never thought he was dead? But why go through all that? If she did know, why not just turn up, announce herself by her maiden name and ask to see him?"

"Perhaps she wasn't sure of the reception she'd get."

"Maybe; but that faint looked awfully real—as though she really was staggered to see him. Couldn't the accident have been faked for another reason?"

"Such as?"

"Well, there are two European diplomats and an American millionaire here—due to return to their own countries almost as soon as they leave Alderley. If she wanted to make contact with one of them, this might be her last chance. You know, I was joking with Richard yesterday about my becoming an adventuress. I didn't know a real one was going to turn up."

"Her title's genuine, by the way. I looked her up in the *Almanac de Gotha*. Baron de la Roche was French. He married a Mademoiselle Anilese Periot in 1923. He died five years later. So she fits the bill all right."

"That only tells us there is a Baroness of that name, a widow, somewhere in the world; it doesn't prove the woman who arrived here tonight is she—only that she's got the same Christian name as her. There's no doubt she's *the* girl, is there—the one you were telling me about?"

"None at all. I asked Mummy. They got engaged in France in 1917."

"You couldn't get the whole story, I suppose?"

"Not tonight. I'll worm it out of somebody sooner or later, though."

"Of course," Jane said, "we don't know he's still in love with her now. There was nothing in his behaviour tonight to suggest it."

"Not publicly, anyway."

"Still." Jane went to the door. "It's immaterial to me either way. As I told you, there can never be anything between Richard and me."

"Of course not. All the same, you are concerned for his happiness, aren't you—purely as a platonic friend? You don't want him deceived by a beautiful *femme fatale?*"

"I think he can take care of himself."

"I'm going to watch her like a hawk, all the same."

"You won't be the only one, Gerry. Good night."

Jane returned to her room and went to bed. She turned the light out immediately, but it was a long time before she got to sleep.

12

Double Deadlock

ON Saturday morning it was hotter than ever. But now the heat was sultry and there was a threat of thunder in the air; it was not weather for outdoor exercise and the tennis courts remained unoccupied and the horses unsaddled.

Anilese de la Roche slept late. After a light breakfast of coffee and rolls in her bedroom, she came down at ten o'clock. She then made a telephone call, after which she sought out Lady Burford.

"I am told my motor car will not be ready until Monday or Tuesday," she said.

Lady Burford brightened. An unescorted titled lady, vouched for not only by her brother-in-law, but also by the Darnleys, was a godsend and just what she needed to balance the house party and eliminate the Thirteen to Dinner problem. "Then of course you will stay here," she said decidedly.

"You are too kind. But I can easily hire a car. Or go on by train."

Lady Burford brushed aside these suggestions and it was arranged that the Baroness should remain until Monday at least. She went to telephone Lady Darnley.

"Peabody," said Lord Burford, "you mentioned in your last letter that you'd picked up something rather special in Rome, and you were looking forward to showing it to me."

"That's right, Earl. I sure did."

"Well, how about it? Or have you decided it's not quite as special as you first thought?"

"Not at all, sir. I consider it to be one of the most important purchases I have made for a long time."

"Well, don't sit on it, man. Let's have a look."

"Very well, I'll get it now."

"Take it along to the collection-room, will you? You haven't quite seen all my stuff yet. I've got one more piece, actually, that I think you'll appreciate."

Peabody cast him a surprised glance. "Oh, have you? OK, then. I'll see you up there in a few minutes."

He bustled off. Lord Burford chuckled and rubbed his hands. Gerry, who had recently finished a session on the telephone, was sitting nearby, rather a faraway expression in her eyes. Lord Burford got to his feet, bent down near her and said: "I knew what the blighter was up to: trying to keep his own piece till last—wait till he'd seen everything of mine, then produce this new thing of his and trump me. I was up to him, though. He'll have a job to outshine my *pièce de résistance*." He toddled off.

But Gerry was miles away.

Peabody entered the sitting-room of the Royal Suite, where his wife was writing a letter. "Do you know what that old sooner's done, honey? He deliberately didn't let me see everything yesterday. He kept one really good piece back, just so as to have something to top me. I'll show the shyster, though. He'll have a job to cap what I've got in here."

He went through the connecting door to his dressing-room, opened a large innovation trunk, took out a flat hard case about eighteen inches by twelve and four inches deep, tucked it under his arm, and strode out.

At ten o'clock the four negotiators gathered again in the music-room. They all settled down and got out their papers.

Richard lit a cigarette and looked at Adler. "Well, my friend, have you got anything to say to us?"

Adler scratched his nose. Then: "No, I'm sorry," he said. "I regret I cannot alter my position. Before anything else is discussed, I must have a firm understanding as to what arms and equipment the British government is going to supply, and an agreed timetable for their delivery; also full details of your contingency plans in the event that we are invaded. If I do not get this information, I shall be forced to withdraw."

There was utter silence in the room following these

words. Richard didn't react at all, just sat quite still, looking impassively at Adler.

Thornton's heart was in his mouth. Never in all his years of diplomacy had he felt quite so tense. He's over-reaching himself, he thought. The Minister cannot possibly stand for an ultimatum like that, no matter what his instructions were. It would be too much of a capitulation. He's going to have to call Adler's bluff. Because the Duchy *can't* withdraw. They've got to have our help.

Eventually Richard spoke. He displayed no annoyance or disappointment. "We seem to have reached deadlock, then. I certainly can give no firm commitments or any information such as you require until something is forthcoming from you in return."

Adler shrugged. He seemed quite unperturbed. "Then where do we go from here?"

"I don't see we can go anywhere from here. There's little point in continuing the talks."

"Are you proposing to let me leave here and report to the Grand Duke that after travelling half-way across Europe especially to talk with you, you sent me home with nothing?"

"I am proposing nothing of the sort. All I propose is that you show yourself willing to negotiate—to give something in return; not just to make demands. If not, I'm afraid you'll have to report just that."

There was silence again for a moment. Adler stared hard at Richard, as though he were trying to read his mind. Then he cast a quick glance at Felman, before looking back at Richard and saying: "Then I suggest we adjourn now and spend the rest of the morning reconsidering our respective positions. We would both look foolish were we to break up now and have to report complete failure to our chiefs. Perhaps we can reconvene after lunch. Would that be acceptable to you?"

"Perfectly."

"Then now you must excuse us. Felman and I have much to discuss." And Adler got to his feet and hurriedly left the room, Felman on his heels.

Richard looked at Thornton. "Whew, I thought we were in real trouble, then."

"Certainly his last words came as a relief."

"What the deuce is he up to, Thornton? And what's

he going to do now? You try a forecast. Mine don't seem too accurate."

"I would hazard the hypothesis that when he made that telephone call yesterday he was instructed to have one further attempt to—er, well, to get something for nothing. He has attempted, and failed. I think now he will make another call to report this, and will be told to settle this afternoon. I would suggest, Minister, that in order to help him save face, we prepare to make some small concession—simply to preserve the pretence that we are meeting him half-way."

"Right. You put your mind to it, will you? Something that means nothing, but seems to."

"Very well."

"I think I'll go and stretch my legs. I've spent most of my time indoors the last few days. I'd like to get a little sun before the weather breaks—which looks as though it might be soon."

Peabody found Lord Burford waiting for him in the collection-room, in his hands a case very similar to the one Peabody himself was carrying. Lord Burford placed his casually down on a table. "Ah, got it? Right, let's have a look."

Peabody said: "I'm sure yours is the more interesting item, Earl. Mine can wait until I've seen that."

"Oh, come along, my dear chap. I've been spouting off about my stuff ever since you got here. Time you entertained me, for a change."

"Well, say you look at mine while I look at yours?"

"As you wish."

They exchanged cases. Simultaneously both cases were opened. Then simultaneously two pairs of eyes bulged, two jaws dropped, and two ejaculations burst forth.

"Good gad!"

"Holy mackerel!"

For inside the two cases lay two identical guns.

They were large, automatic-shaped pistols, ten inches long, with an ammunition clip in the form of an oblong metal box fitted in front of the trigger guard. Both were in superb condition. They were elaborately engraved, with ivory butts, and on the side of each were some letters, and the small figure of a double-headed eagle, carved in relief.

The two men's eyes met. Peabody whispered: "You've got the other one. I was sure it was lost for good."

"So was I. I thought I'd got hold of something unique."

"Where the heck did you get yours?"

"From a little dealer I've known for years. Always found him honest. He came all the way from London just to show me it a month ago. Couldn't—or wouldn't—tell me its provenance, but assured me he had title to it. Naturally, I snapped it up on the spot. You're the first person to see it, outside the family. What about yours?"

"Little guy came to the hotel in Rome. Said he'd heard I was in town and thought I might be interested in something rather special. Rather special! I nearly passed out when I saw it. He wouldn't say where he got it, but he produced documents that seemed to prove he was the legal owner."

Lord Burford said: "Remarkable. May I?" Peabody handed back the Earl's pistol, and Lord Burford took one of them in each hand, balancing and comparing them. "Seems they belong together, what?" He handed both guns to Peabody.

"Sure does. I guess I don't need to say you can name your own price for yours?"

"No, I, er, guess not. Sorry—no deal. Obviously no use offering *you* money, old man; but you're welcome to choose any comparable weapon from my collection in exchange for yours."

"No, sir. I'm not about to part with this baby."

"Looks as if they're destined to stay apart, doesn't it?"

"Unless we can reach a compromise."

"Such as?"

"Well, for a start, would you consider lending me yours for a few weeks? There's the big exhibition in New York City this fall. All the leading collectors in the States are sending exhibits. I cabled, entering this." He held up his pistol. "It would sure give me a big thrill to exhibit the pair. I'd lend you mine in return, later."

Lord Burford scratched his chin. "Like to oblige, old man. But frankly I funk letting it out of my possession. Know you'd treasure it and all that. But you've got these gangster johnnies over there, haven't you? Suppose Capone or someone took a fancy to it?"

"He's in jail."

"Plenty more like him, I hear. And then again the

New York exhibition'll be reported over here, the catalogue will be available; even if you lend me yours afterwards, I couldn't exhibit the pair as my own, as you had. But I'll tell you what. There is one fellow in England who's by way of being a rival of mine—a General Trimble Greene. I'd give anything to fool him into believin' I owned this pair. He's a kind of explorer and he's out of the country at present. But he'll be back in September, just for a couple of weeks, before going off to some expedition to South America. If I could hang onto the pair just long enough to make him drool a bit, there'd be a good chance he'd never see the New York exhibition catalogue, and mightn't find out for years, if ever, that I didn't own 'em both."

"Sorry, Earl, but the exhibition opens September 24th."

"That's all right: I'll be seeing Trimble Greene by the 15th. I'll send off yours so it'll reach America in time."

Peabody shook his head. "I wouldn't want to risk it. On the other hand . . ."

The conversation dragged on inconclusively for several more minutes, until they both realized they weren't going to get anywhere. Then they fell gloomily silent. Ten minutes before, each had been completely happy in the possession of a single gun; now the knowledge of the existence of a second, unattainable, one had cast a cloud over the day.

At last the Earl said: "Fired yours?"

"Not yet. I haven't had a chance to get any ammunition."

"Come along, then. I've got some." He pointed to a section of the room which he had partitioned off as a small shooting range. They took both guns across, Lord Burford stopping to pick up some cartridges at a large cupboard where he stored ammunition and various accessories. They had twenty minutes target practice, after which Lord Burford replaced his gun in the display stand near the door, from which he had removed it before Peabody's arrival. Peabody took his pistol back to his room.

Meanwhile, Gerry had finished her think and gone to find Jane.

"News," she said.

"What?"

"I've been on the 'phone to Pamela Darnley—just after Anilese had rung herself. She told me Anilese is by no means a close friend of theirs. They met her in Monte last year. She told them she lived in Geneva, and she made a few what Pamela thought were purely conventional 'you must look me up next time you're in Switzerland' remarks—which Pamela reciprocated. Then just a couple of weeks ago she had a letter from Anilese saying she was going to be in the area shortly and would like very much to take up their kind invitation. Of course, they had no choice but to say yes."

"She told them she was going to be in the area?"

Gerry nodded smugly. "Exactly. But she didn't say what for."

"Very fishy."

"There's more. I've spoken to Harry Jenkins. He says he can't find anything wrong with the car which would make it suddenly swerve off the road. The bodywork at the front is badly damaged, the radiator's cracked, and the headlight's broken. But all that must have been done *when it crashed*—none of it could have *caused* the accident. He was a bit cagey and wouldn't commit himself; but he did say the damage was 'queer,' that he'd never seen a car damaged quite like it before—and he could hardly believe it had happened just by going into the ditch."

"What did the chauffeur tell him?"

"He was evasive, apparently—said he couldn't remember much about it, suddenly lost control, thinks perhaps he hit a patch of oil. But I've checked and the road's as dry as a bone for half a mile in either direction. And there aren't any skid marks, either."

"Well done. It certainly seems to clinch what you said. But we're no nearer finding out why she did it."

"I'll find out," Gerry said.

At that moment the door opened and Lord Burford entered. He grunted: "Oh, hullo, you two," pulled the bell for Merryweather, and sank down into a chair.

"Daddy, what on earth's the matter? I haven't seen you look so browned-off in all my puff."

"It's that confounded Yankee."

He explained at length about the two pistols. "I'd give my eye teeth for that gun," he added.

Gerry made a few sympathetic noises, but her attention

was obviously elsewhere, and it was left to Jane to be chief comforter.

Having left Thornton in the music-room, Richard strolled out onto the terrace. Here he found his sister-in-law and Mrs. Peabody, who had just been rejoined by Anilese, after she had made her 'phone call to Lady Darnley. This morning Anilese was strikingly dressed in a dirndl skirt and a white blouse with short puffed sleeves under a black bolero.

"Richard," said Lady Burford, "you'll be pleased to know that the Baroness is staying over the weekend."

He smiled. "That's grand."

Anilese stood up. "Richard, when are you going to show me something of these lovely grounds?"

"Now if you like."

"Oh, good. Let's walk round the lake. I adore lakes."

"Enchanté, madame," said Richard.

Thornton did not see Richard again during the morning, nor at lunch. No time had been fixed for reconvening, but Thornton returned to the music-room at two o'clock. Adler and Felman arrived five minutes later. But it was not until after two-thirty, when Thornton was about to send a servant to look for him, that Richard entered. Thornton stared at him. Richard looked white and drawn. For several seconds he stood inside the door, then walked slowly across to his chair and sat down. Thornton expected him to offer some apology for his lateness, but instead, without any preliminaries, Richard looked at Adler and said: "What is the position?"

"Unchanged. Are you prepared to give me the information I requested this morning?"

Richard was breathing heavily, almost as though he'd been running. He raised a hand to his face and ran it down his cheek, as though wiping off sweat. Then, not looking at Adler, he said: "Possibly. I don't know yet. I haven't decided. I need time to think."

It was all Thornton could do to keep back a gasp of astonishment. He stared at Richard, his face a study.

Adler said quietly: "How long?"

"I don't know. Till tonight—possibly tomorrow morning."

"Not later than that?"

"No. I promise."

"Very well."

Richard got to his feet with a jerky movement. He looked at Thornton. "Sorry," he said. Then he hurried from the room.

For ten seconds none of the men spoke. Then Adler broke the silence. "Come on, Nicholas. Let's go and have a game of billiards."

13

Grand Tour

FROM about noon that day the weather had grown even more humid. Gradually the sky became overcast. After lunch, Jane borrowed a bicycle and rode down to the village to do a little personal shopping. By the time she'd finished, the sky was a dark greeny-grey and it was plain a big storm was brewing. She hurried back, put the bicycle away, and went inside. Everybody except Richard was indoors. Surprisingly, he had gone for a long solitary tramp round the estate. In the house there seemed to be that air of restlessness and edginess that Jane had noticed an impending storm often produced. People were roaming round, picking up books and putting them down again, starting conversations and breaking them off quickly, or just sitting and staring out of the windows at the still and leaden trees.

The most obviously affected was Anilese. She seemed disgruntled at Richard's absence and sat by herself, flicking through magazines and politely but firmly rebuffing every attempt to engage her in conversation.

At the other extreme, Martin Adler seemed on top of the world and eager to talk. Jane had a long conversation with him, finding him interesting and well-informed.

Tea was served early, and afterwards Lady Burford made an unexpected suggestion: a guided tour of the entire house for the whole party.

"All of you have seen some of it," she said, "but nobody has seen everything. It would be a pity to have stayed here and missed something important. It seems an excellent time now to make sure nobody does."

It was difficult to refuse such an invitation, and although several of those present—including Lord Burford and Gerry—were somewhat reluctant, everybody went along.

To the surprise of all but Lady Burford herself, the hour was a great success. The charm and tranquility of the old house cast its spell over everyone, seeming somehow to cheer and soothe, and it was a happier group of people who arrived finally in the gun-room—which Lady Burford was careful to make the climax of the tour. Here, his wife having done most of the talking until now, Lord Burford came into his own. Many years of experience had given him a good knowledge of what appealed to the non-expert, and he talked interestingly, with a fund of anecdotes, holding the attention even of the women. Soon he was obviously in high good humour again; so much so that after half an hour he whispered something to Peabody, who left the room. When he returned a few minutes later, the Earl said: "I'll end with my latest acquisition." He crossed to the stand where he had put the engraved pistol.

"In 1918 the famous Danish firearm manufacturers, Bergman Industriewerke, produced a semi-automatic 9mm pistol, model 1910/21. It is commonly known as the Bergman Bayard. It is very unusual in that the rifling inside the barrel is a six-groove left-hand twist—not the more common right-hand twist. Only a thousand of these pistols were made, and they are already valuable collectors' items. Peabody, would you like to carry on?"

"Surely." Peabody stepped forward. "Just before the Bayard was put into production, the firm received an unusual order. It was from a man who said he was acting for a very eminent person, wishing to remain anonymous. This person had heard of the new model and wanted to order a special presentation pair. They had to be elaborately engraved, with ivory stocks, and included in the decoration was to be an emblem in relief. He handed over a drawing to be copied. It was of the Romanov two-headed eagle—the emblem of the Russian Tsars—together with the initials of Nicholas II, the last Tsar.

"Well, the pistols were made—the first Bergman Bayards ever produced—and the man took them away, paying cash. The rest is speculation. Nicholas had by then been deposed and was in exile in Siberia with his family. Had he himself ordered the pistols; or had they been intended

95

as a present to be sent to him—his birthday was in May—
and if so, from whom?"

"Nicholas, of course, was related to the royal house of
Denmark," Lord Burford put in. "His mother, the Dowager
Empress Marie, was Danish, and the aunt of King Chris-
tian. So who was the eminent customer?"

"The gun world has never known," Peabody continued,
"and the pistols were never seen again. Did Nicholas receive them? I firmly believe he did—and had them during
those last months in Siberia. Then, on 16th July, 1918,
he and his entire family were—supposedly—assassinated
at Ekaterinburg. But did that actually happen? It's been
variously reported that one, two, or even all of them
escaped. No one knows their fate for sure. Nor does
anybody know what happened to the pistols. Were they
stolen by the assassins after the Tsar's death? Or did
Nicholas carry them with him—perhaps actually use them
—during the family's escape? The only certainty is that
they disappeared from public view until a few weeks
ago—when I bought this one in Rome."

"And I bought this one here in England." Lord Burford
took his from the stand. "If the ordinary Bayard is valuable, you can imagine the value of these."

The others gathered round interestedly. The pistols were
passed from hand to hand, and the Earl and Peabody
demonstrated how they were loaded and fired.

It was a fine climax to the tour, and the group started
to break up. Jane was one of the first to go towards the
door, and as she did so, she saw that Richard was standing just inside it. At that second he turned and walked
quickly away—but not before she had seen a very strange
expression on his face. She frowned. It looked as though
he'd been listening to the story. But why hadn't he joined
them all openly?

Thoughtfully, Jane went to dress for dinner.

"Richard, can I speak to you for a minute?"

Anilese's voice came from behind Richard in little more
than a whisper, and he turned, surprised. He was walking alone at the tail of the short procession of men on
their way to the drawing-room after dinner. Anilese should
have been already there; instead, she was just emerging
from a shadowy corner of the hall.

He frowned. "What about?"

"You know."

"I was out all afternoon. I can't desert the party again now."

"For a few minutes only. It's very important."

He hesitated. "All right. In the library. In ten minutes."

"Very well. Don't say you've seen me. I'm supposed to have a headache and be lying down."

He nodded, then hurried on towards the drawing-room.

He was able to slip away quite unobtrusively ten minutes later owing to a sudden outbreak of confusion during the serving of the coffee: some people had two cups and others none, while some who wanted black had white and vice versa. The muddle seemed, predictably, to revolve round Algy Fotheringay, but within a short time nearly everyone was on his or her feet, passing and re-passing cups, and while this was happening Richard left the room.

Anilese paused inside the library door and turned. "Understood?"

"Whatever you say."

She opened the door and slipped out, closing it after her.

Richard sank back in the deep leather armchair and closed his eyes. He felt dazed and utterly spent. There was so much he didn't understand. But the time to speculate would come later. First there was something else to do. He looked at his watch, got to his feet, and returned to the drawing-room. He let a few minutes pass, then caught Adler's eye and beckoned him to one side. Adler raised his eyebrows. "You wanted me?"

Richard took a deep breath. "Yes. I promised you a definite decision by the morning. But there's no point in keeping you in suspense. I've made up my mind."

Jane noticed Richard re-enter the drawing-room after a fifteen minutes absence, and she watched his face as he talked to Adler. It seemed to her that in some way he looked different. At dinner he had been very quiet and withdrawn. Now he still looked tired—but like a man who had reached a crucial decision.

He moved away from Adler, caught her eye, and to her pleasure came across and sat down by her. He gave her a smile. "Hullo, stranger. What have you been doing with yourself all day?"

"Brooding, mainly," Jane said.

"That's bad."

"And you?"

"Brooding. But I've been doing mine on the move, which is good for the waistline if not for the soul."

"Oh, for me it's a luxury to be able to sit around and brood. Don't spoil it for me. But what have you got to brood about?"

"Politicians can usually find something."

"Oh, it's politics, is it? I'm sorry."

"I believe the conventional thing for me to say is don't worry your pretty little head about that."

"I don't intend to, but I can still be sorry." She was silent for a moment, then said: "Talking of pretty heads, your friend the Baroness is very beautiful."

He paused fractionally before saying: "Yes, she is, isn't she?"

"She looks as though she's led an interesting life, I think."

He glanced at her quizzically. "Now just how do I take that?"

"Meaning am I being catty? Well, frankly, I could be. Actually, though, I wasn't making any sort of moral judgment. Obviously I know nothing about her character. I meant quite simply that whatever she's been, I'm sure her life has never been boring."

"You're probably right. But why could you be catty— why don't you like her?"

"I didn't say I didn't like her. She's got a lot of charm and I should imagine could be very good company. I should like to know her better, because if you must know I admire her a lot. She's the sort of woman I'd like to be myself. Except for one thing."

"Which is?"

"Well, frankly—"

"Frankly again?"

"Sorry; do I sound too much like a politician?"

"*Touché.*"

"To be blunt, then, if you prefer it." She hesitated.

"Go on: what's the one thing?"

"I don't think you could trust her to pass you the salt."

14

Storm Over Alderley

IT was half-past one the following morning when the
storm broke over Alderley. It was still raging half an
hour later when, just as the stable clock struck two, Gerry
opened the door of her L-shaped bedroom on the inner
corner of the main and west corridors. She had a small
electric torch in her hand. She slipped out, closed the
door quietly behind her and turned right down the west
corridor towards the rear of the house. She was wearing
a dressing-gown and bedroom slippers. On the right almost at the end of the corridor, just before the stairs,
there was a narrow curtained recess, where the maids
kept cleaning equipment. Gerry pulled back the curtain,
squeezed herself in, and drew the curtain again, leaving
just a half-inch gap. She was a little way past the door
to the Baroness's bedroom, which was on the other side
of the corridor. Gerry flashed her torch once at the door,
to get its exact position fixed in her mind, then switched
off.

The clouds that night were so thick that even though
the curtains on the nearby window at the end of the
corridor were not drawn, she could now see virtually
nothing. Then a flash of lightning lit the corridor brilliantly
for a fraction of a second before plunging it back into
what seemed an even deeper darkness.

Gerry settled down to wait.

As it happened, she did not have to wait long. She had
been in the recess no more than three minutes when she
heard the click of the Baroness's door knob. In vain
Gerry strained her eyes. She heard a very slight rustle
of clothing, and groaned inwardly. Why did this of all
nights have to be so maddeningly dark?

Then there came light. The dim light of a torch. Gerry

could just see that it was held by Anilese, and that she was gliding hurriedly away down the corridor. She was dressed in a flowing white *négligée* and her feet were bare. Gerry slipped from her hiding-place and followed.

Like a white ghost the Baroness flitted silently along. She rounded the corner into the main corridor, Gerry about ten yards behind. Then, as Gerry herself was about to go round, she heard a faint, indefinable sound from somewhere ahead of her. She paused momentarily before peering round the corner. The light from the Baroness's torch had vanished. Gerry swore under her breath. She stood still, biting her lip in frustration. A minute elapsed. Then a particularly vivid flash of lightning shining through a high window lit up the main corridor just long enough for her to see that it was quite empty.

The Baroness might have gone anywhere in the house. Gerry had no means whatsoever of telling where. She'd probably lost her chance of finding out anything of importance. But she wasn't going to admit complete defeat yet—at least she could find out what time Anilese went back.

Gerry returned to her niche.

She had hardly time to settle herself, when she heard another noise in the corridor. This time it was clearly the sound of footsteps—and they were approaching. They grew closer.

They sounded like a man's. Then a torch flashed—on and off, quickly. It was held low, and all Gerry could see was the lower half of a pair of trousered legs. Just outside the Baroness's door the torch flashed again. Then there came the click of the door knob, and silence once more. Gerry withdrew into the recess, pulled the curtain, and flashed on her own torch for a quick look at her wrist watch. It was just coming up to seven minutes past two. She resumed her vigil.

About half a minute after this she saw Anilese's white figure returning. Gerry drew well back until once more she heard the door open and close. Now she faced an awkward decision. She ached to know what was being said inside the room. It was unlikely that, even with her ear to the keyhole, she would be able to hear anything significant. But there was a possibility of hearing *something*. It should be worth a try. Yet, even though originally a gate-crasher, the Baroness was now a guest at Alderley;

and both by instinct and training Gerry rebelled violently against the idea of deliberately eavesdropping on anybody, let alone a visitor to her home. So far she'd only spied on what went on in the open corridor.

However, the problem was solved for her, because the next moment the storm, which so far had consisted of heavy rain, lightning, and distant rumblings, now unleashed its full blast. Gerry had rarely heard thunder like it. It would obviously prevent her hearing anything else, however close she got to the door.

Another four or five minutes passed. Then during a momentary break in the thunder, she heard again the click of the Baroness's door. Gerry strained her eyes hopelessly in the darkness. Then, as before, a shaded torch, held low, flashed briefly, showing the man's legs retreating along the corridor. Twice more it flickered, each time revealing the man farther away.

Briefly, Gerry considered following. But it was Anilese she was chiefly interested in, and she stayed where she was.

It was a decision she was bitterly to regret before twenty-four hours had passed.

The probability now was that everything which was going to happen had happened. If so, she'd been wasting her time. Should she pack up? Bed was awfully inviting. She flashed her torch and sneaked another peep at her watch. Not yet quarter-past. She'd stay until half-past, as she'd planned.

"Blast all Baronesses," Gerry said under her breath.

The alarm clock under Giles Deveraux's pillow went off shrilly. He awoke at once and stopped it. Almost two-twenty. Deveraux swung himself off the bed. He was dressed in dark slacks, a sweater, and rubber-soled shoes. He picked up a torch from the bedside table and left the room.

He turned east along the main corridor, stopping momentarily outside the door of each occupied bedroom that he passed and listening intently for a few seconds during the lulls in the thunder. He walked the full length of the main and east corridors and at the far end of the latter took the stairs to the ground floor.

Deveraux was unaware of it, but ten yards behind, a dark figure followed him down.

For several minutes all was still in the east corridor. Then, very slowly, the door of the picture gallery was opened from the inside.

Jane stood inside the door of her bedroom, straining her ears, and mentally cursed the thunder and rain that were preventing her hearing properly. What on earth was going on out there?

She had been awake all night so far. Actually, when she had first gone to her room, she hadn't really expected to be able to sleep. However, after reading for a while she had dutifully turned out the light. But she had soon switched on again and picked up her book.

It had been sultry when she had gone to bed, and she had left the door open an inch in the hope of getting a draught through the room. It was some time later that she had become aware, between thunderclaps, of a lot of movement about the house. She told herself that others, obviously, would be kept awake by the storm and be restless, and it was merely her imagination which made their movements seem somehow furtive.

But then she had heard a sound both strange and alarming: the door of the picture gallery, across the corridor from her room, opening and closing again.

Clearly nobody would be looking at pictures this time of night. On the other hand, the gallery did house a number of valuable paintings. And beyond the gallery were the Earl's guns. So she couldn't just ignore the sound.

Thus it was that Jane, who had put on a dressing-gown and slippers, was now standing with her ear close against her bedroom door, wondering what to do.

Very soon afterwards the noise came again. And following it she was almost certain she heard the sound of foot-steps receding.

Jane took a deep breath, gasped the knob, and peeped out. She could see nothing. She waited, quite still and quiet for several second, then stepped into the corridor.

Giles Deveraux was walking lightly up the main stairs when he heard the stable clock strike two-thirty. As the chimes ceased, he heard another sound. He froze and extinguished his torch, for the sound was that of foot-steps. They were coming along the main corridor, approaching the head of the stairs from the right. Deveraux stood, holding his breath, as the footsteps got closer. He heard them cross the landing and continue along the corridor towards the west wing. He waited until they'd gone about ten yards, then ran quickly up the remaining stairs himself and, hoping against hope he wouldn't run into anything in the dark, turned in the same direction.

He hadn't taken more than half a dozen paces along the corridor when he heard another small noise—this time behind him. He started to swing around, saw a bright beam of light out of the corner of his eye—and felt a glancing blow on the head.

If Deveraux had not started to turn, the blow would undoubtedly have knocked him out. As it was, he avoided the full force of it. However, it was still powerful enough to bring him to his knees, dazed and half-stunned. Before he could begin to recover, he felt hands grab him from behind. He flinched, waiting for another blow, but all that happened was that his assailant tried to pull him sideways. Unable to resist adequately, Deveraux half-fell on his side. The hands took a fresh grip and gave him another heave. Slowly, Deveraux's senses were beginning to come back to him. From the floor he struck out. He had the satisfaction of feeling his fist make contact. But it was a feeble blow and only deterred his attacker for a second. Then he grabbed Deveraux again.

Deveraux was gathering his diminished strength for another punch, when from nearby came a sudden series of bumps and bangs. Although close, they were not particularly loud, and even in his fuddled state, he realized that their source was either Adler's room, or Gerry's. It sounded like some sort of fight. Furniture was being overturned and bodies were crashing about.

The noise stopped as abruptly as it had begun. And at the same instant Deveraux realized that he was alone. He lay still, trying to make his brain work. For a few seconds all was silence. Even the thunder had stopped. Then Deveraux heard hurried footsteps approaching. They blundered past him in the darkness, going east.

It was at that moment he heard the woman's scream.

Gerry heard two-thirty sound from the stable clock, and with a combination of relief and irritation eased herself out of the recess. What a very nasty shape, and how hard and angular carpet sweepers were! She would never feel the same about them again. And all she had discovered was that Anilese had left her room for about four minutes —not the most suspicious of actions—and had received one male visitor, who hadn't even had the indecency to stay long enough to compromise her. What an idiotic waste of time!

Gerry was on the verge of switching on her torch to light herself back to bed, when yet again she heard the muffled sound of footsteps coming along the corridor. She caught her breath and in a panic scrambled back into the recess.

This time the prowler had no torch, so she couldn't even see his legs. She heard him stop outside the Baroness's door. Very, very softly a finger-nail tapped on a panel. A knob turned and there was the almost undetectable sound of the door opening and closing.

Then, in the distance, Gerry heard something else.

She held her breath to hear better. What on earth was it? For a second she'd thought it was thunder. But no: for the moment that had stopped. This was inside the house. It sounded like furniture being knocked about. Though it wasn't in the west wing, and seemed muffled.

Once more Gerry stepped out of her recess. She stood hesitating. Then, her heart in her mouth, she started off along the corridor, switching on her torch.

She had just passed the alcove in which was set the door leading to the western extension, given over to servants' quarters, when the noise stopped short. Gerry stopped too. For a moment there was dead silence. An unnatural silence. Gerry felt hairs prickling at the back of her neck.

Then she gave a violent start as from the floor below came the sound of a woman's scream.

Gerry just couldn't move. The next second she was conscious of somebody approaching. She started to raise her torch, but then it was knocked from her hand and went out as someone crashed into her. She gave a gasp: "Who's that?" There was no reply. And then Gerry's fright was overcome by sheer anger. She made a blind grab—and found herself clutching a man.

The man tried to pull himself free. She hung on like grim death and the next thing she knew she was lurching silently about the corridor, locked with him in a grotesque parody of a tango. Stupidly, for seconds it didn't occur to her to shout for help. When it did she took a deep breath. But this must have warned the man of her intention, for a hand was at once clapped over her mouth.

Suddenly, Gerry realized that she'd quite lost control of the situation. She was being manoeuvred in the direction the man wanted—and could do nothing about it. Then her back was against the wall. Keeping one hand over her mouth, the man held her still with his body and reached out with his other arm. There was a click of a door catch, the man carefully prised himself loose from her grasp and moved her gently to the side. Then there was nothing behind her. She started to topple backwards, but the man held on to her and prevented her falling. Instead, still keeping one hand over her mouth, he lowered her slowly to the floor and released her. There was a click and all was silence again.

Jane stood quite motionless outside her bedroom door, listening. She could hear no sound, other than the almost non-stop rolling of the thunder. She felt in her dressing-gown pocket, took out a box of matches, and struck one. Its feeble glow showed little, but it did seem that there was nobody in her immediate vicinity.

Jane crossed to the door of the picture gallery and opened it wide. She put her head inside and switched the light on just long enough to see that the gallery was empty, all the pictures were present, and the door to the gun-room closed. She thought to go across and try it, but then changed her mind. She closed the door, turned to her right, and started to make her way slowly along the corridor towards the main block. As she approached the corner, she heard the stable clock chime two-thirty.

At the same moment the clock chimed, the match burnt down to Jane's fingers. She hastily shook it out, struck another one, and started to creep forward again. She turned the corner.

Then her heart leapt and the match fell from her hand as from somewhere in front of her came a sudden eruption of noise. It was a muffled bumping and crashing, and seemed to come from one of the rooms at the farther end of the corridor. Jane stood frozen, wondering what on earth to do. It was no business of hers. If a burglar had somehow broken in, there were plenty of men about to deal with the situation. Any second, surely, lights would come on, doors would open, voices would call out.

But seconds passed and they didn't. And Jane knew that she had to do something. She couldn't possibly just go back to her room. She took a deep breath and started to grope her way forward again.

Then the noise stopped. The storm, too, had abated and for a few seconds everything was quiet. She must be near the door of Richard's room. The obvious thing would be to wake him. She took a step, reaching forward to her right, and felt the smooth wood of a door. It gave under her pressure. It was ajar. It was the room where the linen was stored. She had passed Richard's door.

Then Jane's blood froze, as out of the blackness came the sound of a woman's scream.

It was a short, sharp scream, apparently quickly muffled, and seemed to originate from the ground floor. Almost at the same instant Jane heard hurrying, stumbling footsteps coming towards her along the corridor. She sensed rather than saw a dark shape looming up; then someone crashed into her, sending her flying.

Jane ended up gasping for breath in an ungainly heap on the floor.

As she lay there the whole house seemed to be full of muted noises: one set of footsteps blundering away behind her; others approaching from the front; somebody breathing heavily quite close; in the distance, somewhere in the west wing, an indefinable scuffling noise; and in the middle distance, ahead of her, the sound of a groan.

It was all too much for Jane. In a way of which she was always afterwards ashamed, she panicked. She scrambled to her feet and felt wildly for the open door. She almost fell in. She just had the presence of mind to close it behind her softly.

Her heart was pounding. They were coming after her. They mustn't find her. What could she do?

It was not more than half a minute later that her panic subsided. Then she stood absolutely still for a few more seconds, deliberately calming herself down.

There was no danger. She was surrounded by friends. Richard's room was next door. The Peabodys were across the corridor, the Earl and Countess not far away. Nobody was going to hurt her. If there was any burglar about, all she had to do was shout for help.

Jane steeled herself and quickly opened the door again. She struck a match and stepped out into the corridor. The light switch was close at hand. She turned it on.

15

Break-out

THE corridor flooded with light. Jane blinked around, fearful of what she was going to see.

In fact, what she saw was not particularly alarming. About thirty yards from her, past the head of the grand staircase, Giles Deveraux was sitting on the floor, leaning up against the wall and rubbing his head. Jane ran up to him.

"What happened?"

"Somebody beaned me." He stood up, still holding his head.

"He went that way." Jane pointed towards the east wing. "He cannoned into me—sent me flying."

"You didn't see him?"

"No, it was quite dark. Look, you'd better go and lie down. I'll go and get some cold pads—and some brandy."

"No, I'm all right. I want to find out what caused that noise."

"What noise?"

"Didn't you hear? Sounded like some sort of scrap."

Jane stared. "Wasn't that you?"

"Oh no. My little fracas was very quiet—and the other started later."

"Where did the sound come from?"

"Adler's room, I think. Yes—the door's ajar. Let's take a look."

He strode to the door, put his head in and switched on the light. "Nobody in here," he said. "But there's been a scrap in here all right—the furniture's all over the place."

Jane said: "Shouldn't we find out who screamed?"

He spun round. "I thought that was you."

"No, I think it came from downstairs."

"Did it? I was a bit too groggy to mark the direction. We'd better investigate." He turned to the stairs.

Then Jane stopped him. "Wait—listen."

He paused, his head cocked. Somewhere in the west wing could be heard a banging sound, as of somebody pounding on a door.

"Come on," Deveraux said. He started off along the corridor at a brisk stride, Jane trotting meekly at his heels. They turned into the west corridor—and heard a muffled voice calling. Jane paused to switch on the lights. Deveraux pointed. "It's coming from that cupboard."

"I know who it is too," said Jane.

The cupboard in question was on the left and the near side of the alcove in which was the door leading to the western extension and the servants' quarters. A chair, which usually stood near, had been jammed under the cupboard door knob. Deveraux pulled it away and opened the door.

Gerry popped out like an indignant cork. She stared at them. "What the blue blazes is going on around here?"

"You tell us," Jane said. "How did you get in there?"

"Somebody put me there, you chump! Do you think I decided to spend the night there just for fun?"

"Don't get in such a stew. What happened?"

"I heard a noise, started out to investigate, somebody ran into me in the dark, we wrestled, and he shoved me in here. What was the noise?"

"A fight, we think. In Mr. Adler's room. The other man involved knocked me flying. And somebody else tried to brain Mr. Deveraux."

"Jiminy cricket." Gerry's eyes were big.

"Did you scream?" Deveraux asked.

"No. But I heard somebody else scream just before the blister ran into me. It didn't sound like anyone in real danger—just momentarily startled."

Deveraux pursed his lips. "It's time we had a look down there. First, though, I just want to see whether by any chance Adler's gone in to talk to Felman."

Gerry and Jane watched while he walked further down the corridor, quietly opened the door of Felman's room and disappeared inside. He emerged again in a few seconds and came back. "No. Felman's fast asleep with the light out. Come on."

They made their way back along the main corridor

and down the grand staircase, conversing in low tones. "Where on earth has Adler gone?" Deveraux muttered.

"Well, obviously an intruder got in," Jane said. "Presumably he's gone after him."

"An intruder could only have got in before the alarm was set," Gerry whispered. "So he must still be in the house. Do you think I ought to wake Daddy?"

"Not just yet," Deveraux said. "Let's see what we can find out first. We don't know definitely that there is an intruder."

Before they could ask him to explain this, they reached the foot of the stairs. Deveraux asked Gerry to turn the lights on. She did so. They looked round the hall. There was no sign of anything out of the ordinary.

"Right," said Deveraux, "let's do this systematically. You'd both better stay close to me, just in case. I'll lead the way, but you can guide me. Where shall we start?"

At Gerry's suggestion, they went to the rear of the west wing and worked their way back across the house, looking in every room. Nowhere did they find anything wrong. Yet in the minds of all three there was a certainty that something was going to happen. The tension grew, and by the time they'd been searching for twelve or thirteen minutes the two girls at least were getting decidedly jittery.

It was when they were approaching the breakfast-room that Jane stopped dead and grabbed Deveraux's arm.

He turned quickly. "What's up?"

"Somebody in there."

"The breakfast-room?"

"Yes, I heard a movement."

"Sure?"

"Of course!"

Deveraux hesitated, wondering what was best to do.

But Jane had had enough of skulking about in the dark and talking in whispers. Suddenly, she exclaimed: "Oh, come *on*!" Then she dashed forward.

"Wait!" Deveraux hissed. He tried to grab her.

But Jane was already reaching for the knob. Perhaps her palms were sweaty, but her hand slipped as she clutched it and she fumbled for vital seconds before starting to open the door. Then, as she did so, there came from within the room the most tremendous crash and the sound of breaking glass. At the same moment the alarm bell started to clang in the hall.

For two or three seconds Jane stood frozen, her hand on the knob. Then she threw the door wide open and burst into the room. Deveraux and Gerry were on her heels.

The room was in darkness, but light from behind enabled her to see a big jagged hole in the window. She stared, then gave a shout and pointed towards it. "There he goes!" She dashed across the room, but just inside the window tripped and fell sprawling.

Avoiding her, Deveraux ran to the window and looked out "Which way did he go?"

"Towards the lake."

Deveraux took a torch from his pocket, carefully squeezed himself through the gaping hole and disappeared into the darkness. Gerry put her head out and peered after him.

"It's pitch black out there. I can't see a thing. And it's lashing with rain."

She turned to see Jane in the act of putting upright a wooden step-ladder which had been lying flat on the floor.

"Is that what tripped you?"

"Yes." She leaned it against the wall.

"You couldn't tell who the man was?"

"No, I only saw him for a split second. And only in the light from the hall."

Gerry said: "He must have heard us outside and deliberately smashed the window—probably with that." She pointed to a chair which was lying on its side.

Before Jane could answer, Deveraux came back in through the window. He was already soaking. "Hopeless," he said. "This torch is quite inadequate. I can't see more than a couple of yards."

There was a footstep in the hall. They turned to see Merryweather, as dignified as ever in dressing-gown and slippers. "The alarm went off in my room, your ladyship. Has there been a break-in?"

"No, Merry, a break-out," said Gerry.

Deveraux went to the doorway and explained the situation in a few words. Then he said: "Merryweather, I'd like you to organize a thorough search of the servants' quarters and make sure no one is hiding there. At the same time will you check that the women servants are all right and find out if any of them have been up or out of their wing of the house—or if one of them screamed for any reason."

Merryweather flicked a brief glance at Gerry. She gave an infinitesimal nod, and Merryweather said: "Very good, sir." He walked away.

Deveraux turned to Gerry. "Lady Geraldine, no doubt the alarm has woken your parents. I wonder if you would be so kind as to go up and explain just what has happened. Tell your father there's no need to hurry down, but I'd be obliged if he could meet me in the library in a few minutes. Then rouse your uncle and tell him the same. Also, afterwards check that the Baroness is all right. I'm sorry to treat you like one of your own maids, but it is urgent."

Gerry grinned. "Aye, aye, sir." She ran from the room.

Jane was looking at Deveraux, a somewhat quizzical expression on her face. "We're very masterful all of a sudden, Mr. Deveraux."

"Not really, Miss Clifton. Merely efficient."

"Do you have no errand on which to send me flying, sir?"

"If you wish to co-operate, Miss Clifton—on a basis of equality, of course."

"Oh, I would not presume to such eminence. Simply issue your orders."

"Very well. I'd like to know whether the other guests in the east wing are in their rooms. That's Thornton, Fotheringay and Evans. Will you go and see? There's no need to wake them."

"I tremble and obey." Jane salaamed, turned away and started to walk off in the direction of the east wing. Over her shoulder, she said: "I'll go up the back stairs. It'll be quicker."

Deveraux watched her retreating form for a few seconds. Then he looked at his watch—it showed two-fifty-three—and went back into the breakfast-room. He crossed to the window, looked round on the floor and saw for the first time that among the few fragments of broken glass which had fallen inwards, a pair of wire cutters was lying. A pot plant, normally kept on the window-ledge, had also been put on the floor against the wall. Deveraux went up to the window and shone his torch round the frame. From the top right-hand corner two electric wires ran straight up and disappeared behind the picture rail. Deveraux fetched another chair from against the wall, stood on it, and satisfied himself that the wire was intact. Then he got down, replaced the chair, and left the room.

Lord Burford ran his fingers through his hair. "Extraordinary. Absolutely extraordinary. One of me guests knocked on the head, me daughter shut up in a cupboard, and someone smashing a window to break out of the house in the middle of the night after trying to put the burglar alarm out of action."

"I'm only assuming that," Deveraux said. "But the step-ladder and the wire cutters would indicate that that's what he intended if we hadn't disturbed him."

"It wouldn't have done the bounder any good, of course," Lord Burford said. "Cuttin' the wires would have set the alarm off anyway. The point is, though, what shall I do now?"

"Naturally, George, you must call the police." Lady Burford, wearing a dressing-gown and shingle-cap, spoke positively.

"I was just wonderin' my dear, as it seems so far that Deveraux here is the only person hurt, whether, if no other harm's done, we ought to leave the decision to him. I'm prepared to forget about the broken window, but naturally, my dear chap, you'll want the johnny who bopped you traced."

"It's not that, Lord Burford. The thing is that three people must have been involved in what happened. The man who hit me was not one of those who were fighting. One of those men locked up Lady Geraldine and may or may not have been Adler. It may have been Adler who went through the window. Or it may have been an intruder, who got into the house and hid before you locked up. Or it may have been one of the other guests— we should know that any moment. If it was Adler, why did he do it? If it wasn't, where is he? In either case, he's the envoy of a foreign government, and ought to be searched for immediately. Finally, unless there were two intruders, it seems an inevitable conclusion that one at least of your guests is not what he seems to be."

Just then Merryweather entered. Lord Burford turned to him a trifle irritably. "Yes, Merryweather, what is it?"

"Mr. Deveraux instructed me to make some enquiries among the servants, my lord." He looked at Deveraux. "I have searched our quarters thoroughly, sir. No one is concealed there. The housekeeper has woken all the maids. None of them has been out of bed tonight and none has screamed or heard a scream."

"Thank you. Tell me, are all the girls reliable?"

"I have always found them entirely so, sir, and I am confident her ladyship will say the same." He cast a quick glance at the Countess, who gave a decisive nod. "Most of them are local," Merryweather continued, "the youngest has been in service here for two years, most of the others considerably longer. Likewise the male staff."

Deveraux nodded. "Many thanks."

"Right-ho, Merryweather," Lord Burford said. "Better not go back to bed yet, though."

"Very good, my lord."

Merryweather turned to leave, and was nearly knocked over by an excited Geraldine. She addressed Deveraux breathlessly. "The Baroness isn't in her room. Her bed's not been slept in, though most of her things are still scattered around."

Deveraux swore under his breath.

Lord Burford said: "Have you told Rich?"

"No, I thought I'd let you. I called him before I went to her room. He should be on his way down any moment."

Before the Earl could reply, Jane hurried in. She too was out of breath. She said: "Sorry to interrupt, Lord Burford." She turned to Deveraux. "Mr. Thornton was already awake and I woke Mr. Evans accidentally. They're both coming down."

"And Fotheringay?"

"Well, Algy's asleep—" She broke off.

"Yes?"

"Well, it's awfully odd. He's asleep on the floor with all his clothes on."

Lord Burford clapped a hand to his brow. "This is getting like one of those Greek tragedies where messengers keep rushing in with more and more impossible tidings. Is the feller ill?"

"He doesn't seem to be. He's breathing normally and he looks quite stupidly peaceful. But I couldn't wake him."

"No smell of drink?"

114

"None at all."

"Extraordinary. Have to get the chap a doctor, I suppose." Then, as John Evans appeared in the doorway behind Jane, Lord Burford said: "Come in, my boy. Tell us what ghastly news you've got."

Evans came into the room, looking puzzled. He had dressed in slacks and sweater. He said: "I'm sorry, I'm not quite sure what's been happening."

Gerry started to explain. Suddenly Evans went pale. He said: "The alarm's out of action—and a man's got out of the house?"

"Yes, we don't—"

"Holy smoke!" Uncharacteristically, Evans interrupted. "Mrs. Peabody's diamonds! The Wraith!"

And he spun round and dashed from the room, leaving the rest staring at each other blankly.

16

Robbery

EVANS shook Peabody's shoulder and whispered urgently. "HS, wake up, sir."

Peabody opened his eyes and blinked. "John? What's the matter?"

"There's been something going on here, sir. An intruder. He slugged Deveraux and got away. The alarm was set off. I think we ought to check on the diamonds."

"Jumping jehosophat, yes." Peabody sat up and got out of bed, switching on the bedside lamp as he did so. Mrs. Peabody murmured in her sleep and turned over, but didn't open her eyes.

Peabody padded barefooted across the room to the dressing-table, and opened a drawer. He lifted out his wife's jewel-case. "She's left the key in the lock," he said. He turned the key, lifted the lid—and drew his breath in sharply.

"They've gone!"

"What?"

"And look."

He pointed into the box. Lying inside was an oblong of glossy white cardboard bearing a picture of a sheeted ghost.

"Well, that settles it," Lord Burford said. "We've got to call the police. Rich—will you?"

Richard, who had joined them during Evans' absence, nodded. "Right away." He left the room. Lady Burford, pale and shocked, murmured something about getting dressed and followed him.

Lord Burford said helplessly: "I just don't know what I ought to do while we wait for them." He looked hopefully at Deveraux.

"I suggest we have a look for Adler and the Baroness," Deveraux said.

"Do you think there's much point?" Gerry asked. "Alderley's pretty big."

"I know. Obviously if either of them is deliberately hiding we wouldn't have much chance of finding them. I'm only suggesting a quick look in each unoccupied room upstairs, as we did down here, just to make sure neither of them is lying unconscious anywhere. After all, we know there was someone in the house prepared to use violence."

"Very well," Lord Burford said, "we'll do it."

"You could get some of the servants to do it, if you prefer?"

"No, no. Quicker to do it ourselves. Besides, I want to be doing something—not just sitting around twiddlin' me thumbs. Come on, let's start. You'll lend a hand, Evans?"

Evans, who had come back down to break the news of the robbery, leaving Peabody to rouse and inform Carrie, gave a nod. "Of course."

"Good. Geraldine—we ought to get the doctor for Fotheringay. Will you see to it after Richard has phoned the police?"

Gerry nodded, and Lord Burford led the way out, Deveraux, Evans, and Jane following. They started up the stairs. Lord Burford suddenly noticed Jane. "Oh, I don't know whether you ought to come, my dear. The intruder might still be in the house. Could be dangerous."

Deveraux said: "With respect, Lord Burford, I doubt very much if there's any intruder here now."

"But only one man escaped through the window. You said yourself three people were involved. We don't *know* there was only one outsider here."

"I agree; but after the breakfast-room window was broken and the alarm set off, anyone could have left the house by any other window or door."

"My word, I didn't think of that."

"In fact, afterwards it would be advisable to examine all the downstairs windows and doors to see if any of them are unlocked."

They went up to the top floor. Lord Burford paused irresolutely. "Don't quite know how we should set about this." He glanced at Deveraux, on whom he was every minute coming to place more reliance.

"I think in the same way as the young ladies and I tackled the ground floor—go to the end and work our way back. Only now we can split into two pairs and meet back here. I suggest one of each pair should be someone familiar with the house."

"Jane knows the house as well as the family, so you go with her and take the west wing; Evans can do the east with me."

"Right. Nobody sleeps up here, do they?"

"No. There are some empty bedrooms, a couple of bathrooms, and the rest store rooms. My family's acquired quite a bit of junk over nearly three hundred years. We'll see you back here. Come along, my boy." And Lord Burford trotted off, Evans at his heels.

"At the double, B squad," Deveraux said, and started off in the opposite direction. Jane hurried after him.

"Mr. Deveraux, may I ask a question?"

"Certainly, Miss Clifton."

"How was it you came to be involved in this business in the first place?"

"I was hit on the head."

"But why were you hit on the head? I mean, what were you doing up and about?"

"The storm kept me awake. I decided to go down to library and get a book."

"A highly conventional reason. But why dress first?"

"Now I have to let you into a guilty secret. You see, Miss Clifton, I am not a gentleman by birth."

"Really? I would never have guessed. How wonderful our education system is!"

"For a member of the lower orders, a stay at a place like Alderley is a somewhat daunting experience. I have been anxious to do nothing *infra dig*. Now it seemed to me that to go downstairs in one's dressing-gown might be considered not the action of a pukka sahib. I pondered the problem for some time, and although I thought it unlikely I'd meet anyone, I decided to play safe. Hence the slacks and sweater. I was not quite happy, even then, and seriously considered putting my dress suit back on—after all, it was still nearer evening than morning. Eventually, however, I decided that would be going too far.

Right, this seems to be the end of the corridor. Will you take the doors on the right or the left?"

Five minutes after starting the search they were joined by Gerry, who told them the doctor was on his way. They met Lord Burford and Evans as arranged, and went down to the first floor where they met Thornton. The situation was explained to him and he helped with the remainder of the search.

The result of it all was negative.

"Do you think we ought to wake Felman and tell him his boss has disappeared?" Lord Burford said. "He might be able to throw some light on it."

Deveraux nodded. "Yes. I'll go and do it now." He hurried off.

Jane said: "I wish someone else would have a look at Algy. I'm a bit worried about the poor mutt."

Thornton, Evans, and Gerry went with her. They found Algy still sleeping soundly. They lifted him onto the bed, removed his shoes and jacket, covered him with an eiderdown and left him.

Lord Burford meanwhile had gone to dress. The others met Deveraux again at the head of the stairs. "I've told Felman everything we know," he said. "He can't throw any light on it."

Deveraux and Thornton then went downstairs, while Jane and Gerry retired to their rooms to throw on a few clothes, and Evans went to report to Peabody. The girls joined Deveraux and Thornton a few minutes later for a check of the ground floor windows and doors. None was unlocked.

"Not that that proves much," Deveraux said. "Anybody wanting to get out and leave no trace could have heard the window breaking and gone through it after we left."

The storm had now passed, the rain had stopped, and while they were making their tour of the ground floor windows they saw the clouds dispersing and the moon beginning to break through.

They went then to the drawing-room. Gerry rang for Merryweather and ordered coffee. "Bring lots, Merry," she told him.

Ten minutes later Richard came in again. He looked pale and drawn. Jane hesitated for a few moments, then went to speak to him. She found him bewildered, almost

119

dazed, quite different from his usual decisive self. While she was talking to him, Felman entered the room and came across. Richard seemed to pull himself together. He said: "My dear fellow, this is a most incredible business. I just don't know what to say."

Felman shook his head. "It doesn't make sense, sir. I must say, I wish I'd been woken before."

"Yes, you should have been. I realize that now. I ought to have called you immediately my niece roused me. But, of course, until we knew for certain that Adler was not in the house there seemed little point."

Jane said: "Mr. Deveraux did look in your room a couple of minutes after we found Mr. Adler's room empty, just to see if perhaps he'd gone to you for assistance. But you were asleep and there didn't seem to be any real reason to wake you."

Thornton, who had approached the group, touched Richard on the sleeve and drew him aside. "Minister, may I ask if you've notified the PM?"

"Not yet. Frankly, I don't know whether I would be justified in waking him at 4 a.m. with the information I have at present. If Adler's disappearance is voluntary, it may not necessarily be a matter of great concern for the British government: if he's gone off on his own for some private reason, it will be more your government's worry, Felman. Should it turn out he's been kidnapped, by anarchists or Bolsheviks for instance, it'll be a different matter."

"I'm just wondering whether I should contact my Embassy immediately," Felman said.

"It's up to you, of course. If you want my advice, however, I should wait a little longer and hope to find out something definite. It's not as if they could do anything at the moment."

"No doubt you're right." But Felman's voice and expression made it clear that actually he had grave doubts.

While they had been talking, Lord and Lady Burford, Mr. and Mrs. Peabody, and Evans had come into the room. Mrs. Peabody's eyes were red with weeping. The atmosphere in the room was very grim, with nobody feeling in the mood to keep the conversation alive. Algy Fotheringay's incessant drawl would for once have been welcome.

17

Enter Inspector Wilkins

IT was not long before there came the sound of cars pulling up outside. Lord Burford got to his feet. "The police. I'll see 'em in the library. You'd better come too, Rich."

Richard followed him out to the hall just as the front door bell sounded. They waited while Merryweather emerged from his domain and opened the door to admit two men in plain clothes and two uniformed constables. The first man was something of a surprise to both Lord Burford and Richard. He was short, rather plump, had a drooping black moustache, and wore a worried expression. He spoke to Merryweather and came forward looking round him in a lost sort of way. Somehow he did not inspire confidence. The second plain-clothes man was a brown-skinned young giant with an amiable expression.

Merryweather, in a tone which both Lord Burford and Richard recognized as being one of deep dismay, said: "Detective-Inspector Wilkins, my lord; and Detective-Sergeant Leather."

Lord Burford went forward. "Inspector, I can't say how glad I am to see you." He held out his hand.

The oustretched hand seemed to disconcert Inspector Wilkins, who as Lord Burford advanced had started, quite noticeably, to bow. He stopped himself suddenly in mid-movement—without, however, fully straightening up. The result was that he shook hands in an awkward half-stoop, as though he were reaching forward as far as he could to prevent Lord Burford coming too close. "My lord," he said in a deep sepulchral voice.

"Will you come to the library?" Lord Burford said. "We can talk there."

Inspector Wilkins sprang upright. "Certainly, my lord. Er, will your lordship be requiring the constables as well?"

Lord Burford looked blank. "I don't know, my dear chap. That's up to you. Do *you* want 'em?"

"Oh no, your lordship."

"Then I suggest they wait here."

"As your lordship pleases."

"Come along, then."

"Yes, my lord. Come along, Leather."

Lord Burford led the two detectives to the library; Richard brought up the rear. Inside, Lord Burford said: "This is my brother, by the way. Now, as to what happened . . ." Prompted occasionally by Richard, the Earl, who had received accounts of their activities from Deveraux and the girls, then gave a rather rambling but comprehensive résumé of the night.

When he'd finished, Wilkins sat silently for several moments. Then, very slowly, he started shaking his head from side to side, saying as he did so: "Oh, dear, dear, dear, dear."

Lord Burford stared. "Think it's bad, do you, Inspector?"

"Bad from my point of view, your lordship. Too complicated for me to unravel—and too big. Foreign envoys. International jewel thieves. American millionaires. European aristocracy. It's a job for the Yard. And the Chief Constable won't like that at all. He likes his men to tackle anything and everything that comes along. He won't be happy." And Inspector Wilkins was again looking somewhat blank. "But you *will* tackle it, won't you? I mean, until Scotland Yard gets here. You're not going to just go away?"

"Oh no, your lordship. I'll keep the pot boiling. Go through the motions, as it were. But don't expect me to solve anything. I'm not sanguine, not sanguine at all."

"Then what do you want to do first?"

"Well, sir, I'd better have more detailed descriptions of the two missing persons—and photographs, if they should be available."

Richard said: "It's possible their passports, carrying their photos, will be in their rooms. If not, I can probably give you as detailed a description of both of them as anybody. I can take the sergeant up to look, if you like."

"Thank you, sir. While you're doing that, I suppose I

ought to go and have a look at the jewel-case and this visiting-card. And then at the broken window." The prospect seemed to depress Inspector Wilkins still further.

"Very well, then, come along," Lord Burford said, "I'll show you."

"As your lordship pleases."

"Incidentally, my dear chap, I'm not a judge."

"I'm so sorry, my lord. Force of habit, as it were, after spending so much time in court."

They made for the door. Then Inspector Wilkins stopped short. "No," he said.

Lord Burford stared. "What d'you mean—no?"

"I don't want to see them. There's no point. They wouldn't mean anything to me. Jack"—he spoke to Leather —"after you've got the photos or the descriptions, give 'em to Smith. He'll know what to do. Afterwards go and have a squint round Mr. and Mrs. Peabody's rooms, and then at the broken window. Just see if anything strikes your eye. Don't touch anything. I may go and have a look later. But first, my lord," he said to the Earl, "I'd like to have a word with the rest of your guests and particularly with Mr. and Mrs. Peabody. It won't serve any really useful purpose, but I find it makes people feel better if they talk to the officer in charge of the case. Perhaps I can cheer them up a bit—convince them we're on the ball, as they put it. But then, Americans are always supposed to think English policemen are wonderful anyway, aren't they?"

Anybody less likely to cheer up the Peabodys would, thought Lord Burford, be difficult to find. But while Richard took Sergeant Leather upstairs, he led the inspector to the drawing-room and introduced him all round. This turned out a somewhat lengthy process, as Wilkins kept getting confused about names, and relationships and exactly who or what each person was. To the Peabodys, however, he was surprisingly tactful and soothing. He got from them the statements that both had been sleeping since before midnight and that neither had heard anything until Hiram had been woken by Evans. Carrie Peabody admitted that she had left the key in the lock of her jewel-box. "I'd been told Alderley was so secure," she said, "it just didn't seem necessary to bother."

"Well, don't blame yourself, madam. No doubt the Wraith would have had a key with him that would open

123

it. If not, he could easily have taken the box itself. The necklace was the only item taken, I gather. I assume there was nothing else of any value in the box?"

"No, it's mostly paste. I brought just the one really good piece to Europe with me for special occasions. I wish I'd chosen anything but my diamonds. It's not only the value—they are insured—but they were Hiram's present to me when he officially made his first ten million." She dabbed at her eyes. "They mean more to me than all the rest of my jewellery put together."

Wilkins nodded sagely. "Sentimental value. Of course. I know exactly how you feel. A few months ago I lost the truncheon which was issued to me when I first joined the force twenty years ago. I was highly distressed. I found it eventually. The dog had buried it in the garden. Perhaps we'll be as fortunate with your necklace, ma'am."

He addressed the the room at large. "Ladies and gentlemen, I understand that several of you have had unusual adventures during the night. But I've had a very clear account from his lordship and Mr. Saunders and I don't think I need to question any of you further tonight. So if you want to go back to bed, as far as the police are concerned you can. Thank you. Now, perhaps, your lordship, we could return to the library?"

"Of course."

They started to move towards the door. Then Wilkins stopped short. "Whoa," he said.

Lord Burford turned in surprise.

"Oh, I beg your lordship's pardon. The whoa was for myself." He turned round again. "I've changed my mind. I do that a lot, I'm afraid. I would like to speak to Mr. Deveraux tonight, if I may." He looked at Evans. "So if you could accompany his lordship and me to the library, sir."

"I'm not Deveraux."

"Oh, aren't you? I'm sorry. Then where . . . ? He looked round the room vaguely.

"Here." Deveraux stepped forward.

Wilkins looked pleased. "Ah, good. Come along then, sir."

Evans said: "Do you want me, too?"

"No, I don't think so, sir. Nothing personal, you understand. Of course, if you'd like to come along, I'd have no objection, personally."

"No, really, thanks."

"OK, then. Well, good night, ladies and gentlemen. I'll be speaking to you all tomorrow—or later today, I should say. Right, my lord."

In the hall, they found Richard, Sergeant Leather, and Merryweather waiting. Leather came forward and spoke to Wilkins.

"We found both passports in the bedrooms, sir. I've given them to Smith. Neither of the rooms looked as though the people had intended to do a flit, by the way. Their things are still scattered around."

Wilkins nodded. "We'll make a proper search later. Fingerprints arrived yet?"

"Yes, sir, they're up in Mr. and Mrs. Peabody's rooms."

"Take 'em to the breakfast-room after. Oh—wait." Wilkins clapped a hand to his head. "Has Smith gone?"

"He just went out a few seconds ago."

"Stop him, quick." Wilkins waved his arms about agitatedly. "Cockerill," he called to the other constable, who was still standing near the door, "go after him. Tell him to wait." Then, to Leather: "That Wraith card: did you see it?"

"Yes, sir. It looks just like the pictures I've seen of the others."

"Go and see if they found any prints on it. If not, put it in an envelope and give it to Smith. Tell him I want it sent up to the yard pronto for comparison. And Jack, as soon as it's light, you and Cockerill take a look round outside."

"What for, sir?"

"Oh." Wilkins looked blank. "Well, footprints chiefly, I suppose. But anything out of the ordinary. Detect, man, detect."

"Yes, sir." Leather nodded and hurried away upstairs.

Lord Burford came across from speaking to Merryweather. "My butler tells me the doctor's arrived. He's gone upstairs to see Fotheringay."

"Good. Perhaps you'll leave word for the doctor to kindly join us in the library when he's finished."

Back in the library, Lord Burford said: "I don't know about anybody else, but I'm having a Scotch." He crossed to a cabinet. "Deveraux?"

"Thank you, Lord Burford."

"Rich?"

"Please, George."

Lord Burford started pouring. "I don't suppose you do on duty, Inspector?"

"Oh yes, my lord, I do. All the time."

"Oh. I see. How do you take it?"

"Neat, my lord."

They all sat down. There was silence for a few seconds. Then Wilkins leant forward and spoke confidentially. "Tell me, my lord, just between us, how many millions is Mr. Peabody actually worth?"

"I really have no idea, Inspector."

"I've never met a real millionaire before," Wilkins said. "Makes you feel quite funny inside."

Richard said: "Inspector, I'm sure you know your job inside out, but—"

"No, sir."

"No, what?"

"I don't know my job inside out, Mr. Saunders. In fact, mostly I'm out of my depth. I am now. I consider myself extremely fortunate to have reached the rank of Inspector." Wilkins looked and sounded the picture of gloom. "Sergeant, and in the uniformed branch, at that, was the height of my ambition. I'd be more at home in that position, really. I don't rightly know how I came to be doing this sort of work. But there we are. Here I am and mustn't grumble. And I have got one asset—only one, I think."

"What's that?" Deveraux asked.

"I'm lucky, sir. And I sometimes play that luck. I get an urge to do something. I can't really tell why. But somehow it very often seems to pay off. Oh well, better to be born lucky than rich, they say. And it was just a sudden urge that made me decide to have a word with you tonight, Mr. Deveraux. Because I think you can put me straight on at least some of the odd things that have been happening in this house."

18

The Body in the Lake

DEVERAUX ran his finger round the rim of his
glass. "I can't think why you should pick on me,
Inspector. I've already told the Earl here everything I
know, and I imagine he's passed it on."

"He has, sir. But I'd like to hear it from you in your
own words."

"Certainly, if you think it'll help. Well, I was on the
landing, a few feet from the top of the grand staircase—"

"Why?"

"Why? Oh, I see what you mean. I was on my way
downstairs to get a book from in here."

"I see. No doubt the storm had prevented you from
sleeping."

"Quite."

"Fancy—and you an ex-naval officer, I'm told. So you
started to make your way downstairs in the dark. Why
didn't you switch on the light, by the way?"

"There was no need. I had a pocket torch."

"Of course." Wilkins tutted. "Silly of me. Now where
is your bedroom situated exactly, Mr. Deveraux?"

"On the corner of the main block and the west wing."

"So you were going towards the stairs in an easterly
direction?"

"No, actually I was going the opposite way. You see,
I'd got a little way down the stairs when I heard some-
body crossing the landing from east to west behind me.
So I turned round to investigate."

"Ah, now I understand." Wilkins gave a satisfied nod.
Then he frowned. "But exactly why did you want to investigate?"

"I thought to creep about in the dark was rather
suspicious behaviour."

"It certainly was. The man didn't hear you?"

"No."

"And why do you suppose he didn't see the light from your torch?"

"I didn't actually have it on at that time."

"Creeping about in the dark, were you, sir?"

"Not creeping, Inspector."

"No, of course not. I'm sorry. He was creeping; you weren't. Yet you heard him and he didn't hear you. There has to be a perfectly logical explanation for that, but unfortunately it escapes me. Could you enlighten me, please?"

Deveraux looked at him silently for a few moments. Then he chuckled. "Well done, Inspector," he said. "You really got me in a corner. Very neat indeed. Looks as if I'm going to have to come clean. Ah well, I feared I'd have to sooner or later."

He reached into his hip pocket, took out his pocket book, opened it and handed it to Wilkins. The Inspector looked at it without the flicker of an eyebrow, closed it and gave it back. "Thank you, sir," he said. "I thought as much."

During these exchanges Lord Burford and Richard had been looking more and more puzzled. "What the deuce is going on?" the Earl said.

"Well, my lord, Mr. Deveraux has just shown me something which proves that he's in a line of work not all that far removed from my own."

"What are you talking about? Feller's a writer."

"I'm afraid not, Lord Burford. I owe you an apology." Deveraux spoke in a quite unapologetic tone of voice. "I'm under your roof by false pretences, I regret to say. I don't think there would be much point in my showing you this, as it wouldn't mean anything to you. But Mr. Saunders will recognize it, I'm sure." He held the pocket book out to Richard.

Richard looked at it and nodded briefly. "It's right enough, George. Every government minister is familiar with these. There's no need to name Deveraux's department, but as the inspector said, it's allied to the police and I imagine often works in conjunction with Scotland Yard. Thornton told me he knew your face, Deveraux. I suppose he's seen you in Whitehall sometime."

" 'Pon my soul." Lord Burford looked at Deveraux

with something approaching awe. "You mean John Buchan stuff, is that it?"

"Well, rarely so heroic, sir, but something like that."

"And you're not a writer at all?"

"No."

"And there ain't going to be any book?"

"I feel a frightful cad, but no, I'm sorry."

"But I heard you talking about a pen-name—something George; naturally I noticed it specially."

"Jonathan George. He's a friend of mine. Allowed me to use his name. Andrew Lewis doesn't exist."

"Why are you here?" Richard asked him.

"I'm here on the Prime Minister's instructions."

"The PM sent you?"

"He ordered my chief to send someone."

"Why wasn't I informed who you really were?"

"Because it was important nobody else knew. And it is difficult for the average person to behave naturally to somebody in my line of work. If one person knows the truth, usually the others guess it."

"I understand that. No doubt it's a sensible policy. But I wish I'd known, all the same."

"I think everybody here will now have to be told that I'm not what I first claimed to be," Deveraux said. "But with the approval of you all, we'll let it be thought I'm a Scotland Yard man."

"Then mind you remember to call everybody 'sir' or 'madam'," Wilkins said.

"I'll do my best—sir."

"Are you able to say why the Prime Minister wanted you here?"

"I think I'm bound to, if we're going to make any progress," Deveraux said. "I'll tell you everything I know, Wilkins, on the understanding that it's top secret stuff. Mr. Saunders here and Adler, who is a very important man indeed in his own country, have been engaged in highly crucial talks in the last few days. Exactly what the talks are about, I have not been informed myself; but I do know that a successful outcome is considered vital. I don't think Mr. Saunders can tell us more than that, or indeed that we need to know more. But you'll realize it puts a different complexion on Adler's disappearance."

Wilkins gave a deep sigh. "Bad," he said. He looked at Richard. "Would it be improper to ask if anything took place during these talks which could account for Adler's disappearance?"

Richard shook his head. "Nothing. I can tell you that the negotiations were not proceeding as smoothly as we could have hoped; we had run into difficulties. But it would have been absurd to suppose that this could be sufficient to cause Adler to cut and run."

Wilkins drummed on the arm of the chair with his fingers. "What was your brief, Mr. Deveraux?"

"I was told that a lot of people want to know what's decided here—or perhaps make sure *nothing* is decided. The PM wanted somebody on the premises just to keep an eye on things. My orders were simply to be alert for any unusual occurrence or suspicious circumstances, make sure nobody overheard any part of the talks—and just be here in case of emergency. Which I was—with singular lack of success."

"Why exactly were you up tonight?"

"I've been making patrols of the whole house at irregular intervals during the nights. There were several reasons. Firstly, my department notified me on Friday that the telephone authorities had informed them that a call had been made from this house to a public kiosk in London at two-twenty-five that morning. This indicated that something fishy was going on here, and if one call had been made around that time, another one might be. So I decided to check the telephone room now and again each night. Secondly, I wanted to keep an eye on the music-room. There was always a chance that if a spy was present, he'd try to plant a microphone there and run a lead to another part of the house. I checked in the room Friday and Saturday morning early, of course; but just finding a microphone wouldn't be enough: I'd have to know who planted it. The only way would be to catch him red-handed. The planting would obviously be done at night, and if I checked the room frequently, there was a remote chance I'd catch him at it. Again, I made a habit of checking up on the guests—going to their doors, listening carefully, watching for lights, occasionally opening a door and peeping in. It was all a waste of time as things turned out.

"Tonight I left my room just before two-twenty. I went along the main and east corridors and down the stairs at the end. I checked in the 'phone room, then went back upstairs. I had intended to have another hunt round up there and then go down again and look in the music-room and 'phone room once more later. But near the top of the stairs I heard footsteps approaching. I decided to follow them. Then—wham. Of course, as soon as I got to my feet I should have raised the alarm and rung the police. I ought to have realized I needed help. My only excuse is that for some time I was still a bit groggy—my mind not working at full effectiveness. And what with releasing Lady Geraldine, investigating the scream, and so on, there always seemed to be other urgent things needing to be done."

"Quite understandable," said Wilkins.

Lord Burford, who had begun to look a little restless, said: "Look, this is no doubt all very important, but shouldn't one of you be doing something now, instead of talking about what's already happened? I'm personally not so much concerned with Adler and the Baroness as with Mrs. Peabody's diamonds. The Peabodys are my guests, and I'd like to see some action taken to try to recover the jewels before it's too late."

"Oh, my lord, that's all been taken care of." Wilkins was eager to explain. "The alert went out within minutes of Mr. Saunders' call. We're already looking for the lady and gentleman—*and* the necklace. All the usual steps for major crimes have been taken—road blocks set up, and so on. I'm sorry I didn't tell you before, but I thought you'd have realised."

Lord Burford looked a little abashed. "Oh, I see. Sorry."

"I'm afraid it will all be a waste of time, though," Wilkins added.

"Why do you say that?"

"Well, it was half an hour after the alarm was set off that we were called."

Richard said: "We 'phoned as soon as we knew definitely what was wrong. Until then it was merely a question of a broken window and a couple of scuffles in the dark. It could have all been misunderstanding—an accident, or a practical joke, say."

"I appreciate that, sir. I'm merely pointing out that if a getaway from Alderley had been planned for tonight, anyone with a fast car standing by, and with open country roads all round, could have been thirty miles away before we started looking. The other point is that, as regards the necklace, in a rural area like this, no thief is going to carry round something as hot as that when he can bury it and collect it when the hue and cry has died down. So if we were to catch the thief, he'd be unlikely to be in possession of the loot, and we couldn't prove anything. I'm not sanguine, my lord, not sanguine at all."

"Then what do you propose to do now?" Lord Burford asked.

"I don't really know, my lord. Let me think."

But Wilkins was saved from having to think very long because then the door opened and Merryweather announced: "Dr. Ingleby."

Ingleby was a tall young man with a mass of ginger hair and a cheerful manner. He had been the Alderley medical attendant now for three or four years, and was also the assistant police surgeon; so he needed to be introduced only to Deveraux. He accepted a drink and sat down.

"How's the patient, doctor?" Lord Burford asked him.

"Sleeping like a baby. And likely to continue to do so for some considerable time."

"Can you tell us what's the matter with him?" Wilkins asked.

"It depends on how precise an answer you want. He's drugged, of course, but I can't say with what. A sedative of some kind—sleeping tablets, say. Do you know if he was in the habit of taking them?"

Lord Burford shook his head. "I should think it was extremely unlikely."

"I can't find any empty bottle in his room certainly."

Deveraux said: "And if he didn't take them himself . . ."

"Precisely," said Wilkins.

Lord Burford said: "Who on earth would want to dope Fotheringay?"

"I doubt if we'll know the answer to that," Deveraux said, "until after we've answered a lot of other questions."

"He will be all right, will he?" Lord Burford asked.

"Oh yes. He's had a pretty big dose, but by no means a lethal one. Though I expect he'll sleep most of the day."

"That," said the Earl, "is the first bit of good news I've had tonight."

Dr. Ingleby turned to Deveraux. "Are you the chap who took a blow on the head? Let's have a look." He did so, then said: "You'll live. Take a couple of aspirin before you turn in." He looked at his wrist watch and got to his feet. "Nearly four-thirty. I must go."

"Lord Burford stood up, moved across to the bell and rang it. "Good of you to have turned out so promptly, Doctor."

Then he looked up in surprise as, far too soon to be answering the bell, Merryweather entered. "Excuse me, my lord," he said, "the police sergeant wishes to converse with Inspector Wilkins."

The next second he was almost elbowed aside by Leather, who hurried into the room without waiting for an invitation. He spoke urgently to Wilkins.

"Could you come at once, please, sir? It's very important."

Jane let her gaze fall in turn on each of the other occupants of the drawing-room. Strange that nobody had yet taken up that funny-looking policeman's invitation to return to bed. Though both Thornton and Evans looked as if they'd like to. Of the others, Lady Burford was clearly far too indignant at the very idea of such events taking place at Alderley, to consider sleep; Mr. Peabody was annoyed, too, but chiefly, Jane thought, with himself: it must have been a long time since anybody had made a sucker out of Hiram Peabody; Mrs. Peabody was obviously still extremely upset; and Nicholas Felman plainly anxious.

It seemed, in fact, that the only person in the house was thoroughly enjoying the whole situation was Gerry. In spite of everything, Jane grinned as she looked at her friend's bright eyes and eager expression. There was nobody with a greater capacity for enjoying life than Gerry.

Jane's train of thought was broken by the entry of Lord Burford and Richard. Everybody stared at them expectantly. It was as though they'd all been waiting for this moment, had known that the events of the night were not yet over.

Lord Burford paused inside the door and looked round the ring of faces. At that moment Jane knew what he was going to say.

"I'm afraid I've got bad news." His voice was grave. His eyes sought out Felman. "Felman, I'm very sorry to tell you that Mr. Adler is dead."

Felman got slowly to his feet. His face was blank. He said: "Dead? But where—how? I don't understand."

Richard came forward. He said: "One of the constables has just found his body. He—it—was floating in the lake."

"In the lake? You mean he's been drowned?" Felman sounded utterly bewildered.

"No, not drowned."

It was Inspector Wilkins who said this as he came into the room. "The doctor thinks he was dead when he entered the water," he said. "Adler was shot. This is now a murder enquiry, ladies and gentlemen."

19

Murder

THE telephone at Alderley had never been used so intensively as it was in the hour following the discovery of Adler's body. Calls from Richard to the Prime Minister, from Deveraux to the head of his department, from Wilkins to his chief constable, followed in quick succession. Then Felman put through a long distance call to the Duchy. Later, came return calls for Deveraux and Wilkins. The instructions were explicit: to avoid undue publicity Scotland Yard was not, at least for the time being, to be called in; Wilkins and his men were to conduct the investigation, with Deveraux's collaboration and advice.

The reactions of the rest of the party to the news of Deveraux's real reason for being at Alderley were mixed, varying from excitement on the part of Gerry, to a decided annoyance on her mother's.

Meanwhile, the routine of murder investigation proceeded: photographs were taken; the Burfords, their guests and servants were fingerprinted; more policemen arrived and began a search of the park; away from Alderley, the hunt from Anilese de la Roche was intensified.

Wilkins left at seven a.m., when most of the house party staggered to bed for a few hours sleep. He returned at eleven and after spending a quarter of an hour with Leather, who'd remained, met Deveraux in the music-room. With the automatic suspension of the political talks, Lord Burford had told them to use it as an operations room.

"Well?" Deveraux said, "what have you got?"

"Very little," Wilkins shook his head glumly. "First, the Baroness's driver has hooked it. He was staying at the *Rose & Crown* in the village, but he paid his bill and

135

left late yesterday afternoon. A man answering his description caught the five-forty-two to London. He was alone. The car, of course, is still at the garage. Second, Adler must have died instantly. When Ingleby first saw the body at just four-thirty rigor mortis had already set in. Now, as you probably know, it doesn't normally occur until at least four hours after death; but as Adler didn't retire until one a.m., and was seen alive by several people right up to them, Ingleby says this must be one of those instances—which occur sometimes in cases of violent death—of rigor setting in instantaneously. They call it a cadaveric spasm. He estimates—and he stressed he couldn't be too exact—that when he saw the body, Adler had been dead approximately two hours."

"With what sort of margin for error?"

"At first he said about twenty minutes. When I pressed him to give an absolute minimum, he said he'd be prepared only to swear Adler was not killed later than three a.m."

Deveraux looked thoughtful. "When Miss Clifton first heard the sound in the breakfast room, I'd just glanced at the luminous dial of my watch. It was two-forty-eight and a half. So we can say the alarm went off at two-forty-nine. We do *know* Adler was in the house until then, don't we?"

"Yes; Leather's just told me the alarm has been checked: it had not been tampered with, and it worked perfectly. No one could have left the house before then without setting it off."

"Therefore, we can pin the time of death down pretty precisely. What else have you got?"

"Something on that Wraith card: there were no prints on it and we rushed it to the Yard. I had a 'phone call at the station just before I started back here. It's genuine."

"Genuine?"

"In the past, thieves wanting to divert suspicion onto the Wraith have had similar cards done—based on the reproductions in the papers. But this isn't one of those: it's identical in every respect with the cards left at the actual Wraith robberies: same quality cardboard, exactly the same size of card—and the drawing of the ghost run off from the same printer's block: there's a slight flaw in it. Now, nobody other than a few big chiefs at the Yard has ever had access to those cards. They've been described and photographed, but it's quite impossible that anyone could copy them so exactly. So this one has to be from the same batch as the others."

"Great Scott!" Deveraux looked staggered. "That means the Wraith was actually in this house last night?"

"Surprise you?"

"It certainly does. I was sure somebody else had seen that magazine article and come here determined to take advantage of it—pinch the necklace and pin the blame on the Wraith."

"You suspected one of the guests?"

"I did, yes. I imagined either that the other trouble here last night was a coincidence; or that the bogus Wraith used the commotion as a cover to steal the necklace. This puts all my theories back in the melting pot."

"Would you like to go over everything that happened last night—help me get it straight in my mind? I found the accounts a little confusing before."

"I'm not surprised," Deveraux said.

He carefully ran through all the events of the night as he knew them up to Wilkins' arrival. Then he said: 'Since then I've spoken briefly to everybody and asked them if they can throw light on any of it. But apart from the two girls, nobody admits to doing, seeing, or hearing anything."

"What about that scream?"

"That must have been the Baroness. Both the girls were on the first floor at the time. Lady Burford and Mrs. Peabody say they were asleep in bed. There's no reason to doubt them. So unless it was one of the servants . . ."

"Leather's been round with that butler chappie and spoken to each of them. They all swear they were in bed in their quarters all night. He believes 'em."

"So do I. In fact, old man, I'm quite certain none of the servants was involved in any way in either the murder or the robbery." *

Wilkins was silent for a few moments, digesting all he'd been told. Then he said: "Isn't it a bit fishy that all these people claim to have gone on sleeping with so much noise going on?"

"Not really. Plainly not everybody's telling the truth about being asleep in bed, but we mustn't assume they're all lying. Alderley is tremendous solidly built, with thick

* AUTHOR'S NOTE: in this, Deveraux was right.

walls and massive close-fitting doors, many of them with curtains behind them. There are deep rugs and heavy hangings everywhere. From the bedrooms you wouldn't hear much unless it was something really loud and happened in a room adjoining yours or in the corridor immediately outside. Last night there was very little noise actually *in* the corridor. When I was attacked, the only sound was a sort of scuffling. Likewise with Jane and Gerry—neither of them screamed or shouted. The three of us who were in the corridor all heard the noise in Adler's room, but I wouldn't expect anybody else to have done—don't forget Gerry's room is one side and Lady Burford's boudoir the other. The scream came from downstairs and was quite faint. On top of everything else, remember the thunder: that could have muffled a lot of other noises.

Wilkins grunted ruminatively. Then he asked: "Got any theories at this stage?

"Not really. It seems to depend on who went out through the window. Let's assume that it was the Wraith. He'd broken in here during the evening, hidden, come out around two or quarter-past, entered the Peabodys' room and taken the necklace. He'd planned to break out through the breakfast-room—either not knowing about the burglar alarm, or thinking he could circumvent it somehow—was interrupted, had to break the window, and got clean away. It may have been he who hit me and made the Baroness scream. If it was, Adler and the Baroness must have left later—after the alarm was set off."

"Then what happened?"

"Take your pick. They ran into the Wraith, who shot Adler and kidnapped the Baroness. Or the Baroness was the Wraith's accomplice and went with him freely."

"The weakness of that theory is that the Wraith has never used violence—and several times he could have made escape much easier for himself if he had. Nor has he ever been known to have an accomplice."

"Right, let's say that neither Adler nor the Baroness had anything to do with the Wraith, and that she shot Adler herself. Or, that some third person, an outsider, shot him, and that the Baroness left with this man—either willingly or under duress."

"And suppose it wasn't the Wraith who broke the window?"

"Then it must have been Adler. In which case, the Wraith and Anilese both got out later. That would clearly point to them being accomplices. Perhaps Adler saw them outside and tried to stop them: if the Wraith wouldn't use violence, perhaps the Baroness would. Or the same outsider met him and shot him."

Deveraux paused. "Or somebody from the house followed him out, shot him, and came back. In which case the killer's in this house now. And that's the nastiest thought of all."

He spread his hands. "Are those enough theories? I could probably go on. There are things I haven't touched on yet. The scrap in Adler's room, for instance—why didn't the innocent party call for help? Who drugged Fotheringay—and why? I haven't even speculated—and I must say I think this is highly commendable of me—on why *I* was attacked."

Wilkins managed a wan smile. "Perhaps," he said, "we're speculating too much. I doubt we're going to get much further without some more facts."

"Yes, I agree. Such as an identification of the murder weapon."

"Oh, I'm sorry, I should have told you. We know something about that. The bullet was a 9mm; and there was something rather unusual about it."

"What's that?"

"Apparently it was fired from a gun with left-hand twist rifling."

"What?" Deveraux almost shouted this.

"What's the excitement? Do you know of a gun like that?"

"Not *a* gun. Two. Come on. I'll explain as we go."

They found a somewhat bleary-eyed Lord Burford devouring a late breakfast of devilled kidneys in the dining-room—the breakfast-room window still being out. Richard was with him. drinking black coffee.

"Any news?" Richard asked.

"Not yet, sir," Wilkins told him.

"Gentlemen, this is a desperately worrying business. I don't mind saying among the four of us that these talks Adler and I were engaged in are extremely urgent. And we were already behind schedule. The draft treaty should have been signed by this time. Now Adler's dead. Heaven knows how long it will be before the Duchy can get an adequate replacement here—and then we'll have to start all over again. The delay could be vary grave." He broke off. "I'm sorry. What was it you wanted?"

"We've got some information for Lord Burford, sir. Lord Burford, they've dug the bulleet out of Adler."

"Oh yes."

"It's a 9mm—fired from a gun with left-hand twist rifling."

Lord Burford dropped his knife and fork. "But that's—"

"The same as your Bergman Bayard. Very uncommon, isn't it?"

"It certainly is. You don't think mine was used to shoot Adler?"

"I don't know. But I think it would be advisable to check on it as soon as possible."

"Yes, of course. I'll take you up."

He led Deveraux and Wilkins upstairs and through the picture gallery to the gun-room. He opened the door with one of the keys on a ring from his pocket and went in. They followed him, Wilkins staring round in wonder. Lord Burford hurried across to the case where he had displayed the Bergman and gave a sigh of relief. "It's all right. It's still here." He opened the case and made to lift it out.

"Don't touch it, please," said Wilkins. He took a pencil from his pocket, inserted it in the barrel, lifted the pistol to his nose on the pencil, and sniffed. He shook his head. "Can't smell a thing. You say Mr. Peabody's got one the same?"

Deveraux nodded.

"We'd better go and have a word with him, then."

Lord Burford, who had had his eye thankfully on the precious firearm, suddenly gave what could only be described as a yelp. "Wait a minute!"

He made a grab for the gun. Wilkins tried to snatch it away, but was too late. It was in the Earl's hands.

Wilkins gave a groan. "Oh, my lord! Fingerprints?"

But Lord Burford wasn't listening. He was peering at the pistol with popping eyes, turning it over and over in his hands. Then he lifted a reddening face to Deveraux.

"This ain't mine."

Deveraux's eyebrows went up. "Not yours? You mean it's Peabody's?"

"No! This is a replica."

Deveraux stared at him. "Are you sure?"

"Of course I'm sure, you blitherin' idiot! Think I can't tell the difference between my own and a blasted copy? And it's not mine, either."

Deveraux looked bewildered. "Not your what, Lord Burford?"

"Not my—not my Bergman. It's a replica. Can't you understand? I've never seen it before. The Wraith's stolen my Bergman Bayard Special, blast him."

He wheeled round on Inspector Wilkins, brandishing the pistol under his nose. "Wilkins, you'll get it back for me, won't you? Please. I only had it a month. Hardly anyone's seen it yet. It's priceless—practically unique."

"We'll do our best, my lord. But I shouldn't hold out too much hope. I'm not sanguine. I'm not likely to succeed in tracking down the Wraith when the best detectives in Europe haven't been able to."

The Earl gave a groan of despair. "It's a judgment, that's what it is, a judgment."

"Judgment for what, my lord?"

"What? Oh—things." He looked at Deveraux. "Sorry I snapped. Don't take any notice."

"That's all right, sir. Could you tell us if there's any ammunition missing?"

"I'll see." Lord Burford went to the ammunition cupboard, rummaged in it, took out a box, and counted. He looked up and said: "Ten cartridges missing."

Deveraux looked grim. He said: "Do you always keep this room locked?"

"Yes, always."

"How many keys are there?"

"Two."

"Where is the other one?"

"Peabody's got it."

"Has he indeed?"

"He's been spending so much time examinin' the collection that frankly I got a bit browned-off having to be with him all the time. So I gave him a spare key so he could come and go as he pleased."

"And he had the key overnight?"

"Presumably."

"Where was your key last night?"

"On my dressing-table. I ought to put it in me study

safe, really, I suppose—that's a combination lock. But I don't usually bother."

"So actually anybody could creep into your dressing-room adjoining your bedroom, pick up the keys, come here, take the gun, and replace the keys after, without you being any the wiser?"

Lord Burford looked guilty. "Afraid so."

"Did you take the keys with you when you went down in the night?"

"No."

"When you picked up that bunch this morning, did you happen to notice if they were in exactly the same place as last night?"

But Lord Burford couldn't say. Deveraux sighed. "Well, we'd better have a word with Peabody."

"What—now?" Lord Burford looked a little startled.

"Yes."

"Oh, I, er, don't think he's up yet."

"Then I'll have to wake him, I'm afraid."

Lord Burford bit his lip. "Are you sure you really want to do that? I mean, I'm sure you've got other things to do. Why not let me talk to him for you?"

"That's very kind of you, but I must speak to him myself—and as quickly as possible. It's important."

"Oh, all right then. I'll come with you."

They made their way to the Royal Suite and found Peabody in shirt-sleeves in his dressing-room. His wife, he told them, was still asleep.

"Any news of the necklace?" he asked eagerly.

Wilkins said: "I'm afraid not, sir. We wanted to ask you about another matter. Have you got the spare key to the gun-room?"

"Why, yes."

"Where is it?"

"In the pocket of one of my suits. Do you want it?"

"If you please, sir."

Peabody went to a clothes cupboard, reached in and came back with a key identical to the one on Lord Burford's ring. He handed it to Wilkins.

Deveraux said: "It was there all night?"

"That's correct."

"Did many people know you had it?"

"Why, yes. I made a jocular remark about it at tea yesterday. Took it out and said how I really figured I'd

142

made it to the top now I'd got the key to the Burford collection."

"I remember," Deveraux said. "Nothing to stop anyone coming in here last night while you were asleep in the next room, taking it and replacing it later, was there?"

"None, I suppose. Why, gentlemen, don't tell me somebody's robbed the gun-room?"

"In rather a big way," Deveraux said. "They've stolen Lord Burford's Bergman pistol and left a replica in its place."

"You don't say!" Peabody sounded shocked. "Why, that's terrible. I can hardly believe it. Earl, I'm mighty sorry. I know how I'd feel if I lost mine."

Deveraux said: "Yours is still safe, I suppose?"

"Mine? Sure, it's over here." He went across the room and picked up the case in which he kept the pistol. "Here we are, gentlemen. The new pride of the Peabody collection." He opened the case. Then he gave a gasp of horror. "It's gone!"

Lord Burford gave a squeak. "What! Don't say the case is empty?"

Peabody turned and held up the empty case for them to see. His face was a blank mask.

In a whisper Lord Burford said: "The bounder's got 'em both. The Wraith's nabbed the pair."

"But no replica left in place of this one," Deveraux said.

"You can see what happened," Wilkins put in. "He found out either about his lordship's or Mr. Peabody's gun, decided to try for it at the same time as he went for the necklace, and had a replica made to leave in its place. It wasn't until later, when it was too late to get a second replica made, that he discovered there was a pair of pistols under the same roof."

Peabody gave a groan. "The New York exhibition. I cabled, entering mine."

"Don't worry, sir," Wilkins said unexpectedly. They all looked at him. He spoke to Deveraux: "I was wrong. The Wraith didn't take both those guns."

"I tend to agree with you," Deveraux said. "Tell me how your mind is working."

"Whoever took his lordship's gun took ammunition as well—so he intended to use it. Now the Wraith is not a killer. He'd only want the gun for its value. So although he may have stolen *one* of the pistols, he didn't steal them both: the other was taken by the murderer to shoot Adler. And if the killer's got an ounce of sense, he isn't going to have hung on to the gun after the shooting. He'll most likely have thrown it away in the grounds—probably in the lake. So I reckon it will turn up."

Lord Burford frowned. "But surely it's *my* gun you're suggestin' was taken by the killer. The ammunition was stolen from the same room; on the other hand, we know the Wraith was in this suite, so it must have been him took Peabody's gun."

"It would seem so, my lord. But there's a weakness in that argument: it would be the Wraith—not the killer—who'd want to stop the gun's absence being discovered until he had a chance to sell it. The killer would realize that as soon as the bullet was removed from the body we'd identify the murder weapon and would spot the substitution. So it was the Wraith who had the replica made. Now the replica was substituted for *your* gun. Therefore the Wraith has your pistol, and the killer used Mr. Peabody's. My theory is that the Wraith came to this suite, stole the necklace, but didn't know of Mr. Peabody's gun, went to the collection-room and took your lordship's pistol. Then later the killer went there also, after your gun, discovered it missing, remembered that Mr. Peabody had a similar one, so came along and took that, pinching some ammo from the collection-room before he left it."

Inspector Wilkins looked round with the nearest approach to pleasure on his face that he had yet displayed. But the reaction he received was not encouraging. Peabody seemed to have developed a sudden interest in the catch of his case, while Lord Burford intently studied the pattern on the carpet.

Deveraux said: "Well, that's an interesting theory, Wilkins."

"I think so," said Wilkins. "It implies quite a coincidence. But I suppose no more coincidence than the one involved in his lordship and Mr. Peabody buying the two pistols independently in the first place, as you were telling me."

"Actually," said Lord Burford, "that's not quite so much a coincidence as you might think."

"No," Peabody said, "we've discussed this. Granted that the pair were only recently discovered, got split up almost

144

immediately, and were then sold separately to dealers—well, then the Earl and I are two of the most obvious people in the world for the dealers to offer them to."

They left Peabody to finish dressing and Lord Burford went downstairs to continue his breakfast.

Deveraux said: "What now?"

"Well," Wilkins said, "the butler was asking me about cleaning up the breakfast-room and boarding over the window temporarily. I think I can let them, but I suppose I'd better have a look at it first, just for the sake of form."

20

The Bloodstained Egg Cosy

DEVERAUX and Wilkins went down to the breakfast-room. Glass was still scattered around, the chair lying where it had fallen, the step-ladder against the wall, the pair of wire cutters on the floor next to the pot plant.

Wilkins righted the chair, stood on it, and examined the burglar alarm wire where it went behind the picture rail. He got down, picked up the wire cutters aimlessly, and kicked a piece of glass with his foot.

"No interesting prints in here, I suppose?" Deveraux asked.

"Just those you'd expect, where you'd expect them."

"Have your boys found out where the step-ladder comes from?"

"Cupboard outside the butler's pantry. Easy enough to find—the obvious sort of place to look."

He went to the window and gazed out. "The bloke turned left, did he?"

"Yes."

"Well, that ties up with the body being found in the lake."

"No footprints anywhere?"

"No, but that paved path runs almost straight down to the lake and if he kept to that he wouldn't leave any." He turned round. "What's this about a secret passage?"

"Oh, I'll show you."

Deveraux went to the cupboard door, opened it, and turned the knob as Gerry had demonstrated. The panel slid back.

"My, my, my," Wilkins said, "how very romantic." He

put his head through the opening, looked into the darkness, then withdrew and said: "Do you think it's a coincidence it should be *this* room—the one with the entrance to the passage—that was involved?"

"I'm not sure. Whoever broke the window might have come down through the passage in order to avoid me and the girls. But then he would have had to go and get the step-ladder. Why bring it back here? There are other windows nearer that cupboard where it's kept, which he could have escaped through."

"Unless he had the ladder already here, waiting for him."

"That means he would have had to move down earlier in the night, put it here ready, and go back up again. Why?"

Wilkins sighed. "Don't ask me. I'm baffled by the whole affair. One thing I'm getting more and more sure about, though, is that the clue to Adler's behaviour lies in these political talks. Saunders and Felman must know something they haven't told us. Yet we've hardly spoken to them so far. Shall we now?"

"Good idea."

"How do we set about that, do you know? I mean, what's the etiquette? Should we go and search for them, or just ring for the butler and ask him to fetch them?"

"A nice point. I think we can certainly go to our ops room, ring for the butler and tell him to ask Felman to join us. As regards Saunders, I'm not so sure. I think I'd wait for inspiration. Let's get Felman over first, though."

They were about to go out when Sergeant Leather entered. He was carrying a small object, which he handed to Wilkins.

"We've just found this, sir," he said.

Wilkins held the object up. It was made of wool. At one time it had been white, but was now darkened with dried mud and earth. There was also a small reddish-brown stain, which Wilkins put his finger on. "Blood?"

"Looks like it, sir."

"Where was it?"

"One of the men found it caught waist-high on a lavender bush by the side of the path that runs down to the lake."

"It's quite dry."

147

"Yes, sir. So it wasn't out there during the storm. It wouldn't have dried out yet."

"Anybody know what time the rain stopped?"

"Between about two-fifty and three-forty," Deveraux said.

Wilkins said: "Go and find out exactly, will you, Jack?"

"Yes, sir." Leather left the room.

"Now," Wilkins said, "what is this thing? An ear muff? A doll's hat?"

"May I?" Deveraux took the object and examined it. "I fancy it's what is known as an egg cosy."

"What—one of those things you put over a boiled egg to keep it hot?"

"That's it."

"I believe you're right. What the dickens was it doing out there? And where did all this mud and stuff come from? I wonder if it's from the house."

"We can soon find out." Deveraux rang the bell.

Just then they heard footsteps in the corridor and Gerry came in. "Good morning," she said.

"Ah," Deveraux said, "just the person we want. Can you identify this beautiful thing?"

Gerry took it gingerly. "Ugh! What is it?"

"We believe an egg cosy."

Gerry frowned. Then her face cleared. "Oh yes. Mummy bought some at the Sale of Work a couple of years ago—along with a load of other equally useless stuff. We always get lumbered with a lot of junk. No doubt they were crocheted by one of the old pussies in the village. I doubt if they've ever been used. Ghastly things." She raised it to her nose and sniffed. "Smells of lavender."

"Yes, it was found caught on a lavender bush outside. Where was that kept normally?"

"I've no idea. Merry would know."

The next moment Merryweather arrived.

"Merry, where are our egg cosies kept?" Gerry asked him.

"In the right-hand drawer of the sideboard, your ladyship."

Deveraux turned round and opened the drawer. Inside, together with various napkin rings and table mats, were a number of white pristine replicas of the bedraggled object in Gerry's hand. He took one out. "How many here normally?"

148

"Six, sir."

"Sure?"

"Yes, sir. Unfortunately, I see them most days."

"Only five here now." Deveraux put the clean cosy back and closed the drawer. "Any idea," he asked, "why that particular one her ladyship is holding should have been attached to a lavender bush outside, smeared with earth and stained with blood?"

"None at all, sir."

"Lady Geraldine?"

"Search me. I can't find it in my heart to grieve over its suffering, either."

"I don't know why everyone dislikes them so," Wilkins said, "I think they're very nice."

"Mr. Wilkins," Gerry said, "you are very welcome to them." She went to the sideboard, took out the five egg cosies and handed them to him with a ceremonial curtsy. "Compliments of the management."

"Why, thank you, your ladyship. That's very kind. I'm extremely partial to boiled eggs and these will be most useful." He put them in his pocket.

"Well," Gerry said, "on this cordial note I leave you." She tossed the bloodstained egg cosy to Deveraux and went out.

Merryweather said: "Will that be all, sir?"

"Yes, thank you, Merryweather. But you might ask Mr. Felman if he'd kindly join us in the music-room in ten minutes."

"Very good, sir." Merryweather made for the door, then stood aside to allow Sergeant Leather to enter before withdrawing.

Leather said: "I've 'phoned the meteorological office. They estimate the rain must have stopped here at between two-fifty and three."

Deveraux frowned. "Within minutes, that is, of my coming back in. And as we already know nobody left the house before the window was broken at just before two-fifty, the information doesn't really add anything."

"I suppose," said Wilkins, "that the most likely explanation is that somebody was running carrying it and either threw it away, or it caught accidentally on the bush and he didn't have time to stop for it."

"And as it was kept in this room, the somebody must have been the man who went through this window—we know he spent some time here; we know he was running in the dark towards the lake. But why in heaven's name would he want to take an egg cosy with him?" Deveraux turned away and started to prowl aimlessly round the room.

"To carry something in?" Wilkins suggested.

"What could you get in it? Not a diamond necklace, certainly. And why would you want to carry *anything* in it?"

Sergeant Leather gave a discreet cough. "Sir, the man might have been intending to knock or tap something— perhaps using the wire cutters as a makeshift hammer. The egg cosy would be a good thing to muffle the sound."

Wilkins looked impressed. "Well thought out, my lad."

Leather flushed, then emboldened went on: "He might have had it in his hand when he was disturbed, sir. Then he broke the window and jumped through, cutting his hand and staining the wool. He ran down the path as you say, and either dropped it or threw it away as he was passing the lavender bush. That would explain everything, I think."

"Not everything," Deveraux said. "It's an ingenious theory, but it doesn't explain the earth and mud."

"He might have tripped and fallen on a muddy patch with it in his hand, sir."

Deveraux smiled. "I wish I could agree with you, Leather, I really do. But look at it. He handed him the cosy. "If that's what had happened, you'd surely find a great heavy patch of mud on one side, and virtually none on the other. But you don't. The stuff has been lightly and evenly smeared over every part of it. It's been done deliberately and systematically. And I think I can prove it. Look at this." He picked up the pot plant. "Examine the surface of the soil. It's been disturbed. It's had something rubbed on it. See all those little marks? And if you look really closely you'll spot lots of tiny scraps of white wool."

Wilkins took a magnifying glass from his pocket and together he and Leather closely scrutinized the soil. Wilkins said: "Yes, you're quite right."

"It doesn't mean your theory's all wrong, Leather," Deveraux told him. "Far from it. But it doesn't go far enough. He must have had a reason for deliberately soiling it. What do you think, Wilkins?"

"Nothing."

"What do you mean—nothing?"

"I've stopped thinking about it. I reckon I've spent quite long enough on a dirty egg cosy. It doesn't mean anything. If I keep on trying to work it out, I'll go crazy."

Deveraux laughed.

"Leather," Wilkins said, "get it confirmed that this *is* human blood, and if so, which group. After that I'm going on with this investigation as though it had never been found. And now, Mr. Deveraux, we'd better get along. We mustn't keep Mr. Felman waiting."

21

Mr. Felman's Bombshell

THEY beat Felman to the music-room by about a minute. He looked pale and tired when he came in, but there was a decisiveness in his manner that Deveraux hadn't seen before. When Wilkins explained what they wanted, he nodded briskly.

"Yes, it's true. I've got a lot to tell. But not to you two alone. Mr. Saunders must be present. I was just going to seek him out when I got your message."

Wilkins cocked an eyebrow at Deveraux, who nodded and rang the bell again. When Merryweather came Deveraux said: "We'd be glad of a few words with Mr. Saunders, Merryweather. Would you ask him where would be convenient?"

"I've no doubt he will join you here, sir."

"Tell him I think he might like to have Mr. Thornton present, too," Felman added.

"Very good, sir." Merryweather withdrew.

They sat in silence for a few minutes. Then Richard and Thornton arrived. When everyone was sitting down, Felman said: "I'm afraid what I'm going to say may be a shock. I hope, though, that it may not be an altogether unpleasant one. The truth is"—he took a deep breath—"the man killed last night was not Martin Adler."

A stunned silence greeted these words. It was broken by Wilkins. "It said on his passport he was," he remarked calmly.

"His passport was a fake. He was an impostor."

"Oh no." Richard breathed the words. He sank his head in his hands and closed his eyes.

"I knew it!" Thornton's normally pale face was flushed and his voice raised. "He never rang true. Never. I was a fool! I let myself be convinced he was genuine, merely because I thought he had to be."

"Would you mind telling us who he really was?" Wilkins said.

"I'm afraid—well, he was a spy." Felman looked at Deveraux. "You may have heard of him. His real name was Batchev."

Deveraux drew his breath in with a sharp hiss. "Not—not Stanislaus Batchev?"

"That's right."

Deveraux's face was a study. "I don't believe it!"

Felman shrugged. "That's what he told me his name was. I have no reason to doubt him."

Richard raised his head and opened horror-stricken eyes. "I've been negotiating with a foreign agent."

"Don't worry," Felman said, "he didn't get the information he wanted. His mission failed. His death was the best thing that could have happened, for both our countries."

"What—what was he after?"

"What he kept demanding during the talks—full details of your government's commitment. I needn't be more specific, I'm sure."

"Who was he working for?" Thornton asked.

"He didn't say. He was a freelance, apparently, who worked for the highest bidder."

"I can guess who that was," Richard said grimly.

"Whoever it was, they knew what they were doing," Deveraux said. "Stanislaus Batchev is—was—a legend in my line of work. He was probably the greatest undercover agent in the world." He stood up suddenly. "And I lived in the same house as him for nearly three days and didn't spot him! In frustration he punched his right fist into the palm of his left hand.

"Perhaps it'll be some consolation," Felman said, "if I tell you I don't think he spotted you, either."

"May I ask, sir," Wilkins said softly, "if you knew who he was and what he was after, why you co-operated with him?"

"It's very simple. His accomplices are holding my sister Anna a prisoner."

Richard stared. "Oh, my dear chap!"

"I think you ought to tell us the whole story, sir," Wilkins said.

"There's not a great deal to tell. It started on the Orient Express. On the last night as I entered my compartment I was knocked out from behind. When I came round I was bound hand and foot and gagged, lying on the bunk. Batchev and another man were standing over me. Batchev had a gun. He told me Martin Adler was dead, that they'd stripped him of all identifying documents and thrown him out of the train when it was crossing a bridge over a river. Batchev said he himself was going to take Adler's place at the talks, that I had to go along with him to show him the ropes—and that Anna would be held in safety until the talks were over and he was out of England; but that if I didn't co-operate she'd be killed. He then showed me a photograph of her tied to a chair with a masked man holding a gun to her head. I had no choice but to agree. He had a full set of false identity papers, including a passport in the name of Martin Adler, but with his own photo and description. He needed me because I knew all the arrangements, and could brief him and help him along during the talks."

"What a fantastic risk to take!" Deveraux said.

"Yes; he could only hope to succeed because the negotiations were being held here—in a rural area—and because Martin had been going to meet only two British representatives, neither of whom knew him by sight. If the talks had been arranged for London, where he'd be almost certain to run into politicians, diplomats, and journalists who knew the real Martin, he could never have attempted it."

He turned to Richard. "You can see now why the talks went the way they did. You thought he was just being deliberately obstructive in not giving you the information you wanted. But he couldn't: he didn't know it. He was hoping to find some documents which would help him among Martin's things. But I told him all the facts had been in Martin's head. So Batchev had to bluff. He knew he couldn't hope to keep the deception up for long. His only chance was to try to force you to give him what he wanted quickly, without offering anything in return himself. I was in a terrible quandary. I had to think of Anna's safety, but at the same time I couldn't risk letting Batchev get away from here with all that secret information. As long as you held out, it was all right. Thank heaven you didn't give way."

Richard expelled his breath. "If you only knew how close I came."

"I was trying desperately all the time to work something out. He warned me not to attempt to inform our London Embassy, as a very highly-placed official there was in his pay. This may have been bluff, but I couldn't risk it."

"Was there no way you could have got in touch with the Grand Duke direct?" Deveraux asked.

"How? A letter would have taken too long, a cable isn't private enough. I could have tried to put through a telephone call; but you can't lift the receiver and get the Duchy instantaneously: the operator calls you back. I couldn't be sure Batchev wouldn't be standing by me when it came. He stuck pretty close to me, you know. He actually warned me he'd be checking on me at intervals during the nights, so I couldn't even try to call then."

Richard said: "What's the position now? You've been through to the Duchy this morning?"

"Yes, I spoke to the Grand Duke himself and told him the full story. The police are going to start an immediate search for Anna. The only question is, can Batchev's death be kept secret until she's safe? If his men should hear he is dead, I'm afraid they'll carry out the threat and kill her."

"Well, naturally," Richard said, "we ourselves wanted to keep the fact of—as we thought—Adler's murder quiet until all the facts were known and, if possible, the killer apprehended."

"That's what I anticipated. May I ask who knows about it so far?"

"Apart from the people who've been in the house, only the Prime Minister, the Foreign Secretary, Deveraux's chief, and the Chief Constable of the county. Obviously none of them will have talked."

"Neither will any of my men," Wilkins said decidedly, "nor Dr. Ingleby."

"And I made Merryweather personally responsible for keeping the servants quiet," Richard added. "That leaves just my relatives and the guests. I don't think there are any real dangers there. I can vouch for George, Lavinia, and Gerry. Peabody wouldn't be where he is today if he couldn't keep his own counsel, and Evans is a private secretary—one of a naturally secretive breed of beings.

155

That leaves Mrs. Peabody and Jane. Mrs. Peabody will, I imagine, be too upset about her necklace to be very interested in anything else. Jane's a sensible girl; I'll have a word with her. It's fortunate that the person who would be the biggest security risk is still asleep. We can be fairly confident the news won't leak out."

"I know you're bound to worry, Felman," he continued, "so I won't tell you not to; but I'm sure your police will find your sister very soon."

"And," Deveraux added, "although Batchev was quite ruthless, in matters like this he was strictly a man of his word. He wouldn't have been so successful otherwise. Nor would he employ men who would dare disobey him. If he told you he gave orders for your sister not to be harmed, I'm quite sure she hasn't been."

Felman bowed his head. "Thank you."

Richard said: "No matter what precautions we take, with all this police activity here, the press are sure to get onto the fact that something's happened."

"The press will be told that we are investigating a jewel robbery," Wilkins said. "In that respect the Wraith will have served a useful purpose."

Deveraux said: "Are we going to tell the others about the so-called Adler's real identity?"

Richard considered before saying: "I think we've got to. And about the fact—if they haven't already guessed—that he and I were engaged in important negotiations. After all, we are asking for their co-operation in keeping silent, and the truth is going to come out eventually, anyway. Besides, having introduced a spy into the house, I'm more or less honour bound to tell George and Lavinia about him. Gerry will undoubtedly worm it out of her father. That would leave only the Peabody's, Evans, and Jane in the dark—which seems both mean and unnecessary."

Wilkins gave a nod. "I agree, sir, and you're much more likely to get people's co-operation if you take them into your confidence."

"Very well. I'll make an announcement at lunch. Now, is there anything else you want of me? If not, I must go and ring the PM and tell him the latest revelation."

Wilkins looked at Deveraux, Deveraux said: "What we hoped, Minister, was that you might be able to tell us something about the dead man that would throw light

156

on his murder. Well, Felman's done that for us—with a vengeance. It changes the whole complexion of the case. We're going to have to start looking at it from a quite different angle. Unless, therefore, you've got anything additional to this that you can give us . . ." He paused expectantly.

"No, I can't think of anything. Can you, Thornton?"

"Nothing material." Thornton said.

Richard got to his feet. "Then, if you'll excuse me, I must go and 'phone Chequers."

Wilkins coughed. "Actually, Minister, there is something else, if you could kindly oblige: the Baroness de la Roche."

"What about her?"

"We have so little information about her. Anything you could tell me would be most useful."

"What—now?"

"Oh no, sir. Any time. After lunch perhaps?"

"Very well. There's little I can tell you about her life in recent years, so don't expect too much."

"Shall we say two-thirty, then, sir?"

Richard, Thornton, and Felman left together. When the door had closed behind them, Deveraux looked at Wilkins and said: "Well?"

Wilkins scratched his nose. "I suppose we've got to check on Felman's story—find out if the police there can confirm that Anna Felman is missing."

Deveraux nodded. "I think perhaps my department can handle that most effectively from London."

"Good. Can you get 'em to send down anything they've got on Batchev? Particularly names of known enemies. Blimey, there'll probably be hundreds. You know, Mr. Deveraux, I'm not—"

"I know, old lad. You're not sanguine, are you?"

22

Behind the Sliding Door

BEFORE lunch Richard had a quiet word with his brother, and at the close of the meal—at which everybody except the still slumbering Algy was present—he stood up and made his announcement about the true identity of the man who had been murdered, about Felman's sister, the importance of the talks, and the necessity of secrecy.

Felman, of course, immediately became the focus of attention and sympathy. This did not seem to please him. He looked decidedly ill at ease, until Gerry, seeing his embarrassment, insisted on taking him riding.

Jane meanwhile went out to the terrace where Deveraux was drinking his after-lunch coffee. He smiled as she approached. "Hail, fellow sleuth."

Jane's answering smile was somewhat mechanical. She sat down and said: "This man Batchev: I suppose he was a killer himself?"

"Almost certainly."

"That makes it seem not so bad—that he should *be* murdered here."

"It'll certainly be far less embarrassing to the British government for a notorious spy to have been murdered than a distinguished foreign envoy, under their protection. If it can be put around that sinister bearded Russians or fiendish inscrutable Chinese were seen prowling around the area yesterday, so much the better."

"What nationality was he?"

"Unknown. Probably from the Balkans originally, but I doubt if he had a home country in the true sense of the word."

"He sounded just like an American."

"Oh, he could assume any nationality almost at will.

We believe he spent a couple of years in the States quite recently. He was hired by—by somebody to try to co-ordinate some of the dissident and subversive organizations there. He travelled all over America, doing every sort of different job as a cover—reporter, waiter, actor, public relations man, lumberjack. He was very strong physically, much stronger than he looked. The FBI tracked him down eventually, and he only just got out in time. But he passed as an all-American boy for quite a time first. He had quite a lot of charm and was reputed to be very attractive to women. I don't know whether you felt that."

"Oh, yes. He wasn't really my type, but I can easily see how a girl could fall for him. You seem to know a lot about him."

"Well, he's been a bit of a legend for years. Actually, though, I 'phoned London this morning asking for any data we had on him. They rang back before lunch. So I've got it all at my fingertips."

"I see. Must be interesting work, yours."

"Police work, do you mean?"

Jane looked at him quizzically. "If that's what you like to call it. Tell me, Mr. Deveraux, don't all Scotland Yard detectives start as uniformed bobbies? Would I have ever seen you, say, on point duty at Marble Arch?"

"Of course. Every February 29th—except in Leap Years."

"That's what I thought. Don't worry, I'm not going to press the point. May I ask if you're making progress?"

"Some. But it's all very puzzling."

"The business of the missing guns is strange, isn't it? Did I mention that I heard someone leaving the gallery just before I left my room in the night?"

"No, you didn't." Deveraux looked interested.

"Sorry. It didn't seem frightfully important in relation to the other things. Is it?"

"I don't know. What time was this?"

"A few minutes before two-thirty. I suppose it must have been the thief?"

"Very probably. You didn't see anything?"

Jane shook her head regretfully. "No. I looked in the gallery. Everything seemed OK. Then I made my way to the main corridor with the aid of matches. Suddenly all that bumping and banging started. It stopped. I heard the scream, and someone crashed into me. Then the whole place seemed full of movement and noises—people all round me. I'm afraid I panicked. I dashed blindly through the nearest door. After—"

"Which door was that?"

"The linen-room."

"Where the secret passage comes out?"

"That's right."

"There was nobody in there?"

Jane hesitated. "No."

"Sure?"

"Well, I didn't see or hear anybody. Mind you, I didn't switch the light on."

"You said before that there were people all round you?"

"That's an exaggeration, I suppose. What I meant was that I heard several lots of footsteps—some close at hand, some farther away."

"The close ones being the man who crashed into you?"

"Those first, but others after."

"How close?"

"Oh, within touching distance—if I'd wanted to touch."

"Man or woman?"

"I don't know. Certainly quite light enough to have been a woman."

Deveraux leaned forward: "Jane, tell me—could they have either come out of or gone into the linen-room?"

He seemed quite unconscious of having for the first time addressed her by her Christian name. It didn't escape Jane's attention, however, and to her surprise she felt a sudden stab of pleasure. She had to force herself to concentrate on answering his question. "I don't think so."

"Why do you say that?"

"I—I don't know. I didn't hear the noise of the door opening or closing."

"Would you necessarily have heard it—if it was done carefully?"

"Perhaps not. Is it important?"

"Who can say what's important? If we knew definitely that somebody used the passage last night, it might in the final analysis turn out to be a vital piece of the jigsaw. I'm only clutching at straws really."

Just then Sergeant Leather approached. "Excuse me,

sir, Inspector Wilkins' compliments and could you spare him a few moments?"

Wilkins was waiting in the music-room. He said: "I'm expecting Mr. Saunders along in a minute. I wondered if you wanted to be present."

"Do you want me?"

Wilkins pulled at his ear. "Frankly, no. You see, there may be aspects of his relationship with the Baroness that he'd find easier to discuss with me, an outsider, than with a social equal."

"My dear Wilkins, you flatter me. I've got no earls in my family."

"You know what I mean. You're an educated man, an officer and a gentleman, etcetera; you were staying here as a guest; no doubt you've got mutual friends."

Deveraux gave a nod. "I see what you mean. Perhaps it's a point. I'll steer clear."

"Right."

"As long as you know I won't be sticking my meddling nose in, you'll be able to be a bit more ruthless, push him a bit hard, eh?"

"We—ll . . ." Wilkins spread his hands.

Deveraux grinned. "And you're the geezer who had the bally crust to say you'd be happier in the uninformed branch!"

After Deveraux left her, Jane remained sitting thoughtfully on the terrace for several minutes. She was casting her mind back to those few moments the previous night after she'd been knocked down. She closed her eyes and tried to re-live it all: scrambling to her feet, half-falling into the linen-room, leaning up against the wall, heart pounding, ears straining.

Yes. Jane gave a firm nod to nobody in particular. It might get her into trouble, but she'd do it. It was time she did something, anyway, and didn't just sit back waiting for other people to do things.

She went indoors and upstairs to her room where she collected her handbag. She returned to the main corridor, entered the linen-room, crossed to the wall, put down her handbag, placed her hands on the sliding panel, and pushed sideways. It slid smoothly back. Jane opened her bag, took out a box of matches, and struck one.

"Planning a little arson?"

The voice came quite without warning from behind her. Jane jumped and spun round, dropping the match.

It was Deveraux. He was standing in the doorway holding an electric torch. Jane gave a gasp. "Oh, you idiot! You scared me half to death."

He grinned. "Sorry." He came across. "What's up?"

"Well, after I told you I hadn't seen or heard anything in here last night I started thinking. And I suddenly remembered that, although that was quite true, I had *smelt* something."

"What was that?"

"Scent."

"Really?"

"Yes: the Baroness's scent. She was wearing it last night. It's quite distinctive. Perhaps you noticed it."

"I did indeed."

"This passage is very cramped, as you know. It occurred to me that it's the kind of place where somebody might leave a clue—rub against the side, catch their clothing, drop something. I thought it might be worthwhile having a look."

"You should leave that sort of thing to the professionals, you know. An amateur blundering in is just as likely to destroy clues as find them."

Jane flushed. "Oh, really! I am not an absolute fool and I'm not in the habit of blundering. This strange idea that a reasonably intelligent person can't carry out a perfectly straightforward task just because he or she doesn't do it for a living is beyond me."

"All right, all right." Deveraux raised his hands in surrender. "I accept that you're quite capable of doing anything you set your mind to, and I apologize. Since you got here first I wouldn't dream of trying to stop you now. However, as you can see, I did have the same idea"—he held up the torch—"so would you graciously allow me to collaborate?"

"You know," Jane said, "you've got an absolute genius for getting my back up. OK. May I borrow your torch?"

Deveraux handed it to her. "If I may suggest: look very carefully round from the outside before you actually step in."

"Would you believe that actually had occurred to me?"

Jane hung her bag over her arm, switched on the torch, leaned in through the gaping black square, and shone the torch downwards—straight onto the dead staring eyes of Anilese de la Roche.

Jane uttered a half-strangled scream and hurled herself backwards into Deveraux's arms. He gave an exclamation.

"What on earth—?"

She turned and buried her face in his jacket. "Her—Anilese—in there."

"What!"

Deveraux grabbed the torch from her hand, strode to the opening and looked in. He gave a long silent whistle. Then he stepped into the opening and for a few seconds was out of her sight.

Jane leaned up against the wall, her eyes closed, fighting nausea. She managed to regain her equilibrium, then opened her eyes to see Deveraux emerging from the passage. His face was grim. In one hand he was carrying an object draped in his handkerchief.

He said: "She's been shot. Through the heart. Some time ago, I should think." He came up and put his arm round her shoulder. "Gosh, you poor kid. What an experience. I could kick myself for letting you look first."

Jane said: "I'm all right. It was just the shock—those eyes."

"I know. Try not to think about it. You need a drink. Come on downstairs."

Still with his arm around her, he led her out of the room. Jane had to admit to herself that, infuriating man that he was, he was capable of being very comforting.

"What's that you're carrying?" she asked.

He lifted his hand, shaking back the handkerchief to reveal a familiar-looking pistol. He was gripping it near the muzzle.

"One of the missing guns?"

He nodded.

"Do you think she committed suicide?"

"In a fit of remorse after shooting Batchev? Be nice to think so, wouldn't it? Very nice."

They went downstairs to the drawing-room, where they found Lady Burford and Mrs. Peabody. The Countess took one look at Jane's white face and jumped to her feet. "My dear, what *is* the matter?"

Deveraux said: "She's had a nasty shock, Lady Burford.

I'm sorry to have to tell you that the Baroness de la Roche is dead—shot."

He interrupted their exclamations by saying: "Jane found the body. I think she could do with a little brandy. Could you tell me where the Earl is, please?"

"He's lying down. I'll send a servant to wake him."

"No, don't bother, please. Mrs. Peabody, is your husband around?"

"He's on the terrace, I think."

"Thank you." Leaving Jane there, he hurried outside, where he found Peabody sitting, looking broodingly out over the park. Deveraux went up to him. "Mr. Peabody, we've just found this." He held the gun out, still holding it by the end of the barrel. "Could you say if it's yours or Lord Burford's?"

"Holy cow!" Peabody reached for the gun.

"Don't touch it. Can you tell just by looking?"

Peabody put on his spectacles and peered at the pistol while Deveraux twisted it about in accordance with his instructions. Then: "Yes, it's mine," Peabody said. His face lit up. "Gee, that's swell. What a relief! Can I have it now?"

"Not just yet, sir, if you don't mind. Thanks for your help." Deveraux turned and walked rapidly off.

"Say, where did you find it?" Peabody called. But Deveraux had already disappeared through the french windows. Wilkins was not going to like having his interview with Richard Saunders interrupted, but it couldn't be helped.

23

Lady Geraldine's Confession

LIKE a ghastly re-enactment of the previous night, the fingerprint specialists and photographers, the doctor and the ambulance men came and went. Finally Wilkins went too. Only two constables were left on guard duty, Wilkins having arranged for a continuous patrol of the grounds until the alarm system was operative again.

The house party passed an uneasy evening, and with all of them by now pretty well exhausted, physically and mentally, everyone retired early.

The only significant incident took place quite late, when Deveraux was writing up a few notes in the music-room before going to bed. A knock came at the door and Gerry entered.

"Can you spare a few minutes?" she asked. "I've got something to tell you."

She crossed the room and sat down. She looked pale, all her gaiety and sparkle seeming to have gone. "I want to make a confession," she said.

"Splendid. To the murders, the robbery, or all three?"

"Just to withholding information."

"I see. Will it clarify the problems or cloud them still further? Because if the latter, I'm not at all sure I'm strong enough to take it."

"Look," she said, "I know you mean well and you're being flippant to try to make me feel better. Normally I'd play along. I'm a pretty flippant sort of person myself. But I don't really want to be here. I'm not very happy. So could you take me seriously, do you think?"

"Of course. Sorry. What is this information?"

"One thing first." She lit a cigarette. "I haven't told anybody else except Jane any of this, and I don't want to, if I can avoid it. I realize you may have to make it public. If so, I'll be sorry, but I won't object."

"Good enough."

"Well, as you probably know I was very suspicious of the Baroness from the start. I feel a bit rotten about it now she's dead, but I was sure she'd gate-crashed the party for a definite reason, and I didn't believe for a moment she didn't know Richard was here. I decided to keep an eye on her. Saturday afternoon I heard part of a 'phone call she was making."

Gerry wriggled awkwardly. "I know it's not quite— quite to eavesdrop on one's guests. But the door of the telephone room had swung open—it tends to do that. I didn't hide or walk on tiptoe or anything. I just stood still as soon as I heard her voice. As it turned out, I didn't hear very much and certainly nothing incriminating. But it *was* interesting. The first thing I heard was, 'I just thought I ought to warn you.' Then 'No, not yet: I don't want a certain party to see us together again now. I'm going to ask him to come to my room late tonight— about two-fifteen or two-thirty.' Finally she said, 'You cannot make me change my mind, so don't try—just send it.' Then she rang off and I did a bunk before she came out."

Gerry drew deeply on her cigarette. "Of course, I couldn't let things end there. That night I sat up reading until two. Then this is what I did."

Deveraux listened closely to her story without interrupting. When she finished, he said: "Let me get all these comings and goings straight." He picked up a notebook and pencil. "You left your room exactly at two?"

"Yes. The stable clock was striking."

"So you were in position not later than one minute past. The Baroness left her room—two—three minutes after that?"

"Not more than three."

"We'll say at four minutes past. You followed her, lost her, and returned to the recess. You were away until six minutes past. Then half a minute after that, the man arrived. You definitely couldn't identify him?"

"No: black trousers and black leather shoes was all I could see."

"The Baroness arrived back about one minute later, having been gone three or four minutes?"

Gerry nodded. "Just long enough to have pinched the necklace."

"Oh, that's your theory, is it? Well, the more the merrier. But what about the Wraith?"

"Has it occurred to you he might have a woman accomplice?"

"It has. But he's never been known to have an accomplice in the past: and if he did, I can't somehow imagine him letting her do the actual stealing."

"Then suppose the Wraith actually was a woman?"

"My, my, that's an interesting thought. If it's a possibility, I don't know. Everybody's always assumed the Wraith is a man. Whether the police—er, whether *we* know that for a fact, is another matter. However, to revert: at about twelve or thirteen minutes past the man left again?"

"That's right."

"He held the torch low and just flicked it on and off quickly once or twice; finally, there was another arrival, just a few moments after two-thirty. This might have been the same man, or another. He knocked on the door and went in. Then you heard the rumpus in the distance, hurried along to investigate, and the rest is history."

"That's about it."

Deveraux was thoughtful for a few moments. Then he said: "Can we just go through what happened after we released you? I'd like to see if we agree on sequence and times."

They spent some minutes on this, finding that their recollection was virtually the same. "I want to do this with Jane in the morning," Deveraux said.

He studied what he had written for a few moments, tapping his pencil on the arm of his chair. "You'd be ready to swear to what happened while you were in the recess, would you?" he asked.

Gerry looked startled. "Yes—if I had to."

"You may very well have to," Deveraux said.

24

"There's a Killer in the House"

THE following morning Jane spent some considerable time battling with her pride. Eventually she won, and went along to the music-room. She found Deveraux there alone.

He looked up. "Ah, just the person I wanted to see."

"Oh?" She raised her eyebrows.

"Can we go over just what took place the night before last? I'm trying to get the order things happened, and the times, clear in my mind. I should have done this yesterday really, but finding the Baroness's body indoors makes it very important."

"Well, I didn't have a watch, so I'll probably be a bit hazy about times."

However, they managed eventually to get everything worked out, and in accordance with Gerry's account.

Then Deveraux said: "Did you want to see me especially?"

Jane didn't speak for a moment. Then, with quite an effort, she said: "I—I want to apologize."

"What on earth for?"

"Oh, everything. I've been feeling very guilty about you. First of all, after finding you half-stunned, instead of calling the Earl and insisting on your lying down, I let you go haring round the house, chasing criminals. Then, when we heard the man in the breakfast-room, I messed everything up—rushing forward like that, making a noise, fumbling with the knob, hesitating with the door part open. If I'd let you go first, you'd have probably caught him."

"I doubt it."

"There'd have been a good chance. But you never said a word of blame afterwards. Then again yesterday, I was an utter ass when we found Anilese—insisting on going first, then making a fool of myself, screaming and nearly fainting, like a silly little flapper. You should have told me it was my own stupid fault. But you didn't. So I'd just like to say sorry—and thank you."

He smiled. "Well, I won't say it was a pleasure."

Jane said: "Phew. I'm glad to have got that off my chest."- She grinned suddenly. "Mind you, I still haven't forgiven you for nearly drowning me on Thursday afternoon."

Just then Merryweather entered to tell Deveraux he was wanted on the telephone.

A few minutes after Deveraux came off the 'phone, Wilkins arrived. He was clearly bursting with news, so Deveraux decided to get his in first.

"Just had a call," he said. "Felman's story confirmed: his sister *has* been kidnapped. Now, what have you got for me?"

"Hold on to your hat: the bullet that killed the Baroness did not come from the gun you found by the body—*that* was the gun used to shoot Batchev."

"It was *what?*"

"Used to shoot Batchev."

"But—that's crazy! It just doesn't make sense."

"I know. But there's no doubt about it."

"Heaven help us. No prints, of course?"

"Yes, but they were badly smudged; quite unidentifiable."

"Well, at least it takes us one step further," Deveraux said. "It means Batchev's killer came back indoors afterwards. So we can stop deluding ourselves with comforting theories about the Wraith or another outsider shooting him and getting away. We know beyond doubt that there's a killer in the house now."

Wilkins sighed. "I know."

"At least it narrows the field. Anyone we can eliminate?"

"Not from the second murder. Virtually anybody could have killed the Baroness. We just can't pin the time of death down accurately enough to say who's in the clear.

The doc says twelve to eighteen hours before he examined the body—or between ten p.m. and four a.m. the previous night."

"We can narrow it a bit more than that, I think. Geraldine claims to have seen her just before ten past two, and I believe her. However, that can keep. Obviously, what we've got to do is concentrate on Batchev's death. We know he was killed between two-forty-nine and three a.m. It ought to be possible to work out who couldn't have done *that*."

"Let's try. How long do you reckon it would take?"

Deveraux considered. "Well, it wouldn't just be a question of sprinting out, shooting Batchev, and dashing back in again. You'd get very wet. Even if the rain had stopped, your feet and legs would be sodden. So you'd either have to put a macintosh and wellingtons on beforehand (and you couldn't know in advance that the rain was going to stop), or take time after the shooting to clean and dry yourself. Suppose we try a reconstruction?"

The next hour was spent in repeated re-enactments, by Deveraux, Leather, and one of the constables, of every possible permutation of the actions the murderer would have had to perform. Starting and finishing at various points, they went by every conceivable route, including the secret passage, to each possible exit, down to the lake, and back again; they either donned water-proof clothing and rubber boots first and removed them after, or went through the motions of drying and tidying themselves instead. Wilkins timed everything carefully. Afterwards, he dismissed Leather and the constable, and he and Deveraux returned to the music-room.

Deveraux said: "How long?"

"Ten minutes absolute minimum."

"And that's assuming you were quite reckless about the chance of meeting somebody—at just about the time people were starting to move about the corridors."

Wilkins nodded. "Then assuming Batchev was killed exactly at three, anyone who has a minimum period of ten minutes between two-forty-nine and, say, three-five for which they can't account must at this moment be considered suspect. OK?"

"Agreed."

"And you've got the times everything happened fixed pretty accurately?"

"I believe so. I've been over the order in which things occurred with both the girls; at the time I looked at my watch frequently, and the stable clock was chiming regularly—I remember, for instance that it struck three just as Merryweather was reporting the result of his enquiries among the servants."

"Good. So—who can we eliminate?"

"Well, both girls, of course. Neither of them was out of my sight for more than eight or nine minutes—and even that time is fully accounted for: Geraldine went to her parents' room, then to her uncle's, then to the Baroness's before coming down; Jane woke Thornton and Evans, spoke to them both, then found Fotheringay on the floor."

"Right. Anyone else?"

"The sleeping beauty himself."

"Is he still asleep?"

"Yes. The doctor had another look at him last night. He says the sedative doesn't seem to have done him any permanent harm, that he'll wake in his own good time, and we've just got to let him sleep it off."

"Remarkable." said Wilkins. "Now, let's go through the rest." He got out his notebook. "First, Lord Burford."

"He's in the clear. I was with him from two-fifty-seven until three-ten when we split up to search."

"Lady Burford."

"Oh, Wilkins, really—"

"We can't leave anybody out. Lady Burford strikes me as being a particularly ruthless type."

"She's in the clear, anyway: came down with the Earl, stayed till well past three."

"Peabody."

"Not cleared. Evans is supposed to have woken him at about six or seven minutes past three—but he might have been outside and just that moment got back to bed."

"And as Evans works for him and could be lying, we don't really know what Peabody was doing at any time before he and his wife entered the drawing-room later. Which means she's not cleared either. What about Evans himself?"

"I'm not sure. He entered the library not later than four minutes past three. Jane roused him as near as she and I can calculate at two-fifty-five. But it might have been a minute or so earlier—so theoretically he could just

171

have had time. But in practical terms—well, I think I'd put down *cleared—query*."

"Felman."

"Not cleared. He was apparently asleep in bed at about two-thirty-five and again fifty minutes later when I went to wake him. Between, he could have been anywhere."

"Thornton."

"Cleared. Jane went to his room last of the three—after waking Evans and finding Fotheringay and trying to wake him. It must have been two-fifty-eight or fifty-nine by the time she got to Thornton's room. He was in bed. He couldn't possibly have shot Batchev by the lake before three."

"Saunders."

Deveraux didn't answer immediately: "Cleared—I think."

Wilkins looked dubious. "Do you?"

"Well, Geraldine called him at roughly two-fifty-five. He arrived in the library at about seven minutes past three."

"Twelve minutes. Longer than Evans."

"All right. Put down *cleared—query* again."

"I'd sooner put *not cleared—query*. That extra two minutes is important. On top of that, remember, he knows the house and grounds like the back of his hand, which windows open easily and quietly, and so on. He could get down to the lake and back much more quickly and safely than any of the others."

"Yes, I can see that. But if he did, it means he knew exactly where to find Batchev—which implies a rendezvous."

"That could be said of some of the others, too."

"Only of Evans. Not Peabody or Felman. If one of them had been up to something, he could have been ready to take advantage of the first break-out to leave by another window immediately the alarm went off. He would have had to know Batchev was out there *somewhere*, but given that, he would have had up to eleven minutes just to locate him."

"Same applies to Mrs. Peabody."

"I'm sorry, Wilkins, but I'm not for one moment prepared to regard Mrs. Peabody as a serious suspect. Peabody is a possibility—but only just. To my mind it's got to be between Felman, Saunders, and Evans."

"And who's your favourite?"

"It ought to be Felman. Batchev was a man who'd killed Felman's pal, kidnapped his sister—and was in the act of selling out his country. It would almost count as justifiable homicide."

"The drawback being the very fact that Batchev's men are holding his sister hostage."

"Precisely. Would he risk harming Batchev, knowing what might happen to her?"

"He might. If he was a particularly fanatical patriot. Or if his sister means very much less to him than he makes out. Perhaps he hates her."

Deveraux chuckled. "You are the most dyed-in-the-wool cynic I've ever met. Here am I, a member of what's supposed to be a hard, tough, sophisticated service, and that possibility had never crossed my mind."

"Got to think of everything," Wilkins said. "I don't think he did it, mind you."

"Who do you fancy, then?"

"Oh, I'm baffled. I've had a good long talk with everyone here and I still can't see any way out."

They were silent for a few seconds. Then Deveraux said: "Anything on the Baroness yet?"

"Very little. She had no criminal record either in this country or France. After the Baron died she travelled a lot, all over Europe and America. Her home address was officially Geneva, but she'd only got a tiny flat there and she didn't spend much time in it. She arrived in this country ten days ago, and she's been staying at the Ritz."

"What did she live on?"

"Her wits, I imagine. The late Baron didn't die a poor man; but nor did he leave her enough to pay for the amount of travelling she's been doing."

"Did you get anything out of Saunders yesterday?"

"Not much. He knew her in France during the war, but he hadn't seen her since 1917. He thought she was dead. Apparently a house where she was staying was destroyed by a bomb when he believed she was in it. He says it was a tremendous shock when she turned up here. He had no reason to think her story wasn't genuine. She told him very little about her recent life. They spent most of their time together after she arrived reminiscing."

"What did you think of his reaction when he heard of her body being found?"

"Natural enough. Perhaps a little too natural."

"Rehearsed, you mean?"

"I don't know. Politicians do learn to react in proper, set ways; perhaps it would be wrong to read anything into it."

"Do you think he was hiding something?"

"Of course. Everybody hides something."

"I mean, something really significant?"

"Yes."

"Do you think you can get it out of him?"

"Ooh, I doubt it. He's a skilled politician. It would be too much to expect a simple country bobby—"

"Wilkins, you're a humbug. I think you're dying to have another go at him. And I think you should—now."

"Do you really? Well, if you say so, I'll give it a try. But don't expect too much. I'm not sanguine, not sanguine at all."

"Well, before you see him, I've got something else to tell you. It might be useful."

He took out his notebook and, almost word for word, related the story Gerry had told him. When he'd finished he said: "No conclusions from me—you don't need 'em. I'll leave you to draw your own."

25

Cross-Questioning of a Minister

RICHARD came into the music-room where Wilkins was waiting. Sergeant Leather, armed with a short-hand book, sat unobtrusively in the corner.

"Well, Inspector, what is it?"

"I thought you ought to know straightway, sir, that the Baroness was murdered."

Richard closed his eyes. "No—no possibility of suicide?"

"No, sir; not unless someone found her body with the gun lying by it and deliberately replaced the pistol with another." He explained what the ballistics examination had shown.

Richard looked dazed. "It's unbelievable," he said.

"Have you got any idea of who might have wanted to harm her?"

"None at all. I cannot believe anybody in this house could have done it. What motive could anyone have?"

"There you might be able to help, sir. Did the Baroness drop any hint that she might have met one of the other guests before?"

"No."

"That any of them looked familiar to her—or reminded her of someone else?"

"No."

"Did she refer to the other ladies and gentlemen at all?"

"Hardly. She said she was delighted to meet my closest relatives; how kind my sister-in-law was; things like that."

"She didn't mention Batchev?"

Richard shook his head.

"And you never saw them together?"

"Never."

"What would be your explanation of the Baroness having made a telephone call on Saturday afternoon, during which she said: 'I don't want a certain party to see us together again now. I'm going to ask him to come to my room late tonight, about two-fifteen or two-thirty'?"

Richard's eyes widened and for a second he stopped breathing. Then he said: "How extraordinary. To whom was the call made?"

"I would guess to her driver—the man she called Roberts. He was staying at the *Rose & Crown*, but he left shortly after the Baroness made the call, and took the five-forty-two to town."

"I see. And what's *your* explanation?"

"My first thought, sir, was that the 'certain party' she mentioned must be you. But who, I wondered, would that make the man she was going to invite to her room?" He paused, then waited, almost forcing Richard to answer the question for him.

"Well, presumably, since she does seem to have had some connection with him of which I knew nothing, it would be Adler—Batchev, I should say."

"Exactly how my mind worked, sir. But unfortunately, there's a snag to that."

"Oh?"

"Yes. The Baroness said: 'I don't want a certain party to see us together *again now*.' That means the certain party had seen her and this other man together at some time. But you said you never had seen Batchev and her together. Do you follow me, sir?"

Stiff-faced, Richard said: "I follow you."

"I then wondered if you had seen her talking privately or in a clandestine or furtive manner to any of the other guests. Er, had you?"

"Definitely not."

"It doesn't look as though you could have been the certain party at all, does it, sir?"

Richard didn't reply.

"Do you suppose Batchev could have been the certain party?"

"It's patently possible."

"Then the obvious assumption would be that, er, you were the . . ." Wilkins broke off, looking embarrassed.

"I suppose the lady didn't by any chance invite you to her room that night, sir?"

Richard looked straight at him. "Actually, she did."

"Oh? Did she?" Wilkins nodded very slowly. "I see."

"I'm sorry, Inspector. I wasn't attempting to mislead you. Please note that I told you as soon as you asked me. Frankly, earlier I couldn't see that her invitation was germane to your enquiry."

"Because you didn't go, sir?"

"I—I did go. But I didn't see her. She wasn't in her room."

"Oh, really? What time was that?"

"Two-thirty struck while I was on my way along the corridor."

Again Wilkins gave his slow nod. "You may have cleared up one mystery, at least. Mr. Deveraux heard someone crossing the landing going towards the west wing at just about that time. That would have been you, I take it?"

"I imagine so."

"That was seconds before he was struck on the head from behind. You didn't hear any sound at all?"

"I did hear an indeterminate sort of scuffling noise, and a sound like somebody tripping. Certainly nothing to indicate a man had been attacked or was in any kind of trouble. Had I done so, I would naturally have switched the light on and gone to his aid."

"What in fact did you do, sir?"

"I went on to the Baroness's room."

"In the dark?"

"Yes."

"Forgive my asking, sir; I'm sure you were preoccupied at the time, but didn't it strike you as odd that somebody was moving about behind you in the corridor in the dark? Didn't it occur to you to investigate?"

"Well, no. You see, the Baroness had been very insistent that nobody at all should see us again together that night. She made me promise not to mention it to anybody, and to come in the dark."

"May I ask what your reaction was to that request, sir?"

"I thought it was a trifle strange. I imagined she was ultra-sensitive about her reputation."

"Yes, of course. Very natural. And you were prepared

to abide by her wishes even to the extent of refusing to risk being seen merely walking along the corridor—even though this entailed ignoring the fact that someone was prowling about in complete darkness in a house full of priceless jewellery and *objets d'art*? I'd like to say, if I may make so bold, that it's a real privilege to meet such a gallant gentleman."

He didn't give Richard time to answer, but went on: "Did you have any idea what she wanted to see you about?"

"No."

"What exactly had she said?"

"Simply that it was very important she speak to me, and would I come to her room late, after everyone was in bed."

"I'm sure you had a good reason, sir, but would you mind telling me why you didn't suggest to her that you talked down here—in this room or the library? That could not have damaged the reputation of the most susceptible lady."

Richard didn't answer. Seconds passed. Then he seemed to sag. "All right, Inspector. I give in. I had guessed there was a link between her and one of the other people in this house and it was this person she wanted kept in ignorance of our meeting."

"Batchev—Adler as you knew him?"

"I thought it had to be him—or just conceivably Felman."

"I know you can't tell me what took place at the talks, but was it something that happened during them that made you think this?"

Richard nodded.

"The Baroness had been blackmailing you, hadn't she, sir?"

Richard buried his head in his hands. He said: "I can't expect you to believe this. She'd threatened to blackmail me. She brought up something that happened many years ago and told me she was going to reveal it if I didn't make certain concessions in the talks." He looked up. "But she withdrew the threat, Inspector. She spoke to me after dinner on Saturday. She told me that she couldn't go through with it, that I didn't have to worry any more. She also said that if I went to her room late that night she would explain everything. It was her insistence that I should come secretly which made me realize she was frightened of somebody in the house; it followed logically that it was almost certainly Batchev."

"You assumed it was he behind you in the corridor when you were on your way to her room?"

"Yes."

"So you deliberately hurried on?"

"Yes, in case he switched on the light and saw me."

"What did you do when you found she wasn't in her room?"

"It first occurred to me that as she was mixed up with a blackmailer, she might have come to harm. So I looked quickly round the bedroom—in the wardrobe and under the bed—in case she had been tied up or knocked out—or worse. Then I merely sat and waited."

"Did you hear anything outside the room?"

"I thought at one time I heard a distant sort of bumping. It must have been my niece banging to be let out, but at the time I decided it was thunder."

"You didn't hear the sound of the fight in Batchev's room?"

"No. You must remember that I was at almost the extreme end of the west wing and that sound does not carry easily through the doors and walls of Alderley. And then, of course, there was the storm."

"How long did you wait there?"

"Six or seven minutes."

"Then you returned to your own room?"

"Yes."

"Arriving there at approximately two-thirty-eight?"

"About that."

"You didn't see or hear anyone on your way back?"

"No."

"Did you hear the burglar alarm?"

"No, but again I would not expect to. On the first floor it sounds only in my brother's bedroom. The first thing I knew about anything being amiss was when Gerry came to my room. I'd just that moment got back to bed."

"Then you dressed again and went downstairs?"

"That's right."

"But not for about twelve or fifteen minutes?"

"A little less I would think."

"What did you do during that time?"

"After dressing, I just sat and thought—and worried."

"I see." Wilkins scanned his notes and tapped his teeth with his pencil. "Just one more point, sir. On the telephone the Baroness referred to asking someone to come to her room between two-fifteen and two-thirty. You said simply that she asked you to come, er—when, Jack?"

" 'Late, after everyone was in bed,' sir."

"That's it," Wilkins said. "Did she in fact mention the specific time, sir?"

"Yes, I remember now, she did. She must have thought he would be up until then."

"You left it till the very last minute, sir, didn't you? In fact, you didn't actually arrive until a few seconds after two-thirty. I would have expected you to be more anxious than that to hear what she had to tell you."

"I was. But I was sitting up in my room waiting for two-fifteen when I fell asleep in the chair. I didn't wake until nearly half-past two."

"Ah." Wilkins nodded in comprehension. "Very understandable. You must have had a tiring day—with the negotiations and everything. Tell me, do you think Batchev could have known that the Baroness had backed out of the blackmail and that his scheme had failed?"

"Yes. He'd been asking for some quite unreasonable concessions. I played for time and told him I'd let him know later. He must have thought I was on the brink of caving in. Then on Saturday night, after she had told me her decision, I went to Batchev and informed him there was nothing doing. I think he was quite shaken."

"Thank you, sir. I think that's everything. I appreciate your being so helpful."

Richard stared. "Don't you want to know about the blackmail?"

"Not unless you especially want to tell me."

"I certainly do not."

"Then I needn't keep you any longer, sir. If the sergeant types out an account of your movements during the early hours of the night of the murder, you'd have no objection to signing it, I suppose? I'll be asking everyone to do the same."

"I've no objection."

"Thank you, sir."

Richard left the room. Wilkins watched him until the door closed, then turned hastily to Sergeant Leather.

"Quick, my lad—go and find Lady Geraldine. Bring her here, sharp as you can—my compliments, greatly obliged, all that sort of thing. But don't let her talk to Mr. Saunders first. If he should try to speak to her on the way, stop him somehow—tell her I said it's desperately important she comes quickly—anything. We don't want 'em getting together and changing their stories before we've had a chance to get signed statements."

26

Richard's Story

AFTER leaving Deveraux Jane felt restless and full of suppressed energy. She found it almost impossible to stay in one place, and began prowling aimlessly round the house and grounds, getting in the way of servants and gardeners. At last, feeling she would burst if she didn't do something, she went to look for Gerry. She couldn't find her at first, but eventually Merryweather informed her that Gerry was in the music-room—"with the constabulary person, miss."

Jane hung impatient about outside until Gerry emerged, then pounced and demanded a game of tennis.

"Oh, darling, no."

"Why not?"

"I don't think we should, with two of our guests just murdered."

"Tommy-rot. What possible harm can it do them?"

"Nothing. It's just the look of the thing."

"Who cares about the look of the thing! Come on, don't be mean. I just must have some action or I'll go mad."

"Why don't you go for a ride?"

"I don't feel like riding. I want to *hit* something."

Gerry sighed. "Oh, all right. But I don't like playing you when you're in this sort of mood. You'll make mincemeat of me. I might as well play Helen Wills."

Jane and Gerry had played four games when Richard strolled up to the court. He sat down on a bench and watched them. At the end of the set, won by Jane 6–0, an exhausted Gerry begged for a breather. They went across and sat by him.

"You seem red-hot today, Jane," he said.

Gerry said: "She's all keyed-up and she's taking it out on me."

"Why's that?" he asked.

Jane shrugged. "I don't know. All this happening at Alderley, I suppose. Spoiling the party. It's all wrong. Alderley ought to be a haven of peace. It annoys me to see it desecrated like this. I'm angry with the Wraith, and I'm angry with Batchev and with Anilese for bringing their dirt—" She broke off. "I'm sorry, Richard. I shouldn't have said that. It was inexcusable."

"That's all right, my dear. It's true. They were both involved in pretty nasty business. I had my eyes opened about Anilese. Which may be the one good thing to come out of this whole schemozzle." He looked at his niece. "You were quite right about her, Gerry."

"She knew you were here all the time?"

"She did."

"I was sure of it from the very start."

"Why did she come here?" Jane asked him.

Richard had picked up Jane's racquet and was looking down at it. plucking at the strings. "She came here to blackmail me," he said.

Jane stiffened and Gerry's eyes widened. Gerry said: "Blackmail! But she couldn't. I mean, what grounds—" She stopped short. "Sorry."

"What grounds would she have—what was she threatening to reveal? Well, it goes back a long way."

Gerry was red-faced. "Please, Richard, I didn't mean to pry."

"I'd like you to know, Gerry. It seems as though it's bound all to come out shortly, and it'll be better if you hear it from me now. Your mother and father know the whole story, so it's only fair you should too."

Jane started to stand up. "I'll leave you then—"

Richard put a hand on her arm. "No, stay, Jane, please. You're one of the family."

Jane sat down again, concealing the warm glow of pleasure his words gave her.

Richard said: "It's not a long story. I first met Anilese in France in 1917. I was a very green lieutenant, only out from England six months. I was stationed at Amiens. We met at a party given by the wife of some local dignitary. I thought Anilese was the most beautiful creature I'd ever seen. For the first time in my life I fell

183

madly in love. For weeks I haunted her and eventually she led me to believe she loved me too. Almost immediately I proposed. To my joy, she accepted me. Our romance lasted three months, during which time I was promoted Captain.

"Then one day Anilese came to me frantic with worry. She had just heard that a cousin of hers, a young man called Pierre, with whom she'd been brought up and who had been like a brother to her, had been arrested on a charge of spying for the Germans. He had been tried and condemned to death. He was being held temporarily in a British army guardhouse, the local jail being full. Anilese swore to me that she knew Pierre was innocent. She told me a long story about suppressed evidence which seemed to prove it. She convinced me that a fearful miscarriage of justice was going to take place and she begged me to try to save Pierre's life."

Richard paused. Then in a curiously flat voice, he said: "Eventually, after much heart-searching, I agreed to try to help him escape. I need not go into the details. Suffice it to say that I worked out a plan to free him, which succeeded, and very early one morning I myself led him to a *pension* where Anilese was waiting. She had a change of clothes, money, and papers for him. She had obtained a motor car, and the plan was that she was to drive Pierre to Dijon, where he had friends who would get him across the border to Switzerland. I left immediately to return to my quarters, arranging to meet Anilese the next day, after she got back."

Richard stood Jane's racquet carefully up against the side of the bench. He looked up. "Five minutes after I left, the house was destroyed by a stray German bomb. They pulled Pierre's body out of the ruins the next day. Anilese was not identified among the victims, but there were a number of unrecognizable women's bodies brought out; and when I discovered the motor car she had borrowed parked a few blocks away from the *pension,* and when she did not turn up for our meeting the next day, I had to assume that she had been killed. She was officially listed as missing. I was the only person left alive who knew she'd been in the building, and as the body of the escaped prisoner had been found there, I could not admit I knew she had been there too—nor take too great an interest in the house or its occupants. There was naturally a lot of talk about the irony of Pierre's escaping the firing squad only to be killed by a German bomb, and about justice having caught up with him after all. I discovered then that he had unquestionably been guilty of spying.

"You can imagine my state of mind: not only had I helped an enemy agent to escape—and it was purely chance that he hadn't got away—but I had been responsible for Anilese's death as well—for had I not agreed to help, she would not have been in that house when the bomb fell. For a time I was absolutely consumed by grief and guilt. However, my part in the escape was never discovered, and I ended the war with an unblemished reputation.

"A year after the armistice I went back to France, to the town where Anilese told me she had been born and brought up. But nobody there remembered anything of her family. There were no records in the town hall, the church, or the school, or her ever having been there. I told myself that I had misunderstood her, and got the name of the town wrong. I went home, resolving, when I had a chance, to make enquiries about any other places with similar-sounding names. But somehow I never did and, for me, until last Friday, Anilese was dead."

Richard looked from one girl to the other. "Well, that's my story. Not very edifying, is it?"

"Oh, I think it is," Gerry said with a sigh. "I think it's a terrific story. Frightfully exciting and mysterious and sad."

"Did she tell you over the weekend what had actually happened to her?" Jane asked.

"She said she'd left the house about four minutes after me to fetch the car while Pierre was changing. The bomb fell when she was about twenty metres away. She was knocked unconscious by the blast. When she came to, she was in a complete daze. All she remembered was that she had to get to Dijon. She started off on foot, then got a lift. She was put down at a crossroads about half way there, started walking again, then collapsed. She woke up in hospital—and found she'd lost her memory. That's as far as she got. How she lived for the rest of the war, when it was she recovered her memory, why she never got in touch with me—all this she had been going to tell me later."

Rather tentatively, Jane said: "Do you believe her story?"

"I don't know, Jane. Quite possibly some of it's true."

Gerry said: "Perhaps I shouldn't ask, but can we know what happened after she arrived here—when you learnt she was intending to blackmail you, and so on?"

"Yes, you can know. There's not much point in my trying to hide anything any more. I first learnt what she was really after on Saturday morning. We adjourned the talks and I took Anilese for a walk round the lake. Then she sprang it on me. She'd known I was here: she'd known about the talks. Her so-called accident had been faked. And I had to make certain important concessions in the talks—or else. Obviously Batchev was behind it—though at first, of course, that didn't occur to me, because I believed him to be the real Martin Adler. I imagined some outside agency was trying to influence the negotiations. But even before I learnt his real identity I came to the conclusion, incredible as it seemed, that 'Adler' was behind it. How he found out about Anilese and me in the first place, whether *he* contacted *her,* or she him, I'll never know. Anyway, he must have previously arranged with her to hold herself ready to fake the accident if he gave the word. I think he'd anticipated after our very first session that his initial plan of bluffing and browbeating us into giving way was not going to work, and he 'phoned her on Friday afternoon. It must have been Saturday morning on the terrace, just after we broke off the talks, that he gave her the signal to start applying pressure."

Gerry was looking puzzled. "How did Anilese intend to prove you helped Pierre to escape? Wouldn't it have been just her word against yours?"

"Unfortunately, no. She had a letter."

"What sort of letter?"

"A short note I'd written to her at the time, making the final arrangements for the escape—telling her to be at the *pension* with the fresh clothes for Pierre at a certain hour. It was something I'd naturally assumed she'd burnt within seconds of reading it. But no. Perhaps even then she saw its potential."

Gerry gave an exclamation. "While you were actually planning to save her cousin's life!"

"He wasn't her cousin."

They stared. Gerry said: "But—"

"I know. But that was one of the other things she casually revealed on Saturday. She'd never even seen the chap; she'd been paid by his associates to feed me the whole story. And there'd be only my word that Anilese ever told me he was her cousin at all. If the affair came to light, it would be argued that I was paid to do it—or was a German sympathizer myself."

"But that could never be proved," Gerry said.

"It wouldn't need to be, would it, Richard?" said Jane.

He shook his head. "There'd be no danger of my being charged. Not now. But simply a public accusation of that sort would be enough to finish my career, if I wasn't able to clear myself absolutely."

"Where's the letter now?" Gerry asked.

"I've got it."

"You?" They spoke together.

"Yes. Anilese relented, you see. She told me on Saturday evening after dinner that she wasn't going through with the blackmail. She'd been going to leave here first thing yesterday morning."

"And she gave you the letter back?" Gerry said.

"No, she told me it was in London. But she promised I'd get it back today. Sure enough, it came by first delivery this morning. It's postmarked 9 p.m. Saturday."

Gerry looked blank. "I don't understand."

"Anilese's driver, this man Roberts, was obviously a close associate of hers. What their precise relationship was I don't know. But it seems that Saturday afternoon she made a telephone call. It must have been to Roberts at the *Rose & Crown*. I think she told him that the scheme was off, she was backing out, and she advised him to get away. Wilkins tells me that he took the five-forty-two to town. She must have given him instructions to get the letter and send it to me."

"And you haven't destroyed it?" Jane said.

"No, and I don't intend to yet."

"But it's the only proof you helped Pierre to escape," Gerry said incredulously.

"It's also the only proof that I had no motive for killing Anilese. You see, I had to tell Wilkins of her blackmail threat—and that I went to her room in the early hours of Sunday."

"So that was you—" Gerry stopped.

"What was me?"

187

She reddened. "You—you that Mr. Deveraux heard going along the corridor."

"Yes, it was. She told me to come along when everyone else was in bed, and she would explain everything. Only when I arrived, she wasn't there. The police could argue that I had opportunity and motive for her murder. However, if I can prove that Anilese didn't have the letter at the time she was killed, and that by then it had actually been posted to me—well then, it would be much harder for them to maintain I had reason to kill her."

Jane was looking puzzled. "But can you prove you received the letter this morning?"

"Yes. I was waiting for it and I made sure I had a witness. Peabody was with me when Merryweather brought it. He saw me open it. And I got him to initial and date the letter and the envelope there and then. So he can identify it and testify as to when I received it."

"Would showing the police the letter clear you?" Gerry asked.

"I'm afraid not. It would weaken the case against me. But they might still suspect Anilese was holding other material damaging to me and that killing her was my only means of keeping it dark. So I'm not out of the wood by any means."

27

Concealed Weapons

"YOU want me to do *what?*" Deveraux said.

"Take Mr. Peabody for a walk, and when he's at least fifteen minutes away from the house, ask him if he has any objection to our searching his suite and luggage."

"But how do I get him to come for a walk?"

"I'm sure you'll think of something," Wilkins said.

"And what reason do I give for wanting to search their things?"

"I would have thought that fabricating unlikely but convincing lies was much more your line than mine."

"I hope that's a compliment. Very well: mine not to reason why. When?"

"Now, if possible. If he says yes to the search, bring him straight back and, unless I tip you the wink to the contrary, try to get him to take you straight up to their rooms without speaking to his wife and start right away."

"What'll I be looking for?"

"You'll know when you find it."

"And suppose he says no?"

"Don't push it."

"All right, old man, I'll play along. But I'm not promising success. Why can't you ask him, by the way?"

"Because at the same time I shall be asking Mrs. Peabody precisely the same question. *You* only search if she says no to me."

Deveraux achieved his end by the simple process of approaching Peabody when the latter was sitting on the terrace reading a copy of the *Wall Street Journal* which had arrived for him that morning, and saying ingenuously: "Mr. Peabody, would you care to give me your views on this whole affair?"

Peabody was nothing loath. "Sit down, son," he said and waved to a chair.

"Well, sir, I've been sitting down most of the day. What do you say to a stroll round the lake while we talk?"

"Suits me." Peabody got to his feet and they set off across the lawn.

The millionaire seemed positively eager to discuss the case, and was in no doubt that the murders and the theft of necklace and guns were connected. "It's simply too much of a coincidence for all those things to have happened just about the same time, purely by chance," he said.

"I tend to agree with you," Deveraux said.

"Would I be breaching professional etiquette if I asked whether you're satisfied that one of the people presently at Alderley is implicated?"

"It's an inevitable conclusion."

"And you've no doubt got your own ideas as to who it is?"

"Ideas, yes. Certainty, no."

"But you won't want to be cluttered up with other guys' theories?"

"If you've got any theories I'd be glad to hear them."

"Off the record?"

"Certainly."

"Then if you ask me, Felman's your man."

"Why do you say so?"

"He's not behaving naturally. He hasn't from the start. He's jumpy—on his guard all the time."

"He's worried about his sister, of course."

"Granted. But he's also worried about himself. I can feel it. Then again, what do you really know about him? It seems to me everyone else here has got a well-authenticated background. But nobody here knew a thing about him before last Thursday. He arrived here with Batchev. It seems to me he's the only one likely to have a motive."

"Our problem is getting evidence. If we could only search his room, now . . ."

"Why don't you?"

"We don't know how he'd take the suggestion. He might try to claim diplomatic immunity; and the government wouldn't want us to press too hard. I'll tell what, sir: you might be able to help us in this."

"How?"

"You're in more or less the same position as Felman. You're not a diplomat, but you are a distinguished foreign visitor. If we were to ask you for permission to search your rooms, and you agreed, then it would make it that much more difficult for Felman to refuse. How about it?"

"Say, look at that squirrel," Peabody exclaimed.

Deveraux glanced in the direction he was pointing. "Oh yes."

"Interesting creatures. You interested in wild life, Deveraux?"

"Not particularly. About this search . . . ?"

"Oh, the search. Er, when would you want to do it?"

"As soon as possible."

"I see. Well, it's like this. I'd rather you didn't. Not today, anyway. It's Mrs. Peabody—she wouldn't be at all keen to have strangers poking through her things. Of course, if it were really necessary, I could probably talk her into it, but I'd need time. Do you understand?"

"Of course."

"That's mighty accommodating of you. Shall we start back now? My doctor doesn't like me to walk too far."

"Why, yes, of course, Mr. Wilkins, you go right ahead and search to your heart's content."

"Thank you, Mrs. Peabody. That's very obliging of you. I should really obtain your husband's permission, too, but he doesn't seem to be around, and it is rather urgent."

"That's quite all right. Hiram would say the same as me. I'm sure we've nothing to hide. And you're welcome to do anything which might help get my necklace back."

"Then shall we go up?"

"Oh, you want me with you?"

"If you please. madam."

They went upstairs and while Mrs. Peabody stood placidly by, Wilkins and Leather began a search of the suite.

It was in Peabody's dressing-room that they found it. Wilkins was standing on tiptoe, trying to feel if there was anything on top of the wardrobe. His groping fingers touched something that moved, but he just wasn't tall enough to get hold of it.

He called: "Jack."

Leather came across and easily lifted down a small suitcase.

Carrie Peabody said: "Those are just souvenirs of our trip—curios we've bought all over Europe. Do open it."

Leather did so. He lifted out a number of ornaments, and then came to a folded Spanish shawl. Wrapped in it he could feel something hard and bulky. He unfolded it. Resting inside was an engraved Bergman Bayard pistol.

Wilkins gave a sigh of satisfaction, at the same moment casting a sharp glance at Mrs. Peabody. On her face was an expression of blank astonishment.

"Well, madam?" Wilkins said.

She spoke in a whisper. "That's—that's Lord Burford's gun?"

Wilkins nodded. "Can you explain how it happens to be here?"

"No." Her face was white. "I don't—I can't understand it. I—he must have brought it ba—brought it here."

"Lord Burford?"

"Yes."

"You say he planted his own gun in your suitcase?"

She gulped. "I don't want to say anything else until I've spoken to my husband."

"I think perhaps you're wise, Mrs. Peabody. I'll want a few words with him myself when he turns up. But now I must go and show this to his lordship."

"In Peabody's room!" Lord Burford's eyes bulged.

"Yes, my lord."

"But what the blue blazes was it doing there?"

"I don't know. It is definitely your genuine Bergman, my lord? Not a replica?"

"No doubt about it. But what does Peabody say?"

"I haven't seen him since, my lord. Mrs. Peabody—"

"What about her?"

"She claims you must have put it there yourself, my lord."

"WHAT?"

"Of course, the idea of your lordship hiding one of your guns in the luggage of one of your guests is quite absurd, but I had to put it to you as a matter of form. So if your lordship will kindly give me a formal denial, we can get on." Wilkins stopped and waited expectantly.

Seconds passed. "Er—my lord?" Still Lord Burford didn't speak. "Are you all right, my lord?"

"I've got nothing to say."

"Nothing at all, my lord?"

"Not until I've seen my solicitor."

"As you wish, my lord. Then I wonder if I could trouble you once more for the key of the collection-room. I want to have another look round in there after I've seen Mr. Peabody."

Peabody stared. He opened his mouth. Then he closed it again. He gulped. "I'm not saying anything," he said.

"Nothing at all, sir?"

"No. I want to see an attorney first."

"I see, sir. That's your privilege."

Peabody walked off.

"Well, well, well, well, well," said Wilkins. Then he trotted off to the collection-room.

"Did you expect to find the gun there?" Deveraux asked, after Wilkins had told him everything that had happened.

"I'm always ready for anything, Mr. Deveraux. Now you can do me another favour, if you'll be so kind."

Deveraux eyed him suspiciously. "What's that?"

"Search Lord Burford's study."

"You—you mean without his knowledge?"

"That's right."

"You're joking."

"No."

"I can't do that! Suppose he caught me?"

"Leather will be placed in a strategic position where he can see if his lordship approaches. He will then rush excitedly up and say that I want to see him on a matter of utmost urgency."

"What'll you tell him then?"

"Let me worry about that."

"Why can't I worry about it and *you* search?"

"Because I can't search without either his permission or a warrant. I can't see him giving me permission at present, and a warrant to search an Earl's premises wouldn't be got quickly. But you're not bound by the same regulations as me. And you're a guest here."

"That makes it worse!"

193

"Look, Mr. Deveraux, we're trying to solve two murders. We can't afford to be squeamish."

"You really think there's something in the Earl's study that'll help solve the murders?"

"Not exactly." Wilkins tugged at his ear. "Just something that's going to help complete the overall picture."

"You talk as though the case were nearly over, and that you only had a couple of minor points to clear up."

"Yes, I think that's true."

Deveraux gaped at him. "What on earth do you mean?"

"That you're quite right—there *are* still a few minor points to clear up."

"A few!"

"Yes. It's been a very complicated business. Even now I can't explain *every* feature of it. I don't expect to. Hercule Poirot always says that when trying to solve a mystery, any theory you evolve must explain each isolated fact and happening: they've all got to fit into a harmonious pattern with no loose ends. Of course, I'm not in the same class as him—though they do say I look a bit like him—and I can never get that far. At the end of a case there's nearly always something left unaccounted for. But as long as I can explain the main outline of the crime and provide proof of guilt, I'm happy. I'm not an ambitious man."

"Let me get this straight." Deveraux spoke very slowly. "Are you telling me you know who the murderer is?"

"I think so. Of course, I may be quite wrong. It wouldn't be the first time. But to me one person seems pretty clearly indicated."

"But for the love of Mike—who?"

"If you don't mind I'd rather not say until I've got a bit more evidence. I don't want to look silly if I'm wrong."

"But—I thought you were baffled." Deveraux sounded quite stunned.

"I was. I still am about certain things. But you can help me towards getting most of it sorted out by a search of Lord Burford's study. So how about it? Will you oblige?"

Deveraux gulped. "I'll do it," he said. "What will I be looking for?"

"You'll know—"

"Don't say it: I'll know when I find it. OK, let's get it over with."

Twenty minutes later Deveraux entered the music-room. Wilkins looked up. "Well?"

Deveraux brought a hand from behind his back. In it was a white silk handkerchief and in the handkerchief was an engraved Bergman Bayard pistol.

28

Inspector Wilkins Turns Poet

DEVERAUX said: "Tucked down inside the arm chair."

An expression of pure self-satisfaction spread over Wilkins' face. "I knew it," he said. "Mr. Deveraux, I deduced that that had to be there. That was pure reasoning, that was."

"Old man, you have my heartiest congratulations. But how many more of these bally things are there hanging around?"

"No more. There were just the four—a pair of originals and a pair of replicas. This is the second replica. And if we find the fingerprints on this one that I expect to, I'll be a happy man. May I have it?" He took the pistol and handkerchief carefully from Deveraux. "Thank you. I'll return your hanky later. I'm going away now. I've got to dig out a few more facts. I'll be back later this evening, and I hope then we can make an arrest. I'd like you to get everybody gathered in the drawing-room at around nine-thirty. Perhaps you and I can meet here at, say, quarter-to, for a confab?"

"Any instructions for me in the interim, chief?"

"I don't think so. You can spend the time thinking. Keep an open mind and I'm sure you'll reach the same conclusion as me."

"Wilkins, you couldn't give me a teeny weeny clue, could you?"

"You know, Mr. Deveraux, I thought you'd ask that. And I was working on a reply while I was waiting for you. All the following factors are important pointers. Ready?"

Deveraux nodded.

"Then listen carefully." Wilkins cleared his throat, and to Deveraux's amazement declaimed:

> Mr. Deveraux's hearing,
> Lady Geraldine's sight,
> Miss Clifton's keen nostril,
> Batchev's sudden flight,
> Lord Burford's collection,
> Mr. Wilkins's height,
> And last but not least,
> The weather that night.

"I've written it down for you. Here. See you later. So long."

After the departure of Wilkins, the rest of the day passed slowly. The most notable event was the awakening of Algy Fotheringay. This, according to the footman who had been detailed to sit with him, took place at four o'clock. Algy opened his eyes, yawned, saw the footman, and said: "Morning. Would you get me some tea, please?"

But by the time the tea had arrived, he had turned over on his side and gone back to sleep. Shortly after, Dr. Ingleby had called again. This time, after some effort, he managed to keep Algy awake. When Ingleby had gone, and with Algy sitting groggily up in bed drinking cup after cup of tea, Jane and Gerry stayed with him and very carefully and gently tried to explain to him just what had been happening during his coma. Perhaps not surprisingly, he seemed to have difficulty in taking it in, and the effort needed all the girls' patience.

At dinner which, in view of Deveraux's request for a nine-thirty gathering, was taken at eight, the atmosphere was constrained; the imminent return of Wilkins hung like a cloud over everyone and conversation was stilted. Algy, up and dressed, still seemed in a half-trance, and kept asking where the Baroness had gone.

Deveraux was waiting in the music-room when Wilkins and Leather got back. Wilkins came in and flopped into a chair. "My, we've had a hectic few hours, haven't we Jack?"

"Certainly have, sir."

"I've been telling him he's a chump not to get a transfer back to uniformed branch, but he seems set on staying in CID."

"Don't keep me in suspense, old lad. Got the facts you wanted?"

Wilkins nodded silently.

"And?"

"I've confirmed nearly everything I suspected."

"What about the guns?"

"The Baroness was shot with Lord Burford's—the one we found in Peabody's case."

"And—you know who's guilty?"

"I believe so. How about you?"

Deveraux was silent for a moment. Then he said: "I think I do. Thanks to your verse. Tell me one thing: in more than one line, it's in a way *negative*, isn't it—referring to things absent or lacking?"

"That's it."

"And the fact that Batchev's body was found in water is important, too, isn't it? The killer *had* to dump it in the lake?"

"Quite right."

"In that case," Deveraux said, "I fancy I know most of what happened."

Wilkins leaned forward. "Then let's reconstruct it all. Give me the name of the murderer."

"The murderer? OK; perhaps I'll make a fool of myself, but here goes."

Forty minutes later Deveraux said: "Of course, we've got very little concrete evidence."

"That's why I want to do it this way. It's our best chance of forcing the truth out. We can confirm the theory a step at a time. And Mr. Deveraux, I want you to do all the talking."

"Oh no! This is your show, Wilkins. You got there first, right on your own; I wouldn't have tumbled to the truth without your clues. You must handle things."

"But you can do it much better than me. I haven't got the personality to carry it off. I'd probably get muddled and mess it all up. Please do it."

Deveraux gave a shrug. "All right, if that's what you

want. We'd better go in now: they'll be waiting. You know, one thing still bothers me."

"What's that?"

"Even now we haven't got any explanation of that blithering egg cosy."

29

Pistols for Two

JANE sat in the big drawing-room and listened with half an ear to the voice of Lady Burford.

The Countess was giving what amounted to a lecture on the history of Alderley from its erection to the present day. It was doubtful if anyone wanted to hear it. But she had been driven to it by the sheer impossibility of getting any normal conversation going. She was determined to give at least a semblance of normality to the evening, and if her family and guests would not co-operate, she'd do it alone.

It was a fine effort, really, and without it the atmosphere in the room would have resembled that of a morgue. Jane only wished she was capable of helping, of interjecting an occasional comment or question. But she felt far too tense. She looked round the room. So, obviously, did everybody else. Except Algy. He seemed on the verge of falling asleep again.

Jane looked at the clock. It was gone nine-thirty. Would that little detective never come? Did he really know who had killed Batchev and the Baroness? Who would he point to?

Jane let her eyes roam around. Almost impossible to believe that one of the people in this room with her was a killer. Yet there could be no doubt about it: two murders had been committed. Jane gave an involuntary shudder as she recalled again the cold dead eyes of Anilese de la Roche staring up at her from the floor of the passage. She told herself that within feet of her now was the person who had put the life out of those eyes.

Who—in heaven's name, who?

The door opened. Jane gave a slight start and the heads of everyone in the room swung, like spectators at a tennis match, to rest on Deveraux. He came into the room, followed by Wilkins and Leather. Jane scanned the faces of the three men. The only impression she got was one of nervousness. Odd—one never imagined that the policemen might be just as edgy as everybody else on an occasion like this.

Sergeant Leather sat down on an upright chair just inside the door and unobtrusively extracted a shorthand notebook and a pencil from his pocket. Wilkins edged himself sideways along the wall until he reached the corner; here his face was in shadow and he stopped and stood motionless.

Deveraux crossed to the centre of the room, just as Lady Burford said: ". . . and after *that* episode, I need hardly add, Sam Johnson was never invited to Alderley again. Yes, Giles, do you have something to say?"

"I have, Lady Burford. I'm sorry to interrupt." He addressed the room at large. "Inspector Wilkins wanted us all here tonight to try to clear up the very distressing events of the last few days." He reached into an inside pocket, took out a small black notebook, glanced briefly down at it, then looked up and continued:

"During the early hours of Sunday morning two people died from gunshot wounds in this house. That is one of the few undisputed facts of the night—for exactly what else occurred during that period is extremely difficult to determine. One thing, however, is clear: many members of the household were up and about that night. In fact, outside the servants' quarters, it seems that until the time the alarm went off only three people had remained uninterruptedly in their bedrooms. Of the rest, two—Lady Geraldine and Miss Clifton—openly admitted being up. Others have, for various reasons, been less than frank about their movements. But only one of the people in this room committed murder.

"You all know that the man who passed here as Martin Adler was really a foreign agent by the name of Stanislaus Batchev. What you do not all know is that the Baroness de la Roche was brought here by him to assist in obtaining secret information from Mr. Saunders."

Deveraux paused to let this sink in, then went on: "Batchev's scheme was that the Baroness should make use of certain facts in her possession to exert pressure on

201

Mr. Saunders. Mr. Saunders has confirmed that the Baroness did in fact threaten him with these facts."

Every eye in the room turned towards Richard. He didn't move, but sat, his arm folded, his face impassive.

"It seemed at one time," Deveraux said, "that the only person with a strong motive for killing both Batchev and the Baroness was Mr. Saunders. However, he then informed us that the Baroness had withdrawn her threat—that he had had nothing to fear from her and therefore no motive for killing her. Against that, he admits going to her bedroom during the night."

"And finding it empty," Richard said, slowly and decisively.

"That's what you said, sir. You also stated that you arrived there at almost exactly two-thirty. Is that correct?"

"Correct."

"What perhaps you do not know is that Lady Geraldine, who was concealed in a recess across the corridor, has signed a statement in which she maintains that the Baroness, having earlier left her room, returned to it before two-ten, and *had not left it again by the time you arrived.*"

Gerry gave a gasp. "Oh no!" She turned a horror-stricken face to Richard. "Richard—I'm sorry. I just didn't realize."

"That's all right, my dear." Richard's voice was very quiet and controlled. "You were mistaken, that's all."

"Were you, Lady Geraldine?" Deveraux asked her.

"I—I—" Gerry looked round desperately. "I don't know. I don't remember now just what I did say."

For the first time, from the dimness of his corner, Wilkins spoke. "You said, Lady Geraldine, that the Baroness left her room at four minutes past two; that two to three minutes later a man entered her room, and that she herself arrived back about a minute after that; that the man left alone shortly before two-fifteen, and then nothing happened until another man—whom we now know to have been Mr. Saunders—arrived just after two-thirty."

"Well, of course, it's obvious what happened." Gerry spoke excitedly. "The first man must have been Batchev. He killed Anilese and hid her body in the room somewhere—"

"I'm afraid Mr. Saunders has already stated that he searched the room immediately on entering it. The Baroness's body was not there."

Gerry faltered. "Well, perhaps—perhaps he didn't look carefully enough. And what I say would explain Batchev's flight. He had to get away from the house as quickly as possible without anybody knowing. He tried to put the alarm out of action in the breakfast-room. Then, when we disturbed him he panicked, broke the window and jumped out."

"Then," Deveraux asked quietly, "who shot Batchev? And who moved the Baroness's body to the secret passage?"

Gerry sat quite still. She stared at Deveraux, then at Richard, before sinking down into her chair and turning her head away.

"Isn't this a more likely explanation?" Deveraux spoke in a silky smooth voice. "That the Baroness left her room and stole a gun for protection from Lord Burford's collection. She arrived back to find Batchev waiting for her, wanting to know the outcome of her attempt to blackmail Mr. Saunders. She told him then that she was not going to co-operate with him any more—and that if he didn't leave the house she would expose him as an impostor. She had the gun, so Batchev could do nothing to her. He left hurriedly to try to get out without setting off the alarm. Then Mr. Saunders arrived in the Baroness's room. She told him she had been collaborating with Batchev, but was going to no longer, that she wasn't interested in secret information—*but that she was still going to blackmail him for her own benefit.* Not for information, but for money. There was a quarrel. She did not fear Mr. Saunders, so was off her guard. He managed to grab the gun. It went off. The Baroness was dead. He concealed her body in the secret passage—by that time Lady Geraldine had left her vantage point. Then he went hunting for Batchev: because he knew Batchev had the same damaging information about him as the Baroness had. He was looking for him at the same time as Lady Geraldine, Miss Clifton and I were searching the ground floor. He was perhaps in the next room when Batchev broke the window. He realized at once what had happened. He probably had a torch. He shone it through the window and actually saw Batchev running away. The

203

alarm had already gone off, so he was able to open the window and go after him without being heard. He caught up with him by the lake, shot him, returned immediately and got back to his room before Lady Geraldine arrived to tell him what had happened. After she'd left, and before coming downstairs, he put the gun in the passage near the Baroness's body."

Deveraux looked straight at Richard. "What do you think of that reconstruction, Minister?"

Jane watched Richard, her heart in her mouth, and her admiration for him had never been greater as he remained outwardly quite unmoved, an expression of untroubled detachment on his face. Slowly he turned to meet Deveraux's gaze full on. Then a slight smile touched his lips. "Plausible," he said, "except that you know quite well there's not a word of truth in it."

Before Deveraux could reply the voice of Wilkins came again from the corner. "No, sir. That's not quite so. There is some truth in it, though it does leave a number of questions unanswered. And although we didn't really think so, it just *might* have been all true. I asked Mr. Deveraux to put it to you like that to gauge your reaction. I'm satisfied now that that reconstruction is largely false."

Richard closed his eyes and bowed his head. There was a sudden reduction of tension in the room. Jane realized she'd been holding her breath, and she let it out slowly through clenched teeth.

Gerry spoke with a catch in her voice. "I think you're a couple of beasts."

To her own surprise, Jane found herself speaking. "There's something you all ought to know." She flushed, as she saw every eye turn to her, but carried on: "Perhaps it isn't my place to say this, but I'm the only person outside the family who knows it, and if I don't nobody will. The grounds for the blackmail were very flimsy. Richard has never been dishonest, or unpatriotic, or immoral. It was just a case of misplaced loyalty—a long time ago."

"Thank you, Jane." Richard spoke very softly, without looking up.

Deveraux continued. "So, if my previous reconstruction is largely false, what really happened? As you all know, Batchev was killed by a bullet from a Bergman Bayard pistol, the property of Mr. Peabody, this gun later being found by the body of the Baroness. There were fingerprints on it, but they were badly smudged and couldn't be identified. The Baroness was shot with a similar gun owned by Lord Burford, which was later discovered concealed in Mr. Peabody's room. Neither Lord Burford nor Mr. Peabody was able to account for the movement of these guns, though Mrs. Peabody claimed that Lord Burford had planted his own gun in her husband's case. Lord Burford refused either to confirm or deny this. However, what his lordship has told nobody is that sometime around two-ten on Sunday morning, he left his bedroom, went silently to Mr. Peabody's dressing-room, *took Mr. Peabody's pistol and replaced it with a replica of his own.* That is so, is it not, my lord?"

Lord Burford did not answer. To Jane, it seemed he was incapable of speaking. He simply stared at Deveraux and slowly went red.

"It would be advisable to tell the truth, Lord Burford."

At last the Earl managed to reply. "Course I didn't. Certainly not. Ridiculous idea."

"I suggest you did, Lord Burford. I further suggest that you took Mr. Peabody's gun to Batchev's room and forced him to go with you. I suggest that you—as you alone could do—have had the alarm system modified, so that there is one way—known only to you—of leaving the building without setting it off. You shot Batchev, returned to the house and killed the Baroness, who had left her room in the darkness unseen by your daughter. You concealed her body in the secret passage and left Peabody's gun lying near the body in order to incriminate him—a man you hate because you know his collection is superior to your own."

Lord Burford gave a squawk. "No! I didn't! I didn't, I tell you. I didn't shoot anybody. Why should I? I—"

"Family pride, Lord Burford. You overheard Batchev and the Baroness discussing the blackmail of your brother and you were determined not to let his career be ruined by a pair of foreigners—"

"No, it's not true!" Lord Burford was positively squeaking by now. "I knew nothing about the blackmail. I thought Anilese was a lovely gal, Adler—Batchev—a delightful feller. I took Peabody's gun—I admit that—"

"Ah!" Deveraux pounced. "You did?"

205

"Yes—yes."

"What for—if not to shoot someone?"

"Just to show to Trimble Greene—another collector. Wanted him to think I owned the pair. Was only going to keep it until September, then send it on to Peabody in the States, in time for the New York exhibition. Chap who sold me my original sold me the replica as well. Said there'd originally been a pair, but they'd got split up and someone had had the replica made so there'd be a pair again. I thought it might be good enough to fool Peabody, so long as he didn't look at it too closely."

"George!" The horrified exclamation came from Lady Burford. "George—I can't believe my ears! You took Mr. Peabody's gun? You stole from your own guest! I've never been so ashamed in my life!"

"I'm sorry, my dear. I really don't know what came over me."

"I should hope temporary insanity, George. It's the kindest explanation." She turned towards Peabody. "Mr. Peabody, I don't need to say—"

Deveraux coughed. "Lady Burford, I'm sorry to interrupt yet again, but that really must keep. This is a murder enquiry. Lord Burford, let me get this straight: you say you left your replica in the carrying-case in Mr. Peabody's dressing-room and took his original away. What did you do with it?"

"Locked it in the safe in my study."

"Then what did you do?"

"Went back to bed."

"At what time?"

"I got back in my room just after twelve minutes past two."

"How can you explain the gun being found by the Baroness's body?"

"I can't. I've been worried stiff about it. I swear to you, Deveraux, that I killed nobody—"

"I know, Lord Burford. We never thought you did. But I had to find some means of persuading you to admit to the—the borrowing of Mr. Peabody's pistol."

Lord Burford mopped his face with his handkerchief. "Gad," he said.

"Now," Deveraux said, "we still have to explain how your gun came to be wrapped up in Mr. Peabody's shawl, how another replica found its way into the display stand in the collection-room—and how your own replica got from Mr. Peabody's carrying-case where you left it, to the armchair in your study, where I found it this afternoon.

Lord Burford stared. "You found it there?"

"Yes. Have you an explanation, Lord Burford?"

The Earl shook his head blankly.

"Then," said Deveraux pleasantly, "I think it would be reasonable to ask if Mr. Peabody has an explanation." He turned to the Texan. "Well, Mr. Peabody?"

Jane noticed that whereas Lord Burford had gone red when Deveraux had switched his attention to him, Mr. Peabody was now a pale shade of green. "I—er—" he said.

"Mr. Peabody." And this time Deveraux snapped the name. "Did you go to the collection-room in the early hours of Sunday, remove Lord Burford's pistol and replace it with a replica of your own?"

Peabody gulped, then gave a single, jerky nod.

"Hiram!" Mrs. Peabody stared at her husband in horror. "What are you saying?"

"I put it to you," Deveraux rapped, "that you took that gun and used it to shoot Stanislaus Batchev."

"No, sir, I most certainly didn't."

"You know that it was used for that purpose?"

"Yes, but—"

"How do you explain that?"

"I can't."

"I recommend that you try, Mr. Peabody. I think you'd be wise to make a clean breast of the whole thing. Why did you take the gun, if not to kill Batchev?"

"I—" Peabody closed his eyes for two seconds. "I wanted it to put with mine so I could exhibit the pair at the New York exhibition. Naturally, I was intending to send it back immediately after. The guy who sold me the gun sold me the replica, too, as a curiosity. I figure now both replicas must have been made when the two originals were still together as a pair—perhaps for insurance reasons, perhaps by a crook aiming to do a switch. Anyway, sometime, somehow the four got mixed up, and each original got itself paired up with a replica. I'd intended to mention my replica to the Earl, but the shock of seeing his original drove it out of my mind. Then later I got to thinking that maybe my replica would fool him for a few weeks, so long as he didn't examine it too closely. I thought about making the switch during the day time, but I figured if it vanished then, I'd be the chief suspect, as everyone knew I was in and out of the room all the time, and it would be best to do it at night. So during the thunderstorm I just hustled along to the collection-room with my replica—"

"What time was that?" Deveraux interjected.

"Just gone five-and-twenty after two."

"I see. Go on please."

"There's not much else to tell. I switched the guns, hurried back to my room, and went to bed. I put the pistol under my pillow. I didn't put it in my suitcase till the next morning. To tell the truth, I found I'd taken more out of myself than I'd realized. I suppose I hurried more than I'm accustomed to, and on top of that there was the tension. My heart was beating like a steam-hammer. I don't remember anything else till John woke me."

"How long were you in the gun room?"

"A matter of seconds—just in and out again."

Deveraux glanced at Jane. "Now we know who it was you heard closing the gallery door." He turned back to Peabody. "Mrs. Peabody didn't wake up during all this?"

"Er, no, I guess not."

"Is that right, Mrs. Peabody? You slept right through?"

Carrie Peabody looked flustered. "Why—er, I, that is . . ." She took a deep breath. "No, I didn't."

"Because you'd already left the room, hadn't you, Mrs. Peabody?"

She nodded.

"I'm sorry," Peabody said. "I didn't mean to mislead you, but I figured it wouldn't look so good, Carrie being out of the room at the time of the murders. Truth is, I woke up and saw her leaving the room. I guessed she was going to the bathroom and it occurred to me it would be a good time to get the Earl's gun without her knowing. That's why I hurried so. I got back into bed before she returned. Sorry, honey," he added to his wife.

"I see," Deveraux said. "But you hadn't gone to the bathroom, had you, Mrs. Peabody?"

Carrie glanced sideways at her husband, then shook her head again.

"Where had you gone?"

"Down—downstairs."

"Where precisely?"

"To the Earl's study."

"What for?"

She looked up. "To get rid of the gun I'd seen Lord Burford putting in Hiram's carrying-case."

Peabody gave a gasp. "You did *what?*"

"Why?" Deveraux asked.

"Well, heavens to Betsy, why do you think? Listen, the thunderstorm had kept me awake for an hour or more. Hiram had gone to sleep. So I turned on my bedside light and read for a while. Then I started to get drowsy and decided to turn out the light. I looked at the clock first. It was exactly nine minutes after two. I hadn't had the light out for more than a few seconds when I heard the door from the dressing-room to the corridor open. Then I heard footsteps in the dressing-room. I decided to investigate. I got out of bed and crept to the adjoining door, which we'd left ajar. I saw Lord Burford. He had a torch. He took a pistol from the pocket of his robe and put it in the case where Hiram kept his new gun. I must have just missed seeing him *take* Hiram's gun. Then he went out of the room. I was petrified. I couldn't think just what he was up to. I went across to the case and saw that the gun he'd put there was exactly the same as Hiram's own—in fact, it might actually *be* his own. I was in a complete quandry: for some reason, Lord Burford had either planted his own gun on Hiram or had taken Hiram's gun earlier and had now replaced it. I couldn't think of any ordinary reason Lord Burford would do that."

"But for Pete's sake, honey, why didn't you wake me?" Her husband started at her, baffled.

"I didn't want to worry you, Hiram. Not with your cardiac condition. And you were enjoying your time here so much, I didn't want to spoil it for you by getting you suspicious and uneasy, perhaps without cause. Anyway, for about quarter of an hour I just dithered. Then I acted very stupidly. But I've read lots of mystery stories, and when one person plants a gun on another, he's never up to any good. Then we'd been warned about the Wraith coming after my diamonds and we had the Baroness, obviously an adventuress, arriving out of the blue and foreign diplomats and the whole atmosphere of Alderley and some of the Earl's ancestors none too scrupulous about how they treated guests in the old days so I've read and I suppose I'd gotten sort of crime-minded—so I decided I'd just plant the gun back on the Earl and if it turned out the next day it was just a joke or something no harm would have been done but if anything out of the ordinary *had* occurred Hiram would be out of it."

Mrs. Peabody stopped talking and took a breath. She looked round the room, apparently satisfied herself that everyone was paying attention, and started off again.

"I couldn't decide where to leave the gun. I wanted it to be a room which was specifically the Earl's domain. Hiram had been in and out of the gun-room all the time and had the key, so I didn't want to put it there. Eventually I made up my mind just to put it in Lord Burford's study. I made my way downstairs, lighting my way with matches. I went to the study and pushed the pistol down inside the armchair."

"What time was that?"

"The clock struck two-thirty just as I was leaving the study. I was going across the hall to the stairs when the match blew out and I found there were no more in the box. I started to grope my way upstairs in the dark. I hadn't gone up more than about six steps when I heard a noise at the top—first a sort of scuffling, then a louder noise like furniture being overturned. Well, I can tell you, I just froze. A few seconds later I had one of the biggest shocks of my life. Somebody came down the stairs quite quietly and brushed against me without any warning."

"And you screamed," Deveraux said.

"Why, yes. I was just so startled. If I'd known he had my jewels, though, I wouldn't have just screamed, I'd have gone after him."

"You think the man who brushed against you was the thief?"

"Why, surely. He must have bided his opportunity until both Hiram and I were out of the room, don't you think?"

"Perhaps. What happened after you screamed?"

"I just blundered up to my bedroom in the dark, tumbled into bed and went straight to sleep. I may have blacked out. The next thing I remember is Hiram waking me and telling me my necklace had gone. I guess that's about everything. Naturally, ever since I learned of the murders I've felt terrible. I have to admit I've thought the Earl must have done them, but I had no way of proving it and I was sure nobody would believe me if I reported what I saw. Anyway, I'd just like to apologize to everybody: to you, Mr. Deveraux, and you, Inspector, if you're still over there, for not telling the truth before and I truly hope I haven't confused you too much. And to Lord and Lady Burford, for the way Hiram and I have both behaved under your roof. I really am very ashamed."

"My dear, you have no occasion whatsoever to apologize to *us,*" Lady Burford said decisively. "I think you behaved quite reasonably in the circumstances. It is we who should apologize to you. The very idea of George skulking into your rooms in the middle of the night . . ."

"Oh, but Hiram stole his most treasured possession."

"George stole *his* most treasured possession first."

Suddenly Lord Burford banged on the arm of his chair and gave a roar. "Good gad, I've never heard so much nonsense in my life! Nobody stole anything from anybody. Peabody's was a quite legitimate ruse and I don't hold it against him for a moment."

"Well said, Earl." Peabody nodded vigorously. "Ladies just don't understand these things. All's fair in the collecting game. If my wife had only woken me, I'd have known at once what was going on and told her to stop worrying."

"Peabody, I want—"

"Call me Hiram, Earl."

"Very well, Hiram. You must call me George. Hiram— I want to lend you my Bergman Bayard for the New York exhibition."

"I was going to tell you to keep mine to show General Trimble Greene, George. I'm sure—"

"Gentleman, please." Deveraux interrupted rather desperately. "Did either of you—or you, Mrs. Peabody— see, hear, or do anything else other than what you've told me?" He glanced from one to the other and saw three shaking heads. "Very well," he said. "Having got all that out of the way, perhaps we can now start dealing with some real crime."

30

Nightmare

"I now want to turn," Deveraux said, "to another of the puzzling incidents of the night: the fight in Batchev's room. This was something which seemed quite unaccountable. Why should *both* the men involved have wanted to remain undetected? Why didn't the one who had been attacked call for help? One explanation which occurred to me was that one of the fighters was the murderer—and the other the Wraith, who had somehow gone into Batchev's room by mistake. But he couldn't, at almost the same time, have been taking the diamonds from Mrs. Peabody's room, then running downstairs, brushing against her in the dark. One thing we do know is that a few seconds after the fight stopped, someone cannoned into Lady Geraldine in the west corridor. It was obviously someone who wanted to get away from the scene undetected. No one who wanted actually to get out of the *house* would go that way—he'd turn towards the main stairs; in fact, only someone who had a room in the west wing would have occasion to go that way. And only one man did."

Deveraux turned to where Felman was sitting. "Felman, you told Inspector Wilkins that you went early to bed on Saturday night and slept until I roused you just before three-fifteen. That was a lie. At two-thirty you were fighting in Batchev's room."

Felman seemed carefully to weigh his reply. Then he gave a shrug. "Well, if you can call it fighting. It was mostly sound and fury, signifying nothing. No one got hurt."

"It was you who shut me in the cupboard!" Gerry exclaimed indignantly.

Felman bowed his head in her direction. "I regret to

plead guilty, Lady Geraldine. My humble apologies. I used the minimum force. But it didn't suit my purpose to be discovered just then."

"Maybe not then," Deveraux said, and his voice was dangerously soft, "but I wonder why you've kept quiet until now. More than anybody, you had a good excuse for being there: you knew Batchev to be a ruthless spy, who had killed your superior and friend, who had kidnapped Anna, and who was attempting to obtain secret information endangering the safety of your country. It would be quite reasonable for you to have been in his room—perhaps looking for incriminating evidence. The fact that his men were holding your sister would protect you from suspicion of murdering him yourself, wouldn't it?"

"Yes, but—"

"But for the fact that they are not holding *your* sister at all—because you are not Nicholas Felman. Is that what you were going to say?"

For seconds the man they'd known as Felman didn't move a muscle. Then: "You're right," he said. "I'm not Felman. I'm Martin Adler."

"Yesterday morning," the real Martin Adler said, "I told you how Martin Adler was killed on the Orient Express by Batchev and his men. That story was true in every particular but one: it was really Nick Felman who died—though Batchev believed he had killed me.

"The idea originally came from our security service back home. There was a fear that an attempt would be made to stop me reaching this country. The Grand Duke and his advisers seemed to think that my presence here was vital to the success of these talks. So it was suggested that Nick and I switch identities for the trip. Special passports were issued to us. Everybody—including Nick—thought it was a good idea. Except me, that is: I agreed to go along with it just to keep them all happy, but only because I didn't for one moment believe there was any real danger. If I had, I wouldn't have let Nick face it instead of me. As it turned out, they were right and I was wrong. Batchev and his men killed Nick, believing they were killing Martin Adler. I was forced to come along here and watch Batchev masquerade as me, and at the same time masquerade as Nick Felman myself. It was a most wearing—and very weird—experience. Every time anybody here asked me a question about my past life, I had to answer as though I were Nick."

He looked at Lady Burford. "For instance, I've never been to Stockholm, yet I had to answer as though I were Nick, who had. I'm sure I slipped up. I know Batchev did. He was supposed always to answer as me, and he'd obviously researched my life, but several times I heard him talking about places I'd never been. Naturally, to Batchev that wouldn't matter: the real Adler was unknown here and, he believed, dead anyway. The negotiations were a nightmare. I was scared all the time that Mr. Saunders here would give Batchev the dope he wanted. I knew that as soon as that happened he'd vamoose— probably trying to kill me first, so I couldn't expose him. Worse than that, once she was no longer needed as hostage, I could see no reason for them not to kill Anna Felman. However, luckily, Saunders, you held out. The ironic thing was that while Batchev simply didn't have the information you wanted, and so had to stall you, I did have it. It's all in my head. But he'd been told— correctly—that only Adler, not Felman, had this knowledge, so, believing I was Felman, it never occurred to him to ask me."

Richard said: "But why did you keep the pretence up so long?"

"Because," Deveraux said, "he knew that *Felman* was in the clear: that as soon as we confirmed Anna's kidnapping, we'd no longer consider him a serious murder suspect. As Martin Adler, on the other hand, he can offer no reason at all why he shouldn't have killed Batchev."

"Look, for the love of Mike," Adler said, "don't you think Anna Felman's safety is important to *me?* I know the kid—I'm very fond of her. I wasn't going to put her life in danger. I agree I kept quiet for just the very reason you said: I knew I wasn't guilty and I didn't want you wasting time trying to pin the murders on me, and letting the real killer get away. But you don't imagine I thought I could keep it up for more than a couple of days, do you? And I didn't attempt to deceive the Duke on the telephone. I told him what had really happened and what I intended to do. I asked him not to announce Felman's death for the time being—and in the event that a request from the British police for photos of Adler or Felman was received either there or at our London embassy, to ensure that my picture was sent for his and his for mine. In fact, I'm not sure yet how you discovered the truth."

Deveraux said: "Wilkins simply asked Scotland Yard to get a photo of Martin Adler from the London office of your country's leading newspaper."

Adler shrugged. "Well, I couldn't think of everything."

"What were you doing in Batchev's room that night?" Deveraux asked.

"Like you said, I was hoping to get some dirt on him—something that would give me a lever to use against him, or perhaps some clue as to where Anna was being held. It was a forlorn sort of hope, but I felt I had to take any chance, however slight. And I guess I've got to own up to something. It's due to me Fotheringay got drugged."

"What do you mean?"

"I slipped a sleeping-draught in Batchev's coffee that night, so as I'd be able to search his room without waking him. Somehow Fotheringay must have got it instead."

Gerry gave an eager nod. "Yes Batchev suddenly changed his mind after the cup was passed to him, and said he'd have black instead. So Algy took his cup."

"Perhaps he spotted me lacing it," Adler said, "though I don't see how he could have. Nor why it made Fotheringay sleep for so long. Anyway"—he looked towards Algy—"I'm sorry, buddy. I wouldn't have had it happen."

But there was no reply. Algy's head had dropped and his eyes were closed. Gerry leaned over and gave him a poke. He jerked awake and smiled vaguely round.

Deveraux said: "What happened in Batchev's room?"

"Search me, I left my own room at exactly two-seventeen. I imagined Batchev would be well away by then. I opened his door very quietly and slipped in. I was just going to switch on my torch when I heard a broad creak on the far side of the room. I thought Batchev was lying in wait for me. I couldn't understand it when he didn't switch the light on or challenge me. I didn't want to make the first move myself. So I just stood there in the dark, waiting, for over ten minutes. Then I heard two-thirty strike. I couldn't stay there for ever so I started to creep towards the door. The next thing I knew someone had barged into me in the dark. He tried to jump away from me. I figure he was going to put the light on and that idea didn't appeal to me, so I hung on to him. We fairly waltzed around the room, knocking things over right, left and centre. We rolled clear across the bed and he got free of me. He blundered towards the door, but he didn't switch the light on, just ran out. That surprised me, but I wasn't intending to hang around and meditate on the phenomenon. So I high-tailed it out of there at top speed. There seemed to be all sorts of things going on around me in the dark, but I was only concerned with making sure Batchev didn't find out just then that I'd been disobeying orders. I thought it was vital that he carried on thinking he'd got me under his thumb. So I started feeling my way back to my room. Lady Geraldine knows too well what happened next. Fortunately, I'd noticed the cupboard and the chair every time I'd gone to my room, and was able to find them in the dark. Then I hurried on and got into bed pronto. Somebody—you, I guess"—he nodded towards Deveraux—"came into the room and looked at me a few minutes later, but I just lay doggo and you went away."

Deveraux said: "I thought from the first you were the most likely one to have locked up Lady Geraldine, and it occurred to me I might just catch you out of bed."

"No chance. I stayed there until you came back again later and told me Batchev was missing."

"Well," said Deveraux, "that's another mystery at least partially cleared up. Let's now pass on to the next: the theft of Mrs. Peabody's necklace."

31

Arrest

"WE'VE proved beyond doubt," Deveraux said, "that a notorious international jewel thief known by the sobriquet of the Wraith was in this house after the burglar alarm was switched on, on Saturday night, and that Mrs. Peabody's necklace was removed from its box during the same night. But was it the Wraith who escaped through the breakfast-room window, setting off the alarm in the process; or did he simply take advantage of Batchev having set off the alarm to escape quietly himself another way?

"Now, the more I thought about it, the more I found it impossible to believe that a professional thief such as the Wraith would not have known of Alderley's alarm system, or, knowing of it, would have chosen to commit the robbery at a time when he would have to set off that alarm in order to escape. It was just inconceivable. You might say that he could not resist the challenge laid down in the magazine. Which, frankly, is nonsense. The Wraith is, above all, a professional. He's not going to risk his freedom and depart from the methods which have stood him in such good stead for so long in order to answer the challenge of some footling magazine. In addition, there is a further difficulty. Mr. and Mrs. Peabody's evidence shows that one or the other of them was awake and in the bedroom until Mr. Peabody left to go to the gun-room a little after two-twenty-five. There was then a space of about three minutes during which their rooms were empty. Mrs. Peabody met somebody she supposed was the Wraith on the stairs just after two-thirty, and this would tie up with the necklace having been taken during those three minutes. *But nobody could have known that the rooms were going to be empty at just that time.* Are we to assume that the Wraith happened to enter the Peabody's suite at precisely that moment, purely by chance? Or that he was waiting, say in one of the rooms across the corridor, on the off-chance that Mr. and Mrs. Peabody would at some time during the night both leave the room? Each of these alternatives seems equally unlikely.

"At one stage, I must confess, I did seriously suspect Mr. Peabody himself of having faked the theft. But that theory was soon abandoned. For one thing, enquiries in the United States have indicated that his financial position is as sound as a bell, and secondly there is the evidence of the Wraith's calling card. So the question remained: why should the Wraith have behaved in this incredibly reckless way, leaving so much to chance and only avoiding capture through sheer luck? It was an act of insanity."

Deveraux paused and Gerry spoke. "It worked though, didn't it?"

"Precisely, Lady Geraldine. It worked. Improbably, the Wraith got away with the necklace. Or was that merely what we were meant to think? For suppose he hadn't got away at all? Suppose he was still in the house?"

Lord Burford looked puzzled. "You mean hidin' somewhere?"

"No, Lord Burford. We never seriously suspected that, though Inspector Wilkins' men did in fact make quite sure he wasn't. No—I mean still living in the house openly."

The Countess interjected. "I trust you're not suggesting that one of the servants—"

"No, no, Lady Burford. They are all cleared. They've all been with you far too long. No—I mean *here as one of the guests*. Suppose the Wraith had come to Alderley hoping to steal the necklace? Suppose he had then faced the obstacle of a foolproof burglar alarm which would prevent him leaving with the necklace, and so would immediately throw suspicion on to one of the guests when the theft was discovered? Suppose he had just been biding his time, hoping to find a way round this obstacle, when he had been woken in the early hours of the morning and told the alarm had gone off and that a mysterious man had escaped from the house? In those circumstances, there'd be one obvious course: to go straight to Mrs. Peabody's room and steal the necklace there and then—knowing that the Wraith would almost certainly be thought to be the man who went through the window."

Deveraux swung round. "And you did it actually *after* alerting us all to the possibility that the necklace had been stolen—isn't that right, Mr. Evans?"

For long seconds Evans didn't move or speak. Then he slowly removed his spectacles and rubbed his eyes. "That's right," he said. "I took it—just about five seconds before I woke you, H. S." He chuckled. "It was in my pocket all the time. Then when I was searching the east wing with Lord Burford I slipped it inside a vase in one of the lumber rooms on the top floor."

"Is it—is it still there?" Carrie Peabody asked breathlessly.

"No, Mrs. P. I buried it near the lake yesterday. I'd been intending to come back and dig it up on one of the open days later on, when the heat was off. I shall be pleased to point out the precise spot to Wilkins' rozzers on my way out." He looked over his shoulder. "Are you still there, Inspector?"

"I'm here, Mr. Evans," came Wilkins' voice from the corner.

"Well, I hope you're noticing how co-operative I'm being: admitting my guilt, making no show of resistance, giving the exact location of the stolen property. What with it being a first offence, and my having yielded to sudden temptation, I think I might get off with a couple of years in jug, don't you?"

"First offence! Sudden temptation!" Wilkins gave a snort. "The Wraith's been operating for years."

"What makes you think I'm the Wraith?" Evans sounded quite indignant. "You'll never prove that."

"What about the visiting-card?" Deveraux asked quietly.

"I've no intention of revealing my defence at this stage, old boy, but take it from me that I've got a perfectly good explanation for having it. It was my chance possession of that card which first tempted me into *pretending* to be the notorious Wraith."

"Tell that to the judge," Deveraux said.

"I fully intend to."

Wilkins nodded to Leather, who opened the door. Two uniformed policemen came in. Leather spoke to them quietly.

Evans said: "You want me to go with these gentlemen? Right-ho. The good secretary learns unquestioning obedience. Well, good-bye, H. S. It's been a pleasure. Sorry it doesn't look as though I'm going to be able to work out my notice. Good-bye, Mrs. P. Believe me, I really very much regretted robbing you. I seriously considered not stealing your necklace—until my worse self triumphed. Good-bye, my lord, ladies and gentlemen. I'm sorry to leave you all at this stage. I've never been involved in a murder before and I was looking forward to learning who done it. Still, I suppose it'll be in the papers—which no doubt one can consult in the prison library."

He went out with the two policemen. Lord Burford said: "By jove, quite a personality, what?"

Mr. Peabody was white-faced. he said: "I never suspected him for a moment. He actually tried to persuade us not to bring the necklace here."

"That was a very clever bluff," Deveraux said. "He knew that whatever he said, Mrs. Peabody was quite certain to bring it."

"Land's sakes," Carrie Peabody murmured. "Do you think he came to work for Hiram solely to get his hands on my necklace?"

Deveraux nodded. "Twelve months would be no time to wait for such a prize. Doubtless all through your tour he's just been waiting for an opportunity. But until now you must always have been too careful for him."

Jane asked: "How long have you suspected him?"

"I've had my eye on him ever since a conversation I had with him on Friday afternoon. He was very eager to explain that he was thinking of leaving Mr. Peabody and staying in England for a while. He rather dragged it into the conversation. I think he might have already spotted me as a sort of sleuth and was preparing the ground, so that if and when he did the robbery and then immediately left Mr. Peabody's employ, he wouldn't arouse suspicion. Then, he passed himself off as an American on his first visit here, but he came out with the very British slang word 'quid' rather glibly. Again, after the robbery, once we'd accepted firstly that the Wraith would never have stolen the necklace while the burglar alarm was set; and secondly that the murders and the robbery were unconnected (indicated by the Wraith's card and his known dislike of violence), so that the Wraith couldn't have known in advance that the window was going to be broken— both these facts indicating that the robbery took place *after* the alarm went off—well, then, Evans was the obvious suspect."

"Why?" Jane asked.

"Lady Geraldine suggested the Wraith might be a woman. But I checked and found out the police knew this was not so. The Wraith was definitely known to be a man—and fairly young. And at the time the robbery was discovered only two people who fitted that description knew about the broken window and so could have taken advantage of it as I described. They were Evans—and me. I knew I wasn't the Wraith. Therefore . . ." Deveraux spread his hands. "Wilkins made some enquiries into his background today and found it extremely hazy, with at least one of the references he gave Mr. Peabody false. So the picture was pretty clear."

Hiram Peabody gave a sigh. "And he was just about the best doggone secretary I ever had."

32

The Killer

GILES Deveraux crossed the room, poured himself a glass of water and drank it. Then he went back to his place. He looked round the ring of faces. Every eye was on him. Even Algy Fotheringay at last seemed fully awake.

Deveraux said: "Assault, impersonation, suppression of evidence, and thefts of various kinds. We've cleared them all out of the way. And now we can deal with murder."

"Early today, Inspector Wilkins gave me a number of pointers to the truth about these murders. I won't repeat them in exactly the same form that he put them, but they were as follows: Lady Geraldine's sight, my hearing, and Miss Clifton's nostril; then, Batchev's flight, Lord Burford's collection, Wilkins' own height, and finally the weather."

Deveraux went through them a second time, then said: "I should add that certain of them refer to things lacking or missing. Perhaps we can try to explain them together. Who'd like to start? Lady Geraldine?"

Gerry wrinkled her nose. "I've no idea what your hearing or my sight have got to do with it. The significance of Daddy's collection is pretty obvious—the gun that killed the Baroness came from it. Batchev's flight? I suppose it means why did he decide to leave the house so suddenly in the middle of the night. Well, I've already put forward one theory about that. As for Miss Clifton's nostril, Jane's probably got more idea about what that means."

Jane said slowly: "I smelt the Baroness's scent in the linen-room just after I was knocked down. I remembered it later, and as a result we found her body in the passage. That's the only way my nose has been involved. What else was there?"

"The Inspector's height."

Jane and Gerry looked at each other. Jane shrugged. Gerry said: "Pass."

"The weather."

Jane said: "The thunder drowned certain noises—such as what was going on in Anilese's room when Gerry was ouside."

"How did we do?" Gerry asked.

"Fair. Let's go back. Skip my hearing for the moment and concentrate on your sight. You said you saw the Baroness arrive back in her room at about seven minutes past two, and that she had not left it again at two-thirty. This flatly contradicts Mr. Saunders' statement that her room was empty when he arrived."

Gerry bit her lip. She said: "I—I thought . . ."

"You thought I'd forgotten that discrepancy, Lady Geraldine? No."

In a voice hard with tension, Richard said: "You agreed that there was no truth in your original reconstruction which cast me as the killer."

Again from the dark corner, Wilkin's voice cut across the room. "Excuse me, sir, but he didn't. *You* said there was no truth in it. I said there was *some*—though the reconstruction was largely false and didn't answer all the questions. But that that particular reconstruction was at fault didn't mean that you were necessarily innocent of the murder."

Richard closed his eyes. "Oh no."

"But," said Deveraux, "something else does prove you innocent: the very important element of time. I wonder if anybody noticed one vital fact brought out by Mr. Peabody's evidence: that he took Lord Burford's gun—the one used to shoot the Baroness—from the gun-room *a couple of minutes before two-thirty*—and that thereafter it wasn't out of his possession. He didn't shoot her himself or he would never have admitted that. So the killer must have replaced it in the gun-room after shooting her and before Mr. Peabody took it. Which means the Baroness was killed several minutes before that. Therefore, Mr. Saunders couldn't have shot her after arriving in her room a few seconds after two-thirty. By then she was already dead."

Richard let his head fall back. "Thank heaven," he said.

Gerry was looking perplexed. "But when exactly was

she killed? I assure you I saw her going into her room minutes before ten past two."

"I'm not questioning that. I'd say she was killed at about eleven or twelve minutes past."

"But by whom?"

"You answered that question yourself earlier. The Baroness de la Roche was killed by Stanislaus Batchev."

He looked around at the blank faces, as if waiting for some reaction. But it was as if everybody was stunned. Richard spoke first. "In her room?"

Deveraux nodded.

Gerry said: "But who moved the body?"

"Batchev himself."

"He didn't, I tell you. I would have seen him."

"Now we're back to Lady Geraldine's sight. Will you tell us again exactly what you saw from the time you arrived in the recess?"

"I saw the Baroness leave her room at about four or five minutes past two. Then—"

"Hold it there, please. She went to the gun-room and took Lord Burford's Bergman Bayard and some cartridges. She knew that Batchev would be furious when he learnt she was not, after all, going to blackmail Mr. Saunders, and she wanted protection. We assume she picked the lock—a skill she could quite easily have learnt, given the life she'd been leading. She might even have done it earlier in the evening, in preparation. But of course she wouldn't take the gun until the last moment, in case Lord Burford should go to the gun-room before turning in and notice its absence. Please go on."

"About six or seven minutes past, Batchev arrived and went in, then she came back a minute after that."

"And then it must have happened just as you suggested. Batchev accused her of double-crossing him, threatened her, she pulled the gun; then perhaps he grabbed for it, they struggled and she was shot. They were probably locked together. Their bodies would muffle the shot and that, together with the thick heavy door and the thunderstorm, meant you heard nothing. What did you see next?"

"Batchev leaving—alone."

"You didn't know who it was at the time though, did you?"

"No."

"Why not?"

"Because the only light was from his torch, which he held low down. So I couldn't see his face."

"How much of him *could* you see?"

"Well, really only his feet and about half way up his legs."

"Precisely. What you could not see was that Batchev was *carrying the Baroness's body over his shoulder.*"

Throughout the room there was a slow expelling of breath. Gerry stared at Deveraux, opened her mouth—and closed it again.

Deveraux said: "You agree—he could have been?"

"I—I suppose so," she said slowly. "But he didn't seem to be carrying any weight. He walked quite briskly and light-footed."

"He was an extremely strong man—her weight would have been nothing to him."

"But how do you know that's what happened?"

"Given that there is only one door to the room, that the window couldn't be opened more than a few inches without setting off the alarm, and that both you and your uncle are telling the truth, that's the only way it could have happened."

Jane said: "And he put the body in the secret passage himself?"

"That's right."

"Why?"

"We can only surmise, but he must have known that he was going to have to abandon his assignment. His probable intention then was flight as soon as the servants were up and the alarm was switched off—a man of his experience would have a good chance of getting away without being seen—hoping it would be assumed the Baroness had left with him. So it was essential that her body wasn't discovered immediately. I think he thought of the passage simply as a hiding place, and didn't have any intention of using it to take her body downstairs. I believe later he would have collected all her things from her room and dumped them in there with her. But before that he went to replace the pistol in the collection-room."

"Why bother?" Jane asked again.

"Well, it was obviously important to get rid of the murder weapon quickly, just in case anybody else had been disturbed and got up to investigate. He could have left it with the body; but he knew the Earl and Mr. Pea-

225

body were in and out of the collection-room all the time and that its absence would be very quickly noticed. The fact that he and the Baroness were missing would not make anybody necessarily suspect foul play, but if a pistol were gone as well, it might suggest the use of violence and possible murder, and that in turn might lead to a more intensive search being made. Anyway, after hiding the body behind the panel, he made his way to the the gun-room. He must have arrived there just about a minute or so before you arrived in his room, Adler."

Martin Adler nodded.

"Batchev put the gun back," Deveraux went on, "and was no doubt intending then to go and pack his own things. But his plan didn't work out. For he in turn was shot by somebody else."

The tension in the room was mounting again. It was as if nobody wanted even to breathe.

"I mentioned earlier," Deveraux continued, "that outside the servants' quarters only three people in this house had remained in bed all the time prior to the alarm being set off. One of those people was Lady Burford. Another was Fotheringay. The third, strangely enough, was Evans. Which means that one person, other than those who have admitted being up, was also out of bed and creeping about in the dark."

Deveraux stopped, turned, and looked straight at a slight, unobtrusive figure sitting just outside the main circle. "That person," he said, "was Edward Thornton."

Thornton neither moved nor spoke.

Deveraux pointed at him. "There's the man you fought, Adler. There's the man who knocked you down, Jane. There's the man who was paid £10,000 to release secret information about your negotiations, Mr. Saunders."

Thornton looked at him out of cold eyes. "You're mad," he said quietly.

"And there's the man," Deveraux continued remorselessly, "who shot Stanislaus Batchev."

"You fool!" Thornton spat out the words. "Do you think anyone's going to believe that? What motive could I have had?"

"He knew you were a traitor in the pay of a foreign power."

"It's a lie! Anyway, I couldn't possibly have had time

to kill him. Nobody was able to leave the house before ten to three—"

"You didn't leave the house. You shot him in the gun-room at about two-twenty-five, when he went to replace the Bergman."

"But the body was found in the lake, you imbecile!"

"Agreed. You transferred it to the lake later—after the alarm had gone off."

"And just when am I supposed to have done that?"

"Between the times Miss Clifton left your room at about a minute to three, and you joined us towards the end of our search."

"You're not seriously suggesting that I dressed, carried a body from the gun-room downstairs—without being seen—out to the lake, got back to my room, joined you dry and free from mud—all in about fifteen minutes?"

"Certainly not. That was the cleverest part of the whole plan. In disposing of the body, you never left the gun-room."

He looked round. "Remember the pointers: *Lord Burford's collection; Batchev's flight.* Did you all assume that *flight* was used in the sense of *fleeing, escape?* No: it referred, quite literally to the act of flying through the air. That was how the body reached the lake. It was shot there."

The Earl whispered: "You—you don't mean—"

"Yes, Lord Burford—from the circus gun used by Burundi the Human Cannonball."

Richard said: "Great Scott!"

Lady Burford murmured weakly: "I don't believe it."

Hiram Peabody exclaimed: "Jumping jehosaphat!"

The monocle dropped from Algy Fotheringay's eye.

It was at that moment, when Deveraux had the rapt attention of every person in the room, that Thornton acted. Like lightning he sprang to his feet. A small snub-nosed automatic had appeared in his hand. He took two steps towards the door. "Everyone stay where they are."

Wilkins spoke very quietly. "Now don't be silly, sir. This isn't going to get you anywhere." He moved towards Thornton.

Thornton swung round and levelled the gun at him. "I said nobody move. That includes you."

From behind him, Deveraux said: "You can't shoot everyone, Thornton."

Thornton spun round again and pointed the automatic at Deveraux. He licked his lips and cast a quick glance over his shoulder towards Wilkins and Leather. Then his eyes flickered. "Perhaps not," he snapped, "but I can shoot one."

He was standing behind Jane's chair, and as he spoke he leaned forward, grabbed her by the arm and jerked her to her feet.

"If anybody moves an inch, she'll be the first to go."

He threw his arm around her neck, pulled her backwards against his chest, and pressed the muzzle of the gun against her temple.

The first shock lasted a few seconds. Then Jane felt quite calm. The cold metal against her head worried her less than the pressure of Thornton's arm on her throat. She saw the ring of white horrified faces, etched sharp and still as a photograph. She realized that Wilkins and Deveraux had both drawn back, helpless.

Thornton was backing towards the door, dragging Jane awkwardly with him. Closer and closer they got to it, and the pressure of his arm was making her eyes water.

Thornton said: "That's stopped you in your tracks, hasn't it?" He gave Jane another jerk backwards, causing her ankle to knock painfully against the leg of a chair. "Come on, girl. Don't dawdle."

Then Jane lost her temper.

The humiliation of what was being done to her swept over her. How dare he treat her like this? She wouldn't put up with it for another second.

She raised her hands, yanked Thornton's wrist towards her mouth, and bent her head. Taken quite by surprise, Thornton let the pistol slip away from her head, and at that instant Jane gripped his hand between her teeth and bit as hard as she could.

Thornton gave a howl and snatched his arm away. Jane drove her elbow hard into his stomach, then leapt away from him as his gun arm flailed wildly in the air.

Already Giles Deveraux was moving. He sprang at Thornton. With one hand he grabbed the wrist holding the gun, and with the other he landed a crisp right across to the point of Thornton's jaw and sent him flying.

One minute later, Edward Thornton was on his feet again—handcuffed and firmly in the grasp of Sergeant Leather.

Gasping, Thornton addressed Deveraux. "Listen—I admit I took a bribe. The ten thousand was a down payment. I was to receive a further ten when I handed over the details of certain African territory. But I am not in the pay of any foreign power. I was given the money by some Scandinavian. He was acting on behalf of a private individual—a financier who wants to buy up land there in advance, as a commercial venture. It wouldn't harm this country's interests."

"No," Richard said coldly, "only cheat thousands of poor people out of their rights."

"I'd bet my bottom dollar that old buzzard Zapopulous is behind it," Peabody said.

"I don't know," Thornton said. "I only dealt with this Scandinavian. I thought it would be easy. But Batchev wouldn't part with the information. By Saturday night I was desperate. That's when I decided to search his room to see if I could find any papers giving the information. How was I to know he was bogus and didn't have it himself? I tried to drug him so he wouldn't wake: I slipped several sleeping tablets into his coffee after dinner. I didn't realize till the next day that Fotheringay had drunk it instead. And of course I didn't know somebody else had done the same thing."

Lord Burford gave a long low whistle and stared at Algy with something like awe. "By jove, no wonder the feller slept."

"You're very lucky to have escaped with your life, Fotheringay," Deveraux said.

Algy gave a smirk. "I've always been jolly tough. Once—"

"Go on, Thornton," Deveraux said.

"I went to Batchev's room just before two-fifteen. Batchev wasn't there. I couldn't understand it, but I started searching. After about two or three minutes, I heard the door opening. I naturally assumed it was Batchev and I hid behind the wardrobe. Nothing happened and eventually I tried to get to the door. You know what happened then. I managed to get out and ran back to my own room, colliding with her"—he pointed to Jane—"on the way. I went straight back to bed and stayed there until she roused me about thirty minutes later. And that's all I did. I panicked just now because the case looked so black against me. But I swear I am not a traitor. And I am not a murderer. I did not shoot Batchev."

Deveraux looked at him, his face expressionless. Then, before he could answer, Inspector Wilkins spoke again.

"I know that," he said quietly.

An absolutely stunned silence greeted Wilkins' words. It seemed that no one could even gasp. Again it was Richard who produced the first coherent words. "Wilkins—are you now saying it was *not* Thornton who shot Batchev?"

"That's right, sir."

"Then just why did you let Deveraux accuse him of it?"

"I'm afraid it's a favourite ruse of mine, sir—to accuse someone of a major crime to get them to confess to a lesser one. I'm sorry to use it twice in one evening. But as we've got very little evidence, we had to get Mr. Thornton to own up to conspiracy and corruption. Unfortunately, I did not anticipate he would be armed."

He gave a nod to Leather, who opened the door. Two more uniformed policemen came in. "Take him away," Wilkins said.

When the door had closed behind a dazed and speechless Thornton, Lord Burford said: "Are you telling us now Burundi's cannon was *not* used to despatch Batchev's body?"

"Oh, it was used. But not by Thornton."

"Then by whom, man?"

"And," Gerry added, "if it wasn't Batchev, Evans, or Mr. Thornton who went through the breakfast-room window—who was it?"

"Nobody, Lady Geraldine."

"Oh, come on! I saw him. We all did."

Wilkins shook his head. "No. That's what we were meant to think. By Batchev's killer."

"This has gone on quite long enough." The authoritative words came from the Countess. "Mr. Wilkins, please tell us *now* who the murderer really was."

"Very well, your ladyship. I will." He turned and looked straight at Jane. "I'm afraid it was this young lady." His face was sad. "Why did you do it, Miss Clifton?"

Jane met his gaze. For a moment her eyes wavered and dropped. But then she took a deep breath and lifted her head proudly.

"Because he drove my sister to suicide," she said.

33

The Reason Why

"AS some of you here know," Jane said, "my sister was an actress. Her name was Jenny Howard—she changed it officially by deed-poll when she entered the profession and found there was another actress called, I think, Jenny Clinton.

"Jenny died three years ago in the United States. How she died was never made public. She was on a tour with a theatrical company when she met a man who called himself Stewart Baldwin. All I ever knew about him was what I learnt from Jenny. He was supposed to be a free-lance journalist who was doing a series of articles on the tour, and he travelled with the company for about eight weeks. Jenny fell madly in love with him. Then unexpectedly he told her he had to leave very soon on another assignment. He said he wanted to marry her, and asked her to go away with him. She cleared it with the manager and left a week later. She and Stewart were married by a Justice of the Peace in a little town in New Mexico. She wrote home the day after the wedding, saying she was deliriously happy and had no regrets at giving up her career."

Jane drew at her cigarette. "Although my mother and I were both sad that Jenny wouldn't be coming home, we made the best of it. Mother, however, had a strong feeling that the marriage wasn't going to work out, and she asked me to agree not to tell any of our friends about it, for the time being, just in case.

"For about six months Jenny travelled all over America with Stewart, staying in hotels and rooming-houses. During this time she had very little to do, and she used to write to us two or three times a week. She seemed absolutely crazy about Stewart, and she told us practically

231

everything there was to know about him—all his likes and dislikes and habits and ways of talking. She also sent one blurred snapshot of him, which she'd managed to take without his knowledge, as she said he hated to be photographed. Meanwhile, the theatrical company had come home. When people asked about Jenny we simply told them she was staying on in the States for a bit. Of course, the stage people knew about her marriage, but they didn't come in contact with our circle at all."

Jane stubbed out her cigarette. "Then, during March, I came to stay here at Alderley. I'd told Jenny in one of my letters that I was coming, and while I was here I got a letter from her. She sent it here because she hadn't wanted Mother to know, but she was terribly worried and unhappy. They were moving round more and more, and sometimes Stewart would go away for days on end, leaving her in some poky rooming-house. He wouldn't talk about his work, and she couldn't understand what his assignment was supposed to be—he told her it was for some magazine she'd never heard of. Occasionally he'd take her to cocktail parties or receptions and introduce her to lots of people, but they'd never stay long and she wouldn't meet the people again. She said Stewart didn't ever seem actually to write anything and simply told her he was gathering copy. She said she'd just had to tell somebody, as she felt utterly alone and had no friends in America at all. She told me not to take too much notice of the letters she sent to Mother and me at home, but that she'd keep me informed of what was really happening by sending me letters to be called for at the post office."

Jane looked at Gerry. "I got that letter on the day of the Hunt Ball, do you remember? You couldn't understand what was wrong with me."

Gerry nodded, but didn't speak.

"In May," Jane went on, "Jenny discovered she was going to have a baby. She was terribly excited, thinking it might make Stewart settle down. But when she told him he was furious. They had a blazing row and he stormed out. She never saw him again.

"She had practically no money, no home, and no one to turn to. She was frantic. Then two men arrived, looking for Stewart. They were Federal agents—G-men. They told her that Stewart was wanted for subversive activities. Baldwin wasn't his real name; he wasn't a journalist; he wasn't even an American citizen. He'd entered the country illegally eighteen months before. They also informed her gently that a year previously he'd married a woman in Illinois. She was still alive and the marriage had never been dissolved. So Jenny wasn't even legally married to him."

Jane looked at Deveraux. "I realize now what he'd done. He must have been impersonating someone who was known to be married, and for some reason he needed a real wife to produce sometimes for authenticity. Presumably the woman in Illinois had been unsuitable, or perhaps she'd found out the truth and told the authorities about him. He left her before the FBI arrived and got himself a cover by going round with the theatrical company. Probably he realized there might be a good chance of picking up another wife among the young actresses. He took up with Jenny, and then when the time came to renew his espionage work, he married her. When she told him about the baby, he knew she was going to be too tied down to be any further use to him."

Deveraux nodded slowly and Jane continued. "Jenny, I imagine, put on a very good act of being extremely calm and casual about it all. The G-men left, promising to inform the nearest British Consul about her plight."

Jane took another cigarette with a hand that shook slightly. Richard lit it for her.

"Jenny was a very proud person," she said. "We all were. Perhaps too proud. Gerry tells me I am; I don't know. But Jenny was more sensitive than me and more highly strung. After the men had left, she wrote and told me the whole story. She said she couldn't bear the humiliation of coming home with an illegitimate baby, and not even knowing the father's real name. And especially she couldn't face Mother. She went out, mailed the letter, returned to her room and gassed herself."

Jane looked up. Her eyes were moist, but her voice was steady as she continued. "I told Mummy Jennifer had been taken ill and died of a very rare disease. The officials I dealt with were all very good and kept the secret. There were a few lines about her in some of the papers, but none of them said more than that she'd died suddenly. None of our friends ever knew the truth.

"I've carried Stewart Baldwin's photo with me ever since. Just so I never could forget. I had a feeling always

233

that sometime, somewhere, I'd meet him. The very first time I saw him getting off the train last Thursday, I thought he looked vaguely familiar. Then when I was introduced to him on the terrace and heard that phony American accent, the sense of familiarity grew. I puzzled over it most of the next day. I think it was only a kind of subconscious rejection of the possibility of it being him that prevented mè connecting him with Baldwin. It didn't really come to me until I was talking to him on Friday afternoon. He was obviously talking as himself, not as Mr. Adler, and he mentioned once having had an English girl friend who'd lived in the Cotswolds. That was almost certainly Jenny, because we used to live there. I was on the point of mentioning it when he took a drink. Now Jenny had told me that Stewart had the unusual mannerism of closing his eyes momentarily whenever he drank. *Batchev did that very thing.*

"It gave me a terrible jolt. I went up to my room and studied Baldwin's photo. I couldn't be sure even then that Baldwin was him. In the photo he had fair hair and a moustache, and, as I said, the picture was rather blurred and several years old. I didn't then even have the similarity of initials—SB—as an indication. You, Richard, and everybody else, accepted him as Martin Adler, a well-known European diplomat, and I couldn't see how it was possible for him to be Baldwin. So I set myself to finding out. I talked to him as much as I could and I watched him like a hawk. I know all Jenny's letters by heart, of course, and gradually I began to recognize in Batchev little things she had told me about Stewart. I won't go into them all now. They were things like preferences in food and drink, turns of phrase in speech, taste in clothes —Stewart always wore plain neckties, for instance, as Batchev did—smoking habits—always using cork-tipped cigarettes—and so on. Eventually I spotted about ten similarities. Then I was sure."

"An incredible coincidence," Richard murmured.

"Or fate," Jane said. "I did wonder whether he would identify me as Jenny's sister. But of course the surname was different. Whether Jenny told him her original surname I don't know, but if she did there'd be no reason for him to remember it. He must have known she had a sister called Jane, but that's a common enough name.

"Once I knew who he really was, I could have reported

234

to you, Richard, that he was bogus. But I wanted to be sure he was punished for what he'd done to Jenny and I doubted if they'd be able to bring it home to him after all this time. Besides, prison would be too good for him. He had to die. I decided to kill him myself."

34

Execution

"I quite enjoyed planning the execution," Jane said quietly. "It was the three facts of the alarm system, the circus cannon, and the nearness of the lake which were the basis for my plan. I thought that if Batchev's body was found some distance from the house, and he was thought to have been killed at a time when the burglar alarm would prove everybody else to have been *in* the house, then nobody here would be suspected. I knew how to operate the cannon. I was staying here when Lord Burford bought it, and he tested it by firing lengths of timber from the balcony. Fortunately, after that it was only moved back a few feet—not shifted to the side—so that it was still aimed straight towards the french doors. Of course, I couldn't have done it if the lake hadn't been there: if the body had landed on dry ground, it would have been obvious it had fallen from a height—and then the police would have probably thought of the cannon and put two and two together. If it hadn't been for all the other complications, which I couldn't have foreseen, I think I'd have fooled you—you would have thought he'd gone out to meet somebody and been shot by him. The only part of my plan that went wrong was the business of the pistol. I planned to take one of Lord Burford's from the collection, use it to shoot Batchev, put his fingerprints on it, hide it somewhere in the house, and then the next day go and drop it near where the body had been found. I was hoping to make the police think that Batchev had taken it himself for protection, had met and fought with somebody on the grounds, had been shot with it in the struggle, and that the murderer had dropped it while getting away. I'll explain what went wrong in a minute.

"On Saturday after lunch I went down to the village and bought a small reel of black cobbler's thread. In the afternoon Lord Burford showed us all his collection and I decided that as it was one of the few modern style repeating-guns, with cartridges available, the Bergman would be best for me. I went to bed that night normally and tried to read for a bit. I got up at half-past one. I put on a dressing-gown and a pair of cotton gloves, crept along to Lord Burford's room and took the keys to the gun-room from his dressing-table. Then I went downstairs. I fetched the step-ladder, and also a pair of wire cutters from the tool-box that was kept in the same place. I took them along to the breakfast-room and put the step-ladder up by the window. Then I stood on a chair, jammed one end of the thread in the crack of the door, fastened the other end to the top of the step-ladder, and slowly tilted it until it was very finely balanced—just held up by the thread. As soon as the thread was released the step-ladder would crash through the window. I moved the pot plant, put a chair on its side near the window, and threw the wire cutters down on the floor.

"I couldn't, obviously, open the door, so I went upstairs by the secret passage. I went straight to the collection-room to get Lord Burford's Bergman. But it wasn't there. The Baroness must have just taken it. I was absolutely stymied: all the other small guns there seemed terribly old-fashioned and I didn't know how to operate them. It looked as though I'd have to abandon the whole plan. Then I remembered Mr. Peabody's gun, which was identical. I took four cartridges from the cupboard and crept back along the corridor. Then, when I was nearly there, I saw the light of a torch and someone emerging from the Peabody's suite. A second later I saw it was Lord Burford and he had the gun in his hand. He'd said how much he wanted that pistol, so I guessed at once what he was doing. It was vital I found out what he did with the gun. I followed him downstairs to the study and watched him put it in the safe. I hid when he came out, then when he'd gone back upstairs I went in to get it. I learnt the combination of the safe years ago—I sometimes fetched papers and things from it for the Earl when I stayed here as a schoolgirl. But I couldn't remember it exactly at first: it took me two or three minutes to get it.

Then I took the gun, loaded it, and made my way back upstairs.

"My plan then had been to go to Batchev's room and force him to go with me to the gun-room. But just as I got to the top of the stairs I heard a footstep and saw the faint flash of a torch to my right. I thought it had to be Lord Burford again, but then there was a very vivid flash of lightning and I saw quite clearly that it was Batchev. He was walking away from me towards the east wing. I followed him. I watched him go into the collection-room. I could hardly believe my good luck—he was playing right into my hands.

"I didn't see him replace Lord Burford's pistol, because I took a few seconds to pluck up courage to follow him in. I've believed ever since that he'd gone there to *take* a gun. Eventually I went in, closed the doors behind me, and switched on the light. I must have given him a terrific shock, but he didn't show it too much. I kept Mr. Peabody's pistol behind my back and asked him casually what he was doing. He must have thought I'd seen him replacing Lord Burford's pistol, because he pointed to it and said something about finding it in the corridor and deciding to put it back. I walked across as if I was just going to look at it more closely. Then when I got near him I brought Mr. Peabody's gun from behind my back and told him to put his hands up. I believe he thought then that I suspected him of being a thief, was just concerned for the safety of the collection, and that given time he could talk me round. So he decided to humour me a bit, and when I told him to walk down to the far end of the room, he did so. When we got near the cannon I said I wanted to have a look round to make sure nothing was missing, and I told him to lie down on the floor against the wall in the corner, where I could keep an eye on him. He seemed quite relieved at this, because obviously he knew nothing was missing and no doubt he thought that when I realized this I'd apologize, and go back to bed. So it would clearly pay him to co-operate with me.

"Then, when he was lying in the corner, I just suddenly sprang it on him that I was Jenny Howard's sister, and I was going to execute him for causing her death. I've never seen anyone so shaken as he was then. It must have come like a bolt from the blue. Any doubts I might have had about him being Baldwin were removed. In fact, he didn't try to deny it, and when he'd recovered a bit from the first shock, he just tried to convince me I didn't know the full truth about Jenny and that he wasn't to blame. I must say he kept his head quite well.

"I told him nothing he could say would make any difference, and that I was going to give him roughly two minutes and then kill him. I counted off what I guessed were quarter minutes. Towards the end he did get really scared, but there was nothing he could do: I was very careful to stand too far away to give him any chance of grabbing me, yet near enough so that my shot couldn't miss; in that position he couldn't duck or dodge and if he'd rolled, he could only have rolled towards me.

"When I estimated two minutes were up, I said 'That's it,' and I shot him dead."

Jane looked around at the spellbound circle of faces. She said: "Could I have some water, do you think?"

Gerry jumped to her feet and fetched a glass. Everyone was silent while Jane drank. She put it down and went on. "I knew the shot wouldn't be heard: the gun-room is so isolated from any of the occupied rooms. In the past I've been in my bedroom when Lord Burford was using the range, and I haven't heard a thing. I was quite calm. First of all I went across, plugged in the lead running to the cannon's air compressor and switched it on. Then I lowered the barrel right down till it was nearly touching the floor. I went back and dragged Batchev across to it. I was amazed to find that the body was already rigid, as I'd always thought it was hours before rigor mortis set in; but I've looked it up since and found that in cases of violent death it sometimes starts immediately. Actually, it was very lucky for me it did set in so quickly, because I've since remembered Lord Burford telling Gerry and me years ago that it was necessary for a human cannonball to keep completely stiff or he might only fly a few feet. Also, I think the rigidity of the body made it easier to get it into the barrel, even though I still had a bit of a struggle. Luckily, he was quite slightly-built, so I managed it eventually. Oh, before that I held the pistol by the barrel and tried to press Batchev's fingers against it. But their being so stiff made it very difficult and I must have smudged the prints.

"All I had to do after I'd got the body in was to turn

the handle until the barrel was about level as it had been before. Then I went quietly out, turning off the light and locking the door.

"My plan then had been to hide the pistol in one of the lumber-rooms on the top floor, then come down and wake you, Richard, and tell you that I'd seen Adler—as we were then calling him—creep downstairs, take a step-ladder into the breakfast-room, and shut the door. You would have come down with me to investigate. But that plan was spoilt straight away. I'd no sooner closed the door to the picture gallery behind me than I heard foot-steps coming along the corridor. It was you, of course, Mr. Peabody, but I didn't know that then. I darted across to my own room and waited just inside. I heard the gallery door open, and I guessed somebody was going to the gun-room. I was terrified in case they found the body. But it was all right, for a minute or so later I heard the gallery door open and close again and the footsteps go away. I went back out to the corridor. Looked in the gallery, but I decided not to go across to the gun-room again. If anybody *had* found Batchev's body, I couldn't do anything about it—and they might raise the alarm and come back and find me there. Besides, I was pretty sure whoever it was was up to no good, and so wouldn't have turned the light on; again, to find the body they would have needed to go right down to the far end and look into the barrel, and I just didn't think they'd had enough time to do that. So I carried on with my original plan. The gun was burning a hole in my pocket and I knew the bulge would be pretty conspicuous if anybody did see me. So I couldn't turn a light on.

"I made my way towards the front of the house. I heard two-thirty strike—and you all know what happened then. Luckily, when I got up after Thornton had knocked me over, the gun was still in my pocket. But I panicked a bit. There were so many people about that any moment somebody was going to switch on the lights. I had to get rid of the gun before that happened. I was near the linen-room and I thought of the secret passage. I dashed in, opened the panel, dropped the gun inside, and took off my gloves. Naturally, I had no idea that Anilese's body was already there. I went back out, turned on the lights, and found Mr. Deveraux."

She looked at him. "I decided on the spur of the

moment to use you instead of Richard for the next part of my plan. But I didn't say anything about seeing Batchev behave suspiciously in the breakfast-room: for one thing you'd just seen me coming from the direction of my own room; and for another you might have been downstairs yourself and know I was lying. Except for that, however, I followed my plan. After we released Gerry, I was going to suggest we searched downstairs, but luckily you suggested it yourself. Everything worked like a dream. When we got near the breakfast-room I pretended to hear a noise inside. I rushed forward and opened the door. The thread was released and the step-ladder crashed through the window, setting off the alarm. I froze for a second, so that you couldn't rush straight in and see the room was empty. Then I dashed in myself and yelled that somebody was just disappearing outside. You went after him. While Gerry was looking out after you, I stood the ladder up and managed to unhook the thread, bundle it up and put it in my pocket.

"Shortly after you sent me upstairs. I put my gloves on, slipped into the gun-room, opened the window, raised the barrel, and fired the cannon. I was on tenterhooks in case it wouldn't work. But it did. Batchev's body went flying into the darkness. I heard the splash of it landing in the lake. I closed the window, unplugged the compressor, and went out, locking the door. It didn't take more than two minutes altogether. Then I went and checked on Evans, Thornton, and Algy, as you'd asked me to, dropped my gloves off in my room, and came back downstairs. Later on, when everybody was down here after Inspector Wilkins arrived, I pretended to want something from my room, went up and replaced the gun-room key on Lord Burford's dressing-table.

"The only other thing to be done was take the pistol from behind the panel and hide it in the park somewhere the next day. I hadn't meant to go and get it just when I did, but when we were talking on the terrace"—she was addressing Deveraux continually now—"you showed altogether too much interest in the passage, and I thought I ought to remove the gun quickly before you decided to go and search it. Incidentally, I hadn't smelt anything in there: but I had to have some reason for being in the room when you found me, and I'd already said I hadn't *seen* or *heard* anything.

241

"Then we found the Baroness's body. I think that was the most horrifying moment of my life—and utterly baffling, too. I've been as mystified as everybody about who killed her. I didn't think it could be Batchev, because I knew the murder gun was taken after he was dead; what I didn't know was that it had been taken twice."

Jane looked hard at Deveraux. "Was there anything else you wanted to know?"

"Just one thing." Deveraux took the egg cosy from his pocket. "It's not vital, but can you throw any light on this?"

The ghost of a smile crossed Jane's features. "Oh, that. I couldn't get the thread gripped properly in the breakfast-room door: it kept slipping out. I wanted something to fix on the end to stop it—something soft and light which wouldn't make any noise landing. That was the first thing that came to hand. But it was so white I thought that even in dim light it might show up against the dark wood outside. So I rubbed it in the pot plant to darken it. It was still fastened to the end when I put the thread in my pocket. I was nervous we might all be searched, however, and I wanted to get rid of it—it wouldn't be so easy to explain as just a length of thread on its own. So before I raised the barrel, prior to firing the cannon, I reached inside and tried to push the thing into Batchev's pocket. That must have been when it got the blood on it. I thought if it were found there, it would definitely connect him with the breakfast-room and might remove any doubt that it had been he who went through the window—and in addition it would be a good red herring. But I was doing everything so hurriedly I couldn't have put it in the pocket properly. Obviously it fell out as the body flew towards the lake, and landed on that bush."

Wilkins looked at Deveraux. "Simple when you know, isn't it?"

Jane stood up. "And now I suppose you'll want me to come with you, Mr. Wilkins."

Ten minutes later Jane walked down the grand staircase. She had changed out of her evening dress. She was accompanied by Sergeant Leather, carrying her case. Deveraux and Wilkins were in the hall. Deveraux came forward.

"They want to know in the drawing-room if you'd like to see anybody."

Jane hesitated. "No, I don't think—" She broke off and her chin went up. "Yes. Would you ask Gerry and Richard to come out, please?"

Deveraux nodded and went away. A few moments later Richard and Gerry came into the hall. There was an awkward silence for three or four seconds. Then Jane gave Gerry a grin. "Cheer up, darling. You look like death. Don't you realize I won't have to worry about job-hunting now?"

Gerry looked at her. Her lips trembled. Then she flung herself on Jane, threw her arms round her for a second, and turned away, sobbing.

Jane bit her lip sharply, then swung suddenly round on Richard and held out her hand. "Goodbye, Richard."

He took her hand in both of his. "*Au revoir*, Jane. Don't worry about the practical side. You'll have the best Counsel in England, never fear."

"That's sweet of you, Richard, but there's no need, really. I'll plead guilty, of course. Listen, I'm sorry to have put you all through such a ghastly business. Tell the Earl and Countess, will you? Say good-bye and thanks for me, and tell them I'll write if I'm allowed."

"You didn't put us through any ghastly business, my dear. It would have been even worse but for you. *You* stopped him getting away."

"Thanks. It was purely personal, though. Say good-bye to everybody else for me—the Peabodys and Mr. Adler and Algy." She turned to Deveraux, who was standing a few feet away. "Did you think I'd confess when Mr. Wilkins accused Thornton?"

"We thought you might—rather than let him be falsely charged."

"I would have, of course. I was just plucking up the courage—when he acted himself." She paused. "Are you coming now?"

"Not now."

"Then good-bye. This morning I rather slyly apologized for hindering you when the imaginary man went through the window. I'd just like you to know that the other apologies and thanks were genuine."

"I know that."

"I don't really know why I'm saying this. I knew you spelt trouble for me from that first moment when you practically drowned me through driving like a lunatic up the drive—knocking down footbound pheasants right, left and centre. Very well, Mr. Leather, I'm ready."

Wilkins opened the front door, and Jane walked through the doorway and down the steps to the waiting car, Leather and another policeman a few paces behind. "Like a princess and her courtiers," Richard murmured.

They watched the car drive off into the darkness. Then Wilkins shut the door and went back into the drawing-room.

Very quietly, Richard said: "I wonder why she asked to see *me*."

There was a pause before Gerry said. "Why shouldn't she?"

"She's always seemed rather stiff with me. I got the impression years ago that she didn't like me very much."

Gerry looked at him sharply, opened her mouth, then seemed to change her mind. Instead, in a voice that shook a little, she said: "They—they won't hang her, will they?"

Richard put his arm round her shoulder. "Of course not. Not when they learn of the provocation. Not when they learn what sort of monster she prevented escaping—a murderer, kidnapper, spy, and blackmailer. And they'll learn the truth of that from me—whatever it does to my reputation."

"She couldn't get off, though, could she?"

"I think she could—with a clever lawyer and a sympathetic jury. She could change her story, claim she was under stress tonight, not responsible for what she was saying, that really she shot Batchev in self-defense—something like that."

"She won't do that. She'll tell the absolute truth."

"And in this country we don't approve of people taking the law into their own hands," Richard said. "However great a villain the victim. She planned Batchev's murder and carried it out with great efficiency. She'll show no remorse. She's bound to go to prison for a long time."

"It's not right," Gerry said in a choking voice, "for ridding the world of a man like that."

"Perhaps—" Deveraux said, then broke off.

"Perhaps what?" Richard asked.

"Nothing," said Deveraux.

35

Inspector Wilkins Explains

IN the drawing-room ten minutes later, "Deveraux," said Peabody, "how in tarnation did you get at the truth?"

"I didn't, sir. Wilkins did. I was blundering in the right direction, but I was a long way from the truth when he gave me his list of pointers."

"Then," said the Earl, "I insist that before he leaves he explains his deductive process."

"Hear, hear," said Adler.

Looking awkward and embarrassed, Wilkins shuffled forward. He coughed. "Well, my lord, if your lordship insists. Let me say first that Mr. Deveraux is being far too modest: it was he who spotted Evans as the Wraith. I can't say much about my own deductive process, but I can tell you a few things I thought were rum. And I may add that when I came in here this evening I didn't know everything. I had theories, but not the full picture, and no proof.

"I decided quite early on that nearly everybody was hiding something. It seemed to me the first problem to solve was the matter of the pistols, and when I learned of the rivalry over the matter of the Bergman Bayards, I suspected that perhaps something a little, er, unconventional might have been going on. When we discovered the gun in the collection-room was a replica, I decided that Mr. Peabody was the most likely, um——"

"Crook," said Carrie Peabody drily.

"Let's say culprit, ma'am. Then, my lord, after saying that the gun in the collection-room was not yours, but a

245

replica, you added, "And it's not mine either." When questioned you claimed to have meant that it was not your *Bergman*. But, as we'd already established that fact, the remark didn't make sense, and I decided that what you had meant was that *that* replica wasn't *your* replica. As there were a pair of originals, it wasn't unlikely there were also a pair of copies; and if your lordship had one of each, it was on the cards Mr. Peabody had one of each, too. Next, when Mr. Peabody discovered that his pistol was missing from its care your lordship's involuntary exclamation was, "Don't say the case is empty?"—indicating you were extremely surprised not to find *something* in it. Your reaction, sir"—he turned to Peabody—"both to being told of the theft of Lord Burford's gun, and to the theory I put forward at that time, seemed somewhat unnatural.

"Then there was the matter of the scream on the stairs: both Lady Geraldine and Miss Clifton were upstairs at the time and, once it appeared that the Baroness was by then already dead, barring servants, either her ladyship or Mrs. Peabody had to be the one responsible. And it seemed that Mrs. Peabody, a visitor in a strange house, would be the more likely to be nervous. Considering all these factors, I evolved a tentative theory to account for the matter of the four pistols. Then I played a couple of long shots. First I searched Mr. Peabody's luggage. Your unwillingness to allow it, Mr. Peabody, and your readiness, ma'am—followed by your genuine amazement when I discovered the pistol—supported my theory that Mr. Peabody had hidden one gun in the room, and you'd taken another one away—the one put there by his lordship. In fact, you started to say something like 'He must have brought it back again.' I had a good idea you'd want to plant it in a room that was specifically Lord Burford's—which probably meant the collection-room or the study. I had another look in the collection-room myself, then got Mr. Deveraux to search the study. Fortunately, this paid off and my theory was virtually confirmed."

"Well, I'm exceedingly sorry to have made your job more difficult," Lord Burford said gruffly.

"That goes for me too," said Peabody.

"Please don't mention it. It really made the case more interesting—more of a challenge, as it were."

"I guess I fouled things up for you a bit, didn't I?" said Adler.

"Not really, sir. It always seemed most likely that you were one of the fighters in Batchev's room and the man who had incarcerated Lady Geraldine. Your exact motives were not clear, but you've explained those yourself. The matter of your antagonist was more tricky, but once we'd eliminated Batchev himself—who was already dead— and picked on Evans as the Wraith—who has always been purely a jewel thief and who wouldn't have had occasion to enter Batchev's room—well, then the man you fought had to be either Thornton or Mr. Fotheringay here. I'm sorry to say, Mr. Fotheringay, sir, that I did wonder if *you* were the Wraith and the drug had been self-administered, but—Mr. Fotheringay?"

"He's just gone to sleep again," said the Countess.

"Then I can say that Mr. Deveraux assured me that unless Mr. Fotheringay was the most brilliant actor imaginable, he couldn't conceivably be the Wraith. That left Mr. Thornton. There seemed no reason why he should have hidden in Batchev's room, but then I asked the Yard to make some enquiries about him, and they turned up a deposit of ten thousand pounds in £1 notes in his bank account. That brought him right into the centre of the picture. But there was still no way of proving anything. So I decided to try my ruse of frightening him into speaking the truth by accusing him of the murder."

There was silence for a few moments. Then Richard said quietly: "And what about the murders?"

"I must admit, sir, that you were the problem there. From the point of view of motive, you were the strongest suspect. Yet I was quite unable to work out a coherent sequence of events with you cast as the murderer. So I changed my approach and decided to assume, at least as an experiment, that you were telling the complete truth. Taking your evidence then in conjunction with Lady Geraldine's—and I could think of no reason why, as she wasn't the killer herself, she should be lying—"

"How did you know I wasn't the killer?" Gerry asked.

"If you were, why should you have admitted being near the Baroness's room? You could have claimed to have been in your room right up to the time you went to investigate the rumpus. Where was I?"

"Comparing my evidence with Geraldine's," Richard said.

"Ah, yes. Assuming you were both telling the truth, Batchev himself was clearly indicated as the murderer of the Baroness. And when I learnt that Lady Geraldine had been able to see only his feet, then I realized how the Baroness's body had left her room. That explained one murder, but left me as much in the dark as ever about the death of Batchev himself. Of the people present, Mr. Felman (as we then thought he was) had the best opportunity and motive, and when we learned he was really Adler after all, he was a very strong suspect.

"But all the time the main question worrying me was why Batchev had tried to break out at all—and with only a pair of wire cutters to put the alarm out of action. He knew it was an elaborate and virtually foolproof system; he must have known that such an attempt was almost certain to set off the alarm. Having concealed the Baroness's body, with virtually no possibility of it being found during the night, why hadn't he waited until the alarm was switched off at six-thirty, then left quietly by a side door? To try to break out like that was the act of a madman. I just couldn't believe in it, and I started to hunt round for another explanation.

"I told myself that of course he hadn't been meaning to go through the window just then—all he'd actually been doing was work on the alarm. To that end he'd fetched the step-ladder to stand on. Then I asked myself *why*? To be sure, Batchev was not a tall man. But neither am I. Yet I could reach the wire quite comfortably by standing on a chair."

"Inspector Wilkins' height," Adler murmured.

"Precisely, sir. Or rather *lack* of it. So Batchev could have reached it, too. Why, then, go to all the trouble of fetching a tall, heavy step-ladder? What other use could he have possibly had for it? All the thing had done, apparently, was fall over. That pulled me up short. Was that all it had been *meant* to do? If Batchev had been standing on the chair, and not on the ladder, was it the ladder and not the chair which had smashed the window? The window had broken almost exactly as the door opened. Could it have been the actual opening of the door which had caused it? Had we been intended to think Batchev had gone through the window, when in fact he hadn't? No. Because he *had* gone through the window: Miss Clifton had seen him; and we'd found his body outside.

"Then, after the discovery of the Baroness's body, Mr. Deveraux informed me that Miss Clifton had told him she had smelt the Baroness's scent in the linen-room. That struck me as highly unlikely. I couldn't imagine the Baroness using a powerful perfume, and when I asked Mr. Deveraux he agreed it had been a subtle and elusive scent. I didn't believe that a scent like that would have seeped through an oak panel. That meant that if Miss Clifton were telling the truth, she had smelt a trace left from the Baroness's body being carried through a fairly large room approximately fifteen minutes before. That seemed to me impossible—in view of the fact that Lady Geraldine, who has a good sense of smell (she identified the scent of lavender on the egg cosy), did not identify the Baroness's scent when the body passed within a few feet of her as she stood in the recess. It seemed Miss Clifton had lied. And if she'd lied about that, had she also lied about the incident of the broken window? I checked with Mr. Deveraux and learned that only Miss Clifton claimed to have seen the man—and that he himself had not even heard the supposed sound in the breakfast-room."

"Deveraux's hearing, eh?" said Peabody.

"Yes, sir. But again something *not* heard, a sound that was lacking. So I took another closer look at Miss Clifton's evidence. And immediately one question struck me: when, during the night, she'd left her room, supposedly to investigate the sounds she'd heard, *why hadn't she switched on a light?* By then I knew about the movements and motives of everyone else who'd been up, and I realized they'd all had good reasons for not wanting to be seen. But if Miss Clifton were telling the truth, she'd had no such reason. Yet apparently, apart from quickly flashing the gallery light on and off, she'd spent all the time groping about in the dark and striking matches.

"I next asked Mr. Deveraux to go into very precise detail as to their finding of the Baroness's body. Then I learned something else odd. Miss Clifton had been going to take her handbag into the passage with her. I could think of no reason she should do that—unless it were to put something in it. Which meant she must have known there was something behind the panel. And the only thing—other than the body—was the pistol which had killed Batchev. I was then sure Miss Clifton had set up the business of the breakfast-room window just to fool us.

"I still couldn't understand how she'd managed the actual murder, as it didn't seem she'd had time to leave the house and get back again. I thought of all sorts of things: that she'd had an accomplice; that Batchev wasn't killed instantly and had staggered out to die; even that there might be an underground river leading to the lake with an entrance in the cellars, into which she could have dumped the body. Then, when I was looking in the gun-room again, I saw the circus cannon—and something clicked. We checked and found minute traces of blood inside the barrel. That was it."

"Lord Burford's collection," Richard said. "I thought that simply meant the murder weapon came from it."

"*One* murder weapon came from it, sir. The pistol that killed *Batchev* came from Mr. Peabody's collection. From that aspect, both collections were of equal importance, and I would have mentioned both if that had been what I had in mind."

"And the pointer about the weather?" Peabody asked.

"Miss Clifton explained that correctly. The weather was important: you had complete darkness followed by vivid flashes of light; dead silence, then loud claps of thunder. So some minor things were seen or heard, while others, normally more noticeable, were not.

"But to revert: my suspicions that Miss Clifton had engineered the business in the breakfast-room were virtually confirmed when, during enquiries in the village, we learnt that a girl answering her description had bought a reel of cobbler's thread there on Saturday afternoon.

"I was then certain there'd been one murderer—and one murderess. When this evening I asked Mr. Deveraux to give me the name of the murderer, and he said Batchev, I knew he'd reached the truth."

36

Future Plans

THE next morning Richard and Adler commenced their talks. This time there were no snags, and the desire of each of them for a quick settlement was so great that by five p.m. they had reached full agreement.

Also in the morning, the diamond necklace was dug up by a policeman and restored to a joyful Mrs. Peabody, who immediately insisted on Hiram making out a substantial cheque to the local police benevolent fund.

The Peabodys were to stay on at Alderley for a few more days. Peabody and the Earl decided that Lord Burford should retain both the Bergman Bayards until the return of Trimble Greene, and then take them to New York himself in time for the exhibition. The Countess was to go too, and afterwards the Peabody's were to show them something of America.

Algy had managed to build up a somewhat jumbled picture of the events which had taken place while he was asleep. He came rapidly to the conclusion that two dangerous criminals, recognizing in him the chief threat to their nefarious schemes, had both attempted to kill him, and that only his remarkably tough constitution had saved him. This story he was anxious to spread without delay through London society, and by Tuesday lunchtime he had left.

During all this, one person remained downcast. Gerry was very distressed and worried about Jane. She turned down an invitation to accompany the Earl and Countess to the United States, and spent most of the day quietly by herself.

Then came another invitation. The negotiations over, Adler sought her out and, surprisingly diffidently, suggested she visited the Duchy as his guest while her parents were away.

In spite of everything, Gerry was thrilled. But still she regretfully refused.

"It'll be quite safe," he assured her, "thanks to the arrangements your uncle and I have completed today."

"It's not that, really," she said. "Normally it would be wonderful. But I couldn't be happy doing anything like that until I know what happens to Jane."

"I'm sorry," he said. "But I'll keep the invitation open."

It was just after this that Gerry had a long conversation with Deveraux.

Deveraux was dressing for dinner when there was a knock and Richard entered. He sat down on the bed, lit a cigarette, and said: "Perhaps what?"

Deveraux deftly inserted a cufflink in his dress shirt. He said: "We're going to be at war before the decade is out."

"Been listening to Churchill?"

"Yes. Haven't you?"

Slowly Richard nodded. "Yes. Don't quote me, but I'm afraid he's right. I may say so myself publicly soon."

"During this war, and in the period leading up to it, my department is going to become more and more important. It's going to expand. I'm lucky enough to have a certain amount of influence in the service, and over the next few years my main task is going to be recruitment. I've been told that if I find anybody I want, and he's willing, I can have him."

"Very nice. So?"

Deveraux swung round. "Last Thursday I met a girl. Since then I've got to know her well, and this evening I made it my business to find out everything I could about her background and history from your niece. I now know that that girl has got every quality and every qualification I'm looking for. She's cool, courageous, and resourceful. She's self-confident and highly ingenious. She's intensely loyal, lives by a strict personal code, and I'd swear she's completely trustworthy. She's also pretty ruthless and she's prepared to kill in a good cause. She's strong and fit, and could obviously, even untrained, hold her own in a rough-house. She speaks French and German, and she has no close family. I've no intention of letting a girl like that rot away the best years of her life in penal servitude when she could be doing valuable work for her country."

"I thought you might mean something like that."

"Your family has second sight. Lady Geraldine seemed to read my mind quite remarkably."

"Don't worry: she knows how to keep her mouth shut."

"Oh, I'm not sorry she guessed—although naturally I couldn't have told her. She cheered up tremendously—then went off to accept some invitation from Adler."

"How will you get Jane out? If such influence as I have can be any use . . ."

"Thank you, but I don't think it'll be necessary. First, we'll let her serve six to twelve months of her sentence. It'll do her good. She's a bit too arrogant and self-willed at present. She's got to learn to accept discipline—and control her temper. But after that . . ."

Deveraux stood up and put on his coat. "Well," he said, "if you read in the papers that Jane Clifton, serving a life sentence for murder, has died in prison, don't grieve for her. It won't be true." His face went grave. "Grieve only if years from now you hear from me that somewhere in Europe an unnamed British woman agent has been executed by firing squad."

Richard drew at his cigarette. "And supposing she's not shot? Supposing we fight this war and win it, and Jane comes through it? What then?"

"Then," said Deveraux, "if I come through it too, I'm going to marry her."

37

The Final Mystery

THE following morning Richard, Adler and Deveraux left Alderley at the same time. Deveraux and Richard were to drive separately to London, and Adler was to be dropped at the station, and from there go home alone, as inconspicuously as he'd come.

The others came out to see the three men off. They were all standing talking, while the servants loaded the luggage into the cars, when another car came up the drive. It stopped and Wilkins got out. "I thought you'd all be glad to know," he said, "that we've just heard Anna Felman's been found safe and well."

A minute later, while the others were saying good-bye to Adler, Deveraux drew Wilkins aside. "I was going to call in at your station to say so long," he said. "It's been quite an experience working with you, old man. I hope cracking this case will do you some good."

Wilkins sighed deeply. "It looks as though it might mean promotion."

"Isn't that good?"

"I suppose so. But it'll likely mean more cases like this one. There seem to be hundreds of them among the English upper classes these days. And I don't really enjoy them. I'd be much happier working on the new one-way traffic system. I'm not sanguine, not sanguine at all. Still, I mustn't bother you with my troubles. What will the case mean to you?"

"Me? Oh, merely memories, Wilkins. I've just got the one memento." He took from his waistcoat pocket a small woollen object. "Funny, that's how I'll always think of this business—as the affair of the bloodstained egg cosy."

"You know, Mr. Deveraux, I suspected you for a while."

"Did you really? Why?"

"Well, while I believed Batchev had gone through that window, it seemed you'd actually been outside at the same time as him. If you'd had the gun, fitted with a silencer, you'd have had the best chance of anyone to bump him off. You'd have needed an outside accomplice to dump the body in the lake, that's all. But it wasn't long before I ruled you out. Besides, somebody had certainly bopped you on the head—"

"Great Scott!" Deveraux broke in. "Wilkins—who on earth did it? We were so busy solving the murder, we forgot all about that."

Wilkins' mouth dropped open. "Goodness me, so we did. I haven't charged any of them with it."

"I don't particularly want anyone charged. I've got to know, though. But—I don't see which of them it could have been. Not Thornton. Certainly not Jane. Batchev was dead."

"Evans, then?"

"It could have been. But why? It doesn't make sense."

They were standing near Deveraux's car. Nearly everyone else was out of earshot, the sole exception being Merryweather, who had dismissed the footman and was himself strapping Deveraux's luggage onto the rack behind the dickey seat. He turned now and cleared his throat.

"Excuse me, sir. I could not help overhearing your conversation. I am in a position to throw light on the subject."

Deveraux blinked. "You, Merryweather? Are you saying you know who hit me?"

"Yes, sir. I regret to say that it was I."

"*You?*" Deveraux and Wilkins both goggled at him.

"Yes, sir. If I may be permitted to explain. I was suspicious of you. You will appreciate that I had no means of knowing your true standing. There had been that challenge to the Wraith in the magazine. You were a person virtually unknown to the Family, and appeared to have engineered your invitation. It seemed, if I may use a colloquialism, extremely, er, fishy, and I resolved to keep an eye on you. I watched your room on the Friday night and my suspicions were confirmed when you left it and prowled around the house in the dark. I decided not to notify his lordship, as, if you denied it, I would have no proof. I was persuaded that on Friday you had been merely rehearsing and that you intended to steal the necklace on the Saturday night. So I followed you again, hoping to catch you in the act. But you simply continued to walk about the house. I thought that perhaps you were going to postpone the theft yet another night. Then, as you neared the top of the stairs, I heard footsteps approaching, which I recognized as being Mr. Richard's. You stopped and extinguished your flashlight. But then to my amazement you went rapidly after him. I immediately concluded that you were not a thief, but a hired assassin. My first thought was to save Mr. Richard. I dared not call out, as I was sure you were armed. So I rushed forward and struck you."

In a weak voice, Deveraux said: "With what?"

"With a silver salver, I'm afraid, sir."

"Most—most apt."

"Thank you, sir. Fortunately I missed striking a direct blow. Then my own torch failed. I endeavoured to reach the light switch, at the same time keeping a firm grip on you. But you were too heavy. I was about to call for help, when you struck me a blow in the abdomen which winded me. Then the other commotion started and my nerve fled. Mr. Richard was by then clearly safe. I retreated down the stairs, brushing against the lady whom I later learnt was Mrs. Peabody, and retired to the servants' quarters. The next day I discovered that you were a police officer. I would like to tender my most sincere apologies, sir."

Deveraux's lips twitched, but he spoke gravely. "Your apology is accepted, Merryweather."

"I am gratified, sir. You did, I think, say you did not wish to prefer charges?"

"Quite correct."

"That, sir, is a great relief to me. Will that be all, sir?"

"Yes," said Deveraux, "that will be all. Thank you."

"Thank *you*, sir," said Merryweather.